TRUE MONSTERS

Dedication

For the ones trapped in their own prophecies.

I hope you find your wings. Or tail. Or whatever you may have.

REECE

ONE

As soon as the tires passed over the border of the town, the air grew thick, as if it was trying to suck the oxygen from my lungs. My next breath was so sharp my mom turned around from the passenger seat, her eyebrows permanently bent on her pale face. She opened her mouth as if to speak, but pressed her lips into a thin line before turning back around. Her knuckles were white on the armrest.

I looked out the window, expecting to see fog, but only saw walls upon walls of thick pine trees. They glistened with moss, dew drops shining like little glowing eyes, glaring at us as we drove down the road. The trees knit their branches above us, trying their best to plunge us into darkness. Goosebumps trailed down my arm, and I absentmindedly tried to scratch them away as we passed by the town's welcome sign. Moss covered that too – making it almost impossible to read. It hung loosely from its frame, the wood dripping down into the pine straw below.

WELCOME TO TREDECIM

The road spat us out of the trees and into what I assumed was downtown. Old brick buildings lined the streets for about thirty seconds before disappearing altogether, revealing a giant black lake.

"Wow, when you said small town, you weren't kidding. How many people live here, ten?" my stepfather asked.

"Maybe a thousand," my mom said. The car drove around the right side of the lake, where a few more buildings and neighborhoods appeared. Five minutes later, we stopped in front of a what once was white trailer yards from where the water lapped at the grass.

The humidity hit even harder outside of the air conditioning. Sweat instantly beaded on my forehead as I lugged my suitcase out of the car. No sooner had I set it on the ground than the screen door of the house banged open, and a small pink blur threw herself around me.

"*HimynameisAnnie!*"

I staggered backwards as she grinned, her bright smile way too big for her small head. I froze like a deer in headlights as she babbled on.

"I've been waiting for you to show up for *hours*."

"Annie, give the poor girl some space!"

"Okayyy, *mom*." Annie reluctantly released me as her mother walked toward us. She was followed by a tall man I barely recognized from old pictures.

Annie's mom leaned down and hugged me – much more gently than her daughter had. She smelled like fabric softener.

"We're so glad to have you here, Honey. My name is Marie."

I could already tell she was the opposite of my own mother. Marie had soft curves where my mom had pressed creases; gray streaks in her hair where my mom had hair dye. No wonder Dad had chosen her as his replacement wife.

I nodded as she stepped away, locking my hands behind my back. Over her shoulder, my mom's piercing gray eyes bored into mine. I knew what that look meant. She had made me memorize it.

"Nice to meet you," I said, forcing my lips to curve into a smile. The barely recognizable man put his hand on Marie's shoulder and smiled at me. "Hey, Sweetheart."

I nodded, and our little family reunion lapsed into awkward silence. *Why isn't he hugging me?* I thought. Is it because he doesn't want me here? Is it because he feels awkward because he hasn't seen me in so long? Is it because he doesn't like hugs?

The last question was answered as Annie threw herself onto his chest. He caught her and hoisted her up on his hip without even looking at her.

"Well, you all have had a long drive. Brad, Cheryl, would you like to come in and get something to drink?" Marie offered.

"Thank you, but no. We've got other plans for tonight, and better get out of here," my mother said. Neither she nor my stepfather made a move to hug me. I suppose it should have bothered me, but all my body did was sweat in the oppressive heat.

"Remember your appointments," she whispered. I nodded, wishing she would hurry up and drive away so I could mingle with this strange family in the air-conditioned house. At least I assumed it was air-conditioned. She quickly shut herself back into the car without a word or glance at my father. I watched as my mom and stepfather disappeared once more, my chest growing tighter and tighter. I was officially alone with a biological dad and stepmom I barely knew, and didn't want to know.

Marie broke me from my trance by grabbing my suitcase and hauling it up the porch steps. "Come on, Sweetie, you must be tired. Let me show you around the house, and then we'll have dinner in a little bit."

I forced my legs to follow her. You could see almost everything from the back door. There was a living room littered with toys and books across from a small kitchen, where something bubbled in a crockpot. Two doors and a bathroom sat on the right side of the house, Jack and Jill style. One door was crammed with drawings consisting of pink scribbles and glitter, the other plain.

"That one is yours," Marie confirmed, opening it and pulling my suitcase inside. It looked like it had been someone's home office before being converted into a bedroom. A small twin-size bed was shoved into a corner, a small nightstand with a lamp next to it.

"It's not pretty yet, but we can take you into town and get some decorations for it if you like," my father offered. I nodded, my neck beginning to stiffen. I wasn't sure if I trusted myself to talk. My mom had made the conditions of this trip very clear. I couldn't mess up.

"Dinner will be ready in an hour. In the meantime, we'll let you settle in. You can take a nap, go explore, whatever you want to do, and we'll talk more tonight," Marie said, softly shutting my door. I plopped down on the bed, wincing as the springs creaked beneath me.

Go explore, do whatever. My fingers tightened on the sheets. Back home, my mother had me on a tight schedule. Get home from school, work on your homework, study, go to your appointment, eat dinner, watch TV for an hour, sleep. I doubted other teenagers felt such a thing was comforting, but I liked the routine. I liked knowing what was coming. How was I supposed to pass this test if I didn't know what was coming?

I started to unpack my suitcase only to abruptly stop once I realized I didn't have a dresser to put anything in.

I peeked my head out the door to see my father playing a game with Annie, who was losing very badly based on the way she was throwing cards across the table. The sight of them made my stomach tighten even more. I quietly slipped past them and out the back door, taking care not to let the screen door slam shut.

Mosquitos attacked me instantly. I carefully stepped down the wilting porch stairs, walking around the house. The grass needed to be mowed; it tickled my bare ankles as I shuffled through it. The lake seemed to watch me as I moved, although it looked more like a soup with too many vegetables in it. It vibrated in a chorus of frogs and insects, the noise louder than a highway.

I made my way around the back of the house to see a garden under invasion from a herd of deer. As soon as they heard me, their white tails popped up. They jumped back into the woods through a narrow slit in the trees.

I followed them, hesitating once my feet hit the pine straw. I had never been hiking before, let alone seen deer or a garden growing food. My mom and stepdad lived in an apartment in Atlanta, and you would never catch either one in a place without climate control. I thrived in those conditions. I was not confident I would do the same in this shit hole of a town.

I reached out to touch one of the pine trees, running my fingers over its rough bark. My hand came away red. I let the specks stay there, not wanting to ruin my clothes.

I held my breath as if I was going underwater and stepped into the trees, following the path the deer made. They apparently made a snack of the garden pretty often – the trail was worn and easy to follow.

Water dripped from the leaves as birds chirped back and forth. Squirrels rustled in the underbrush. A black snake slithered out in front of me. *Okay, maybe this isn't such a good idea*, I thought. I didn't tell anyone where I was going. What if they called me for dinner, and I wasn't there? Was that something I could get in trouble for?

I turned back around as something snapped beyond the path. I froze, straining to hear any other noises. *It's probably just the deer*, I told myself. There aren't any bears here.

You're not in Atlanta anymore. There are definitely bears out here.

My heart thudded heavily in my chest. I jumped as a pinecone hit the ground near my feet. Laughter sounded behind me, and I spun around to see two teenage boys in the middle of the path.

"Dude, I told you not to scare her!" one said, shoving his friend, who was laughing so hard he was bent over, hands on his knees.

"Did you see her face?" he chortled, wiping his eyes. I stared at both of them. Aliens might have well have landed and asked me to take them to my leader. The laughing one looked like the sort who knew what he would be doing in the middle of the woods. He had dark brown hair to match his dark tanned skin, and he wore a t-shirt and cargo shorts. He smelled like bug spray.

The other one looked like he would be better off inside. Dark black curly hair fell over his icy blue eyes, practically shining against his pale skin. He wore a white t-shirt and gym shorts and, curiously enough, no shoes. Who doesn't wear shoes to go walking in the woods?

The pale one stepped forward, extending his hand. I couldn't help but notice delicate scars wrapped around his wrist. I wanted to ask what had caused him to feel the need to carve at his skin, but I bit my tongue just in time.

"Apologies for my friend. He saw you pull up and well . . . can't resist a little prank. My name is Cyan," he said. Cyan's voice was aloof and soothing, like a lazy river. If he pulled a joint out of his pocket and asked if I wanted to share it with him, I wouldn't have been surprised. I shook his hand. "You look like a vampire," I said, wondering too late if that was an appropriate thing to say. Luckily, he sniggered, brushing his long hair out of his eyes.

"I get that a lot. This is my friend, Jack. We're your neighbors." Jack walked forward and shook my hand, a shit-eating grin marring his face. "Sorry for the scare. Consider it your hazing ritual." *Why would anyone need to be hazed just for moving into a new town?* I thought.

They beckoned me to walk with them, which I did not care to do. As I opened my mouth to tell them off, my mom's warning echoed through my head.

You want to get out of there, don't you?

I grit my teeth and I continued to walk with them down the path as they attacked me with questions. You would've thought they had never met a town outsider before, which, according to their questions, seemed likely.

"Girl, why are you wearing a skirt and a button-up? It's like a thousand degrees. Mother Nature forgot to tell the South it's supposed to be Fall right now," Cyan complained. I looked down at my school uniform. It was Monday, and I usually went to school on Monday, so I had put on the pleated blue skirt and white button-up without even thinking about it.

"Here, have some bug spray. You're making me itchy just looking at you," Jack said. I gratefully applied, wrinkling my nose at the harsh smell.

"You'll get used to it," Cyan said. "You have to wear it almost all the time here." The trail eventually spat us out onto another grass lawn. Cyan pointed at the mobile home to the left.

"That one is mine. The one to the right is Jack's. And yours is down there on the end." Together, our three houses formed a semi-circle around the edge of the lake. Even though the water looked grim and murky, the thought of dipping my toes into cold sludge made me want to drool. Good thing I had packed a swimsuit.

Invite them. Make friends.

"Sure could go for a swim right now," I said. "Maybe we could go together later this week." Jack and Cyan both winced.

"Sorry, no one goes swimming in that lake. Too dangerous," Cyan said.

Dammit. That lake is probably fine, they just don't want to hang out with me, I thought.

Across the way, Marie stepped out on the back porch and waved me over.

"Sorry, I gotta go," I said, trying to keep the irritation out of my voice.

"Nice to meet you. Hey, tomorrow we can take you on a tour of the town if you want!" Jack called out.

Okay, good, they actually are cool with spending time with me. Guess the lake is dangerous, I thought, sighing in relief as I stepped back into the AC.

"Ah, I see you met the neighbors. Jack and Cyan are good kids," Marie said. Our dinner consisted of some sort of cheesy potato casserole from the crock pot and dinosaur chicken nuggets. Annie had made a mountain on her plate, and my dad was currently making his dinosaur nuggets trek up the mountain, only to be devoured by a horrible monster at the top. Annie's giggles bordered on a pitch that could only be heard by dogs.

My mom would have never let me play with my food like that. Let alone help me play with it, I thought. Marie watched the display with an amused smile on her face as she attempted to make small talk. She spilled gossip like my old friends did.

"Just so you know, Jack's father, Mr. Smith, is the town's only police officer, so don't do anything sketchy," she teased, nudging me with her elbow. I pretended to laugh while wondering what would happen if you called 911 when the only cop in town was on vacation.

"Of course, nothing really happens here, so he's got a pretty easy job. Course, if something crazy ever does happen, Cyan's parents both work at the urgent care downtown," she continued. Urgent care? No hospital? What did people do if they had a problem that was more than *urgent?* I had barely been here for two hours and already the town seemed to border on neglectful if not dangerous. *I need to get out of here as soon as possible.*

I helped wash dishes after dinner was done, which earned me a grateful smile from Marie, and returned to the sanctity of my room. No sooner had I shut the door than my dad walked in with another smile. It looked like one of mine – forced, plastic, too positive to be genuine.

"Hey, kiddo, can we talk for a minute?" He sat down on the edge of my bed without waiting for my answer. "I'm really glad you're here," he said finally. The words sounded nice, but I couldn't tell if he was lying. If my mom was scared of me, why wouldn't he be?

"Why didn't you hug me earlier?" I asked.

"I-I wasn't sure if you were the hugging type. Your mother told me some things are . . . you know . . . harder for you."

I stiffened. That was just like my mom. Take a problem she had and make it my problem. She was already tilting the odds in her favor – making me seem strange, unlikeable.

"I like them," I protested, even though my mom was definitely right. He reached over and pulled me into the most awkward side hug of my life.

"I've missed you," he whispered, his chest trembling. I jerked in surprise as water plopped down on top of my head.

"Why are you crying?" I said, my voice coming out harsher than what I meant it to. "I mean, why are you crying? Did I upset you?"

He quickly withdrew. "I feel . . . I guess a little guilty? I wish I could've been there for you more when you were little, but your mom . . ."

This is where their stories differed whenever I asked them what happened. According to my mom, the pregnancy was an accident, something unexpected she was desperate to control. To my dad, the pregnancy was a blessing, a blessing my mom had mostly refused him. Until accident number two, anyway.

"I'm sorry," I said, correcting myself quickly. "I promise I have my . . . symptoms under control. I won't ruin your reputation here." He wrinkled his nose like he had suddenly smelled something terrible.

"I'm not worried about my reputation, Sweetie. I just want you to feel welcome here, by all of us. You can let your guard down. Gosh, you're so much like your mother."

I doubted that was much of a compliment, or what he said was true. My mom hadn't been worried about her reputation at first, either. Now look where I was.

"I'm tired, may I please go to bed?" I asked, not sure if I was actually tired at all. He nodded, getting up and heading for the door.

"Love you," he said.

"I love you too," I lied.

. . .

The next morning, I woke up in darkness. I brushed my teeth and showered in the Jack and Jill bathroom before putting on my school uniform and heading to my laptop. Given the circumstances, my private school had offered to let me complete my schoolwork online. They trusted me to keep my grades up and balance living with a strange family.

I logged on and completed my work in silence. It only took an hour to find myself staring at an empty screen. Turns out not having to sit through six different lectures made school a lot easier.

On the other side of the door, smells of breakfast filled the house. I sighed and leaned back in my chair as something pinged on my window.

I got up and looked outside to see Jack and Cyan waving, two bikes lying on the wet grass. I fumbled with the window until I was able to pry it open. Paint ripped off the ledge as I did so.

"What are you doing in there? Aren't you coming to school?" Jack asked.

"I'm doing my private school classes online," I said.

Jack scoffed. "Oooh, okay, Miss Private School. Scuse me for assuming you were a common folk."

Cyan hit him, straddling his bike. "You can come with us to school if you want," he offered. "We can show you around, introduce you to some people."

I chewed my lip in contemplation. Other than exploring the woods and getting eaten by mosquitoes, I had nothing else to do. I might as well continue my test of making friends. I shut the window and pulled on my shoes before meeting the boys outside. Jack tapped on his handlebars like he was trying to coax me to climb on.

"You ride your bikes to school?" I asked. I suddenly felt much more self-conscious about wearing a skirt.

"It's only two miles up the road. There's not exactly a bus here," Cyan said. Trying my best not to flash anyone, I jumped up on Jack's handlebars and held on for dear life as he pedaled off down the road.

Other kids passed us, most of them pausing to wave or stare. The air had a slight nip to it, and I found myself shivering into my button-up.

"That's the fire station over there," Cyan pointed out. "That's the McDonald's – only fast food restaurant in town, by the way, so dash your hopes now. There's the Diner, but it's only open when Mrs. Eugine feels like it." Cyan continued to play tour guide as we cycled towards an old brick building. The bike skidded to a stop, nearly sending me flying into the grass.

"Here we are," Cyan said. "The town library, aka, school."

The boys threw their bikes in a pile by the stairs before we walked through the front doors. The smell of old books roasting in the humidity hit me like a brick. An older woman with glasses as thick as the air stared at me as we walked past the front desk.

"Don't mind the looks. Everyone's just curious about the newcomer," Cyan whispered. We walked to the back of the library and through a set of double doors that led into a tile hallway. Dozens of kids roamed the hallways.

"This is it," Jack announced. "High school is this hallway, middle school is that hallway, elementary is that one." A tall balding man in a white lab coat walked by, a pile of papers in his hands.

"Is he your science teacher?" I asked.

"He's *the* science teacher. Since we only have like . . . a hundred kids, the teachers teach all the grades and just rotate around. He teaches high school first, then migrates over to the middle school side, then elementary, and they all rotate like that."

Jeez, why don't they just all homeschool then? Or do online school? Surely this can't be an effective system, I thought.

A burly guy pushed through us, a skinny blond following him.

"Watch where you're going, fag," he muttered.

Cyan stuck out his chest, pouting. "If you want to go on a date, just ask!" he called sweetly. The guy shot him a middle finger as he turned the corner.

"That's Henry," Jack said. "Resident jackass. His dad is the Baptist preacher."

"His bark is bigger than his bite," Cyan said. "And Brian – the skinny one – is just his little lapdog." The bell rang, and students scurried off into their respective rooms.

"Whelp, gotta go. We'll show you around downtown after school," Jack promised, pulling Cyan down the hallway.

Realizing I would have to walk home since I didn't have my own bike, I sighed and slowly made my way back into the library. Thunder rumbled outside, the dark clouds sinking lower and lower.

19

"It's not gonna rain, Sweetie," the librarian said suddenly, peering at me over her glasses. "It's always thundering like that."

"Oh, thank you for letting me know."

"You got a library card yet?"

She knows I don't have a card yet, I thought. *I'm brand new.* I raised my eyebrow at her and crossed my arms.

"What do you think?" As soon as the words left my mouth, I knew I probably shouldn't have said them out loud. *Be gentle when you talk to people*, my therapist always chided. Luckily, the old lady smiled and motioned me over. She pulled out an old plastic card from a drawer on her desk, scanned it into the computer, and handed it to me.

"There you go, lass. Hope to see you around town more. Tell Marie and your father I said hello."

By the time I made it back to the house, I was so sweaty and covered with mosquito bites that I took another shower. *First things first*, I thought. *Get a bike. Get bug spray. Keep being nice to the boys.*

I assumed they were only being kind to me because I was new in town, which didn't bother me a bit. It's not like any so-called friends from Atlanta had texted me to see how I was doing. How many of them had even noticed I was gone? How many of them were *relieved* I was gone? I would take my friends where I could get them, and right now, those two were easier to maneuver around than my new family.

True to their word, the boys showed up at my house right after school ended. Surprised they had remembered, I hopped back up on Jack's bike as they pedaled to downtown. We left the bikes in front of the library again as we strolled amongst the old shops. It soon became clear where all the townspeople hung out. The tiny strip included a barbershop-salon combo, a thrift shop, and even a video game store.

We stopped at the thrift shop where I quickly found an old bike and claimed it as my own. The shopkeeper, Mrs. Davis, was so amazed at seeing an outsider, she let me take it for free, even though insisting on paying felt like the proper southern thing to do. My mom has left me a cautious amount of spending money – enough for the occasional treat, not enough to cause damage.

Across the street was the Dollar General, which had everything from clothes to groceries to blessed bug spray. I walked away with a bag full of several bottles, plus a package of pink unicorn stickers lurking by the checkout for Annie. It seemed like something my therapist would smile at if I got my loud step-sibling a gift. It still mystified me why she was so excited to see a stranger she had never met, but then again, how many other little girls her age actually lived here? Did she have any friends?

Jack treated us to ice cream, and we all sat down on the curb to eat. I dug into mine with a spoon as Jack raced to lick his before it melted.

"Of course you're the type to get ice cream in a cup, weirdo," Jack commented, side-eyeing me. Cyan shoved him yet again. Their friendship was beginning to make more sense. They reminded me of how I used to be with my old friends – constant teasing bordering on harassment, but under the surface, a bond I could no longer wrap my head around.

"Does my ice cream in a cup offend you?" I asked.

"No. It matches your uptight personality," he teased. I hid my disappointment with a smile. I wasn't supposed to be uptight. But – if Jack could tease me, that meant I could tease him back. I glanced over at Cyan to see that he had barely touched his cone. Most of it dripped down his fingers, but he didn't bother to lick it off his knuckles. Now that I was thinking about it, the teenage boy was strangely skinny. His cheekbones stuck out from his face like shards of glass, and his fingers looked like bones of gnarled wood stretched too thin.

"Aren't you going to eat your ice cream?" I asked. Jack buried his elbow deep in my ribcage, and as I turned to glare at him, he narrowed his dark eyes.

Don't, he mouthed. I raised an eyebrow. *Don't what? Ask Cyan why he's not eating his ice cream? Why was that such a bad question to ask?*

Cyan shrugged, watching the drips land on the concrete. "What are you, a cop?"

"No," I said. "But Jack's dad is – right? Mr. Smith?" Cyan sniggered as Jack blushed.

"Man, why'd you have to bring that up?" he complained. "Marie told you, didn't she?"

"Marie knows everything about everyone," Cyan said. "What all did she tell you?"

"Not much, to be honest. She said you two were nice," I said. Cyan and Jack exchanged a grin.

"Did she tell you how she ended up here with your dad?" Cyan asked. I shook my head. I knew my dad had moved here after I was born and met Marie and her daughter, but no one had told me how Marie got here.

"Her ex-husband was an abusive fuck. Rumor has it, he laid his hands on Annie, and that was it. She shot him dead, got off with a plea deal, moved here, met your dad, end of story," Jack said.

"Interesting," I said. "I mean – *wow*. That's crazy." To be fair, I couldn't exactly picture the short, round woman ending another man's life. But it made sense why no one had bothered to share the story with me. I wondered if she felt bad about killing her ex-husband. I wouldn't.

I swirled my spoon around in my melted ice cream. "So . . . what have you heard about me?" I asked. The boys exchanged a glance. "Come on, I can take it," I pressed. This was an excellent chance to see how well I was blending in.

"Really not that much," Cyan admitted. "You're Steve's daughter. He lost custody of you when you were little because your mom's a bitch, apparently."

I shrugged. "She is strict."

"Well, use this opportunity to let loose a little bit. Your dad is definitely not strict," Jack said. "We're going to have all kinds of fun adventures this winter."

My watch beeped suddenly, and I sprang to my feet. "Sorry, guys, I gotta go." I threw away my ice cream cup and dashed for my bike, pedaling home as fast as I could. I jumped in front of my laptop screen just in time to accept the incoming video call.

My therapist's gentle face stared at me from the camera. "Good evening, Reece. How are you doing today?"

I nodded, trying to catch my breath. According to the boy's gossip, they didn't know why I was really here. I was in the clear.

. . .

I tossed and turned that night, the thick air seeping in through the cracks in the walls. The room was cool, but the blankets felt too damp to curl up in.

I gave up and opened my eyes, staring at the popcorn ceiling. I crawled out of bed and walked to the window, yawning and popping my back. The lake seemed to suck the light from the Moon. The streetlamps were all broken, along with the old docks oozing into the water.

I leaned against the window, condensation pooling on the glass from my breath. *What's so dangerous about you?* I wondered. *You're telling me no one in this entire town goes swimming, ever? What about summer? Does anyone here have a pool at least?*

A flicker caught my eye. I held my breath as the water rippled by the broken-down dock by the house. A limb shot out from the water, grabbing the edge and pulling itself up. I frowned and stared as the figure stood and walked casually towards the woods.

I guess people do go swimming in the lake, I thought.

TWO

The next morning, I woke up in a sticky sweat. I hopped in the shower only to be instantly wet as soon as I dried off. I completed my assignments before Annie left for school and debated on what I could do to pass the time. My dad worked from home, and every moment I spent in my room was another opportunity for him to walk in and try to talk to me. I wasn't sure what route I should take. He knew what had happened. Would he be suspicious if I acted *too* normal? Would he report negative things to my mom if I didn't act normal *enough*?

I exchanged my skirt and button-up for a pair of shorts and a t-shirt. I lathered myself in bug spray and ventured outside, strolling over to the dock. I tested my weight on the first board and carefully maneuvered to the end, easing myself down to sit at the edge. I dangled my feet above the water, wondering if what I had seen last night was real or just some fever dream. Thunder rumbled above, the sky heavy, but it had yet to rain like the librarian had said.

"Reece! Get off of there!" I spun to see my dad waving from the back porch. I quickly made my way back to solid land, my heart thudding in my chest. "I meant to tell you before – that dock isn't stable. Should stay away from there."

"Is it true that no one ever swims here?" I asked.

He sighed, suddenly looking much older. "Yeah. Kids have drowned. There's who-knows-what at the bottom of that lake – guess people get tangled in it." He pointed to a house across the lake. "Ten or so years ago, two little boys were having a sleepover. Thought it would be fun to go on a midnight swim. One of them never came back up. Found the body a week later. Not pretty."

Jeez, the whole town forbids swimming because one kid makes a stupid decision and drowns? They hadn't gotten over it after all this time?

"Got it. I'll stay away from the docks," I said, burying my annoyance. As I followed him to the house, I couldn't help but notice footprints in the mud, leading towards the woods.

Jack and Cyan came to fetch me right after school. As we biked to town, I debated telling them about the strange figure swimming in the lake, but decided to keep my mouth shut. I didn't need my two new acquaintances thinking I was uptight *and* delusional.

We walked back through all the same shops we had visited the previous day and ate ice cream from the same stand. Jack made fun of me for eating out of a cup again, to which I responded by smearing a sticky finger across his face.

He was about to return the favor when another figure slapped his cone out of his hand. It flew into the street, where a passing car promptly crushed it under its front tire.

"Hey man, what gives?" Jack sputtered. Henry – the pastor's kid – sniggered next to the skinny blond, Brian, I think his name was. His smile was like a shark's.

"Oh, sorry, was that your ice cream? Sorry, I meant to go after the fag's," Brian grinned. Cyan smirked as he threw his uneaten cone squarely at Brian's face. It hit his nose right on target. It stayed there for a moment before falling to the ground between his feet, smearing the carnage down his chin. Brian swiped the excess away and gritted his teeth.

"Sorry, was that not the same kind of cream you prefer?" Cyan teased. Brian took a step forward only to be intercepted by Jack, who looked much larger in comparison.

"If you can't take it, don't dish it out!" Jack said, staring down his nose at Brian. Henry stepped up, and he, unfortunately, was much bigger than Jack. His biceps were the size of my skull.

"Aw, trying to protect your boyfriend?" Henry asked.

Surely this is an instance where I can sound mad, right? Maybe it'll earn me more favor if I defend them. "Why the hell do you care if he has a boyfriend or not?" I snapped. "It's twenty-nineteen. Don't you belong in the seventies with that opinion?"

Brian turned his dark eyes on me. "And you do you think you are, newbie?"

"About a hundred IQ points smarter than you two combined." Cyan and Jack sniggered. I steeled myself for another insult or for a punch to the face – whatever small-town bullies did to newcomers, but nothing came.

"Guess we'll be seeing more of you," Brian said, turning and walking off with Henry. I imagined throwing another ice cream at Brian, the cone sinking through the flesh in his back and popping out the other side. Maybe Marie and I were similar in our propensity to end the lives of bullies.

"Oh, go drown!" Jack shouted after them. As they disappeared around the corner, Jack and Cyan burst out laughing.

"Wow, the uptight private school girl has some spice," Jack said, rubbing his knuckles on my head. I instantly bit my tongue. Was that too much? Was I too mean? I doubted my mom or therapist would approve of that interaction. They definitely wouldn't have approved of my violent ice cream fantasy.

"I'm sorry," I said.

"Don't apologize, that was great," Cyan said.

I relaxed. *You made the right call.* "Does it bother you when people make comments like that?" I asked.

"Nah. I bat for both teams, but I'm extra gay when it annoys other people," Cyan replied through a smirk.

As I biked back home, I pondered the fight – if it could even be called a fight. How could Cyan be so relaxed about being called such a name? What kind of psyche did a guy have to have to attack the only queer kid in town? Well, maybe Cyan wasn't the only one – but still – in a town like this, how many could there be? Maybe the pastor was homophobic, and that was where his son got it from.

Why do they get to be assholes but I don't?

I survived another dinner with my family before going to bed. Part of me wanted to stay up to see if that weird figure would emerge from the lake again, but my body was so exhausted from the night before, I fell asleep as soon as my head hit the pillow.

It wasn't my alarm clock that woke me up the next morning. Voices trickled in from my window. A quick search of the house revealed everyone was outside. I padded outside barefoot in my pajamas to the growing crowd gathering around the lake. Jack stood at the forefront, body stiff as a board. Marie shielded Annie's eyes from the scene.

"What's going on?" I asked. Marie stepped aside, revealing a limp figure on the grass. Brian's glassy eyes stared back at me. Dark black bruises marred his throat. His mouth hung open, almost comically, his tongue lolling in the mud. I bit down hard on my cheek to keep from laughing.

Murmurs rippled, but the crowd seemed to accept the dead body the same way they would've accepted a piece of roadkill – slightly perturbed but not devastated.

I wondered how Henry would react when he heard the news.

. . .

The whole town came to the funeral – teenagers, adults with their kids, old folks who could hardly shuffle – one lady even brought her lap dog. The little Baptist church was barely big enough to fit everyone, but they all squeezed into the corners and pews like they were used to this sort of thing. The casket remained closed.

My therapist had given me some pointers on things to say to grieving people and how to act solemn, but the tips appeared needless. No one was crying. Cyan picked at his cuticles beside me, and Jack stared up at the ceiling, tapping his foot on the ground. The others did a better job of sitting still and pretending to pay attention, but I had the uncanny sense I was stuck in a room full of mannequins. Or people like me.

The pastor droned on at the pulpit, occasionally wiping sweat from his forehead. He babbled on about how good a kid and student Brian was, which I debated silently in my head. He probably didn't deserve to drown, but how great a kid could he have been if he had constantly bullied Cyan? By the time the sermon was done, my butt was asleep, and I was struggling to pretend to care.

The family went off by themselves to the graveyard – a five-minute walk from my house, which didn't sound creepy at all. Cyan and Jack accompanied me as we headed to the parking lot. On the way there, Jack suddenly sprawled on the asphalt. We turned around to see Henry behind him, chest heaving and eyes red around the edges.

"You killed him," he rasped, his hands balled up into fists. *Finally, something interesting,* I thought, biting my lip so I wouldn't smile. Jack scrambled to his feet, brushing off his hands on his suit coat. Others filtering out of the church stopped to stare at the display.

"What are you talking about?" Jack demanded.

"You told him to go drown yesterday. And look what fucking happened!" Henry shouted, his fist barreling towards Jack's face. The crowd gasped as Jack went down, blood flying from his nose. Cyan dove in front of him.

"Dude, seriously? You think Jack killed Brian? You're crazy," Cyan laughed.

"You don't have the right to call *me* crazy," Henry hissed. He wound up his fist again, but was blocked by a uniformed man tackling him from behind. The pastor wasn't far behind, shouting as Henry tried his best to escape their grasp. The crowd watched in shock until the policeman, Mr. Smith, I assumed, handcuffed him and hauled him back to his feet.

"Alrighty buddy, you're going to cool down with me for a while," he muttered, dragging a screaming Henry through the crowd. Cyan and I helped Jack up to his feet as he held his sleeve against his bleeding nose. Another adult swooped in, moving Jack's arm to examine it.

"It's not broken, just bruised. Cyan, take him home and put some ice on it," he said.

Cyan nodded. "Thanks, Robert. Let's go, man."

I took Jack's other shoulder as we escorted him home through the field of stares in the parking lot. We trotted up the sagging wooden steps of Jack's trailer. Cyan fished a bag of frozen peas out of the fridge and tossed it to Jack, who plopped down on the couch with a groan. Jack's place looked and smelled like one would expect with only two men living there. I perched on the edge of the coffee table, moving a pile of grease-stained paper plates to do so. The rest of it was covered in DVDs and video game controllers. The house smelled slightly of wet dog, even though there was no dog in sight.

"Bet you weren't expecting a fight at your first Tredecim funeral," Cyan joked, moving another pile of plates to sit next to me.

"I can't believe he actually punched me!" Jack complained. "I mean – does he seriously think I dragged that asshole into the lake to drown him in the middle of the night?"

"There were bruises on his neck," I said. The boys stared at me. *Probably not a good thing to point out*, I thought. "Never mind. Why would he go swimming?" I asked. "I thought you said the lake was dangerous?"

"It is. Obviously. I don't know why he thought swimming was a good idea. Especially this time of year," Jack said.

"Maybe he was high or something," Cyan said.

"You sure as hell wouldn't catch me in that lake drowning someone - no matter how much I hated them," Jack muttered.

"I'm sure he'll cool off. His best friend did just die," Cyan said.

Are we not going to talk about the bruises on his neck? Did everyone just miss that? I thought. *Was there not an autopsy done on the body?*

No sleep came to me that night as questions ran through my head on a loop. The next morning, I ignored my school assignments and biked to the library. The old woman grinned behind her novel as I walked in, trying to scrape the wet hair off the back of my neck.

"You need a ponytail holder." She wordlessly handed me one before I dove into the dusty shelves. It was a good thing I had brought a Kindle for reading purposes - all the books here seemed to be a thousand years old. Based on the amount of dust on most of them, no one had checked them out for that long either.

I gave up finding anything useful in the texts and settled for an ancient computer. I typed in *Tredecim, Georgia*, only for the engine to suggest *Magicicada tredecim*, which was the scientific name for cicadas. I went back to the books. The old woman materialized beside me, balancing on a cane.

"Can I help you find anything?"

"Do you have any old newspapers?"

A moment later, she appeared with an old box full of little rolls. "You have no clue what these are, do you?" I shook my head. A few minutes later, I had the roll, called a microfilm, properly inserted into a machine beside the computer. Black and white images from an old newspaper appeared on the screen.

"I've got about thirty of those boxes if you want any more. Happy hunting." She disappeared once more, leaving me with the dust.

My dad had said that one kid across the lake had drowned ten years ago. But fifteen years ago, Tredecim had been a normal southern hick town. The building of the McDonald's was featured for weeks. There were even pictures of people swimming in the lake, all smiles.

The tragedy struck five years later. The death of the little boy, just six years old, was covered for months. Pictures of his gravestone, swarmed with flowers and crosses, took the front page. I raised an eyebrow as I recognized another little boy featured in the photographs.

A littler Brian. A caption said he had been a close friend of the victim.

That's ironic, I thought. *Your best friend drowns, and you do the same ten years later?*

News of the drowning eventually faded, as did pictures of people swimming in the lake. Other normal things popped up. An obituary here and there, a restaurant gaining a new manager, small, boring town stuff.

Except something felt off about the deaths. I scrolled back to 2007 and counted the number of obituaries. Including cases of death by old age, fifteen people died. That felt like a lot for such a small town. The next year, twenty people.

I counted the numbers again, subtracting the deaths by natural causes, which weren't that many. And then I counted again, just to be sure. *There's no way*, I thought. *I have to be miscounting.*

Except I wasn't. I quickly went through the rest of the years up until the present day, double-checking my math until I was sweating from something other than the heat.

Thirteen. For the past decade, thirteen people have died every year from something other than natural causes. They had all drowned.

My mind flashed back to the mysterious figure I had seen coming out of the water and the bruises on Brian's neck. I swallowed, my chest tightening.

Something wasn't right.

THREE

I stayed in the library until the boys got out of school. It felt irresponsible to keep my mouth shut. A *good* friend would share the revelation, regardless of how insane it sounded. It would make them think I cared.

I grabbed them out of the crowd of escaping students and pulled them over to the computer. "You'll never guess what I just found!"

The boys didn't smile. Cyan's hair was mussed, and Jack was sporting another bruise on his cheekbone.

"I've been in here all day researching. I found something really weird. Every year since 2007, thirteen people have drowned." I held my breath, waiting for their eyes to go big and thank me for looking out for them, but all they did was stare at me.

"Seriously? You too?" Jack accused, crossing his arms.

I blinked. "Sorry?"

Cyan sighed, running his fingers through his hair. "Reece, people have been messing with us all day. They all think Jack *actually* killed Brian," he whispered.

"Well, someone did."

Jack's jaw dropped.

"I don't think it's you!" I said, crossing my arms. "Whoever the killer is, he's got to be older than us. He's been doing it for ten years –"

Cyan held up his hands. For the first time since meeting him, there was no goofy smile on his face. "Stop, just stop. This is not the time!"

I narrowed my eyes. What do you mean, this isn't the time? Do you hear what I'm saying? Every year, thirteen people die. Not from old age or sickness, but *drowning*. There were bruises on Brian's neck. Don't you think that has to be way more than a coincidence?"

"I'm not a murderer!" Jack hissed.

"I already said I don't think it's you! Unless you've been killing people since you were six years old."

Cyan took his friend by the shoulders and steered him towards the doors. "Reece, I know you're new here and probably bored or whatever, but nothing weird is going on here. You're making connections that aren't there. Brian drowned – that's it. There weren't any bruises on his neck. No one here is killing anyone."

They escaped through the double doors, leaving me speechless. If my therapist had been there to witness the conversation, she would've taken me back through everything word by word and shown me pictures of their faces. *Now, in the future, do you think bringing up such a thing would be appropriate, given how your friend was feeling?*

I ignored my racing heart and stalked back to my computer, shutting it off and collecting the microfilms. I lugged the box back up to the front desk and raced home on my bike.

I burst into the house, wiping sweat off my brow. Marie and my father looked up in surprise as I walked into the living room.

"Can I talk to you guys?"

Jack and Cyan were acting unreasonably because they had had a bad day. But I knew I was right. *Someone* had to appreciate that fact. I explained what I had found at the library and the bruises on Brian's neck. Their faces grew paler the more I talked. Marie sent Annie outside to play halfway through.

"Well?" I demanded. "Tell me that's not weird. We need to tell the police or something!" They exchanged a glance before sighing. I didn't have to be an expert in emotions to know what that meant.

My dad walked over to the coffee table and handed me a newspaper. "Honey, I know seeing all that a few days ago was scary, but there's nothing for you to be worried about. They published the autopsy report in the paper – look."

I quickly scanned the print and frowned. Drowning. Plain, old drowning.

"But that doesn't make sense. I know I saw bruises. And what about the thirteen thing?" I protested.

He shrugged. "Coincidence? Look, everyone knows that lake is dangerous, and sometimes, stupid people go swimming in it. There's no grand conspiracy here."

The newspaper trembled in my hand. My heart thudded in my chest. My dad's eyes grew wide. He gently cupped my face. "Honey, are you . . ."

I pulled away from him and locked myself in my room, trying desperately to breathe. Damn my stupid lungs. Damn my stupid body. Damn my stupid brain.

I *knew* thirteen people dying for the past ten years wasn't a coincidence. I *knew* I had seen those bruises on Brian's neck. Why wasn't anyone else seeing it? Goddammit, I knew I was *right.* Was someone lying? Trying to cover something up? Was the whole town in on a secret I wasn't allowed to know?

I blew through my lips, forcing my lungs to cooperate with me. *Control yourself,* my mom chanted in my head. *Don't embarrass me.*

I wiped my eyes and washed my face in the sink. *Just drop it,* I told myself. You've upset yourself and other people. It's not worth it. Keep pretending to be normal. Everything will be fine.

The next day, I stayed holed up in my room, catching up on schoolwork. I only looked up from my laptop when someone banged on my window. I opened it to see Jack and Cyan, smiling sheepishly.

"Can we talk?" Cyan asked, his voice distorted through the glass. I met them outside, fumbling with my fingers behind my back.

"I'm sorry. I shouldn't have said anything, especially since you two had such a bad day yesterday." I would've rather gutted myself than utter the stupid apology, but I had to play nice if I wanted them to stay my friends.

"We were kinda mean too. Yesterday was stressful. Water under the bridge?" Jack offered.

I forced a smile. "Water under the bridge."

. . .

As the weeks went by, we continued our ritual of riding downtown and eating ice cream after school. Everyone left us alone for the most part. Henry was nowhere to be seen. The town seemed to have gone back to normal, and the air was reluctantly turning cooler. As October ticked closer, Cyan grew more and more excited. He nearly fainted when I told him my mom had never let me celebrate Halloween before.

Halloween was apparently a big deal for Tredecim – an excuse for the town to embrace its run-down, spooky aesthetic with pride. As it lurked closer, the town added more and more decorations. Skeletons

hung from the broken street lamps, swaying eerily in the breeze. Jack O'
Lanterns pierced through the darkness on every porch. Cackling witches
and motorized brooms wandered downtown. Marie and Annie covered
the entire house in fake spiderwebs.

Of course, according to Cyan, the high schoolers didn't go trick-
or-treating; they went off to the woods to party and tell ghost stories,
which sounded a thousand times scarier. He still insisted I wear a
costume.

Annie dressed up as a pink, sparkly unicorn and was vibrating
with excitement as the sun began to sink into the sky. I put the finishing
touches on my costume right as Jack and Cyan came to collect me. They
gasped when I revealed myself.

"Good god, what is that?" Jack sputtered.

"I'm an escaped inmate – you know – from an insane asylum?" I
twirled in my old hospital gown, complete with fake blood stains. The
irony wasn't lost on me, but it would have to remain an inside joke.

"I got that, but what is *that*?"

I held up my replica ice pick, also marred with fake blood.
"You've never heard of a lobotomy? It's where they would stab you
through the brain with an ice pick. It calmed people down."

"That's *disgusting*."

I crossed my arms. "It's way better than yours! That's the most
basic costume of all time."

Jack gasped, putting his hand over his heart. "I look fabulous."
His inflated dinosaur tail smacked me in the knees as he spun. Cyan

watched the display with a smirk, fake blood trailing down his mouth. His icy blue eyes were replaced with blood-red, slitted contacts. A long black cape dragged the ground behind him. He sported a black crop top and black skinny jeans. He had even gotten his nails done with pointy black tips. I briefly wondered what Henry would think of that outfit.

"And you're even more basic," I pointed out.

Cyan shrugged. "*Halloween is the one day a year a girl can wear whatever she wants, and no other girl can say anything about it,*" he quoted, spinning around. "Besides, I look hot as a vampire."

I couldn't disagree.

We headed down the trail into the woods, Jack's dinosaur costume swishing and scraping against every branch in our path, followed by whooshes of air.

"Told you that thing was going to rip," Cyan said as we stepped out into the clearing. A huge bonfire lit up the night, crackling and sparkling. Teenagers from the high school milled around it as they laughed and tossed back drinks.

"Are those drink-drinks?" I whispered, water seeping up through my shoes as we trudged closer. I couldn't exactly risk partaking in something that might make me more honest.

"You don't have to have any if you don't want to," Cyan said as Jack yanked a beer out of a cooler. I relaxed in the warmth of the fire, the cool air damp and heavy on my skin. *I should've brought a jacket.*

Cyan must've noticed me shivering because he extended his cape and placed it around my shoulders. We sat down on a bench as we watched the others chat and get tipsy around the fire.

"Not exactly the most comfortable bench," I muttered. "No one brings fold-out chairs to this thing?"

"That's what we get for having it at the cemetery."

"The *what?*" I looked down at the stone bench we were sitting on and noticed for the first time there was an inscription labeled on the stone.

I groaned. "We're going to be haunted for sure."

Cyan grinned. "I mean, it is Halloween after all. Isn't that the point?"

I think my mother had the right idea when she barred me from celebrating this, I thought. The fact that another teenager had been buried here just a few weeks ago made it seem even more sacrilegious. How many of these headstones would match the ones I found in my research if I looked?

No, don't you dare. You promised to drop it, remember? Fit in. Pass your mom's test.

Cyan managed to find a non-alcoholic soda and shared it with me as we watched the others get drunker and drunker. At one point, people started getting up and telling ghost stories, which I couldn't help but listen to. Turns out, drunk teenagers telling stories was more funny than scary. *Why does Mr. Smith not come out here and stop this?* I wondered. *The whole town has to know we're out here.*

Jack made his way to the front of the crowd, holding up his hands for attention. "Once upon a time, there was a lovely couple who had a son, smart and handsome. This son worked in the town's factory. One night, while he was at work, his father was gifted a mysterious magical artifact – a mummified monkey's paw – infused with magic."

"Psh, this one? Heard it a thousand times," Cyan whispered under his breath.

"The paw was capable of granting the owner three wishes – anything they could want in the world – but at a horrible price. Not believing the outlandish tale, the father wished for two hundred pence. Later that night, the foreman from the factory arrived at their door bearing bad news. During his shift, their precious son had drowned."

The crowd suddenly went silent. Even the fire seemed to pause in its crackling. Some of the teenagers exchanged raised eyebrows. I thought I heard someone whisper Brian's name. *He doesn't drown, I* thought. *He gets crushed in the machinery.*

The fire glinted red in Jack's eyes. "The foreman paid the father two hundred pence as compensation. Desperate to have her son back, the wife grabbed the monkey's paw and demanded it bring back her boy." Jack cackled, hands on his knees like he had done on our first meeting in the forest. His laughter echoed off the trees and headstones. The air grew colder. I didn't realize I was holding my breath until Cyan nudged me with a raised eyebrow.

"The son clawed his way out of the lake to return to his family, but he was no longer their son – just a horrible, bloated monster! The father, terrified of seeing his son's mangled corpse, took the monkey's paw and wished him dead again.

"And more will die," he rasped. "More will die tonight." Jack stumbled as if someone had pushed him, blinking down at the ground. The crowd stared up at him, eyes wide.

"I think I'm ready to go, you?" Cyan asked, getting up. I followed him through the woods, leaving Jack behind and rubbing my arms. *That was unnecessarily creepy,* I thought. *Even for Halloween in a graveyard.*

We stepped back out into civilization to see kids still making rounds through the houses, their pillowcases overflowing with candy. Here, the air felt warmer and decidedly less murder-y. Cyan and I swiped a handful of candy from a doorstep and sat down on my porch to eat it. Off by the lake, Annie swapped treats with the handful of other kids her age.

"So, other than drunk Jack telling stories, how's your first Halloween?" Cyan asked.

I shrugged. "It's okay. Don't think it's my thing though."

"You more of a Christmas girl?"

"I guess."

Annie stood up from her friends and started walking towards the house.

"What's your favorite holiday?" I asked.

"April Fools Day."

"Be so for real."

"I'm serious. Very underrated – very underutilized."

I frowned. Annie had stopped walking towards the house and was now staring at the lake. Her bag of candy fell to the ground. Cyan's eyes went wide as she stepped onto the dock. *She should know better than to go on there*, I thought.

Cyan cupped his hands around his mouth. "Annie, get off the dock! It's dangerous!"

She ignored him and continued walking, stopping about halfway down.

"Annie, get back here!" Marie called from the front door. A cold wind blew my hair in front of my eyes, and by the time I got it out, people had started screaming. Cyan leapt to his feet and bolted for the lake. Splintered wood gaped where Annie had just been standing. I chased after Cyan as he knelt by the hole, shouting. "I can't see her!"

"She can't swim!" Marie wailed. I held my breath as Cyan dove into the black water, creating more screams from the shore. My father ran up, phone pressed to his ear, face pale.

"Over here!"

I looked up to see two soggy figures pulling themselves up on the shore. I bolted with my family to meet them as Cyan attempted to beat the water out of Annie's lungs. She started crying, which meant she was breathing.

Marie hugged her to her chest, sobbing just as hard as Cyan gasped for breath, shaking the water out of his curly hair, his vampire cloak wrapped around him like a blanket. I looked back at the dock.

How did he swim so fast, dragging along a six-year-old? I thought. How did he find her?

"Annie, Annie, are you okay? What happened, Sweetie?" my dad asked.

"You're safe now," Marie crooned, smoothing the hair out of her face.

"It pulled me down," she sobbed. "It grabbed my ankle and pulled me down."

I looked up to stare at Cyan, whose makeup was now running down his face. He had lost one of his contacts.

"Sweetie, that was just me. I was saving you," Cyan said. She batted his hand away.

"It wasn't you. It dragged me down. It had glowing red eyes," she sobbed. I stopped breathing as I moved her hair away from her neck. Several dark bruises, the size of fingerprints, marred her delicate skin.

. . .

The figure coming out of the lake.

Thirteen victims.

Glowing red eyes.

The bruises.

The coincidences tossed and turned in my stomach until I was nauseous. Of course, the reasonable explanation was that Annie had seen Cyan's red contacts in the water and had mistaken him for some scary lake monster. That was what everyone kept telling her anyway. For such a young kid, she was stubborn.

I wanted to point out the bruises, but they had mostly faded by morning. I had the suspicion they would get chalked up to anything other than a crazy murderer lurking in the lake. Annie was uncharacteristically quiet, as were Marie and my father. They sat motionless at the coffee table as Annie watched cartoons, huddled in a blanket.

I headed out the door and shuffled through the grass to see Cyan standing by the dock, staring out at the water. His eyes looked sunken in. I was surprised that he had jumped in after Annie. The thought hadn't even crossed my mind to try to save her. He really was a nice person.

He noticed me and offered a weak smile. "Hey, Reece. How is Annie?"

I shrugged. "She'll be fine. Where's Jack?"

"You haven't heard?"

I shook my head.

Cyan twisted his fingers together. "He found another body at the bonfire last night. Another high schooler. She drowned."

Goosebumps snaked down my arms. Jack's odd storytelling echoed between my ears.

Had she had too much to drink and wandered off? Why had Jack been the one to find her?

Did she have bruises on her throat, too?

49

. . .

I spent the next few days scouring the newspapers. Deaths in town were apparently so common that they barely took up more than a slot on the obituary page. But I did find out who the town mortician was. Dr. Davis – the science teacher. Go figure.

It wasn't hard to find his address. I banged on his front door on a Saturday morning. He answered in his pajamas. I thought for the millionth time about how I had promised myself to let it go, but my curiosity was consuming me. I knew I was right. Someone else had to know, too.

"You're Steve's kid, right? What can I help you with, miss?"

"The girl that died – did she have bruises on her neck?" I asked.

He furrowed his brow. "Now, why would you think that?

"Brian had them on his neck, and my little sister had them too when she fell into the lake. She said something grabbed her and dragged her down. Cyan jumped in and saved her."

Dr. Davis chuckled. "I'm sure you and your sister are imagining things. There's nothing strange going on here. Those poor kids drowned – that's it."

"I didn't say anything strange was going on. I asked if there were bruises on the girl's neck."

He started to close the door. "Tredecim is a safe town!" he chided. "There's nothing weird going on here. Leave it be." He slammed the door shut.

I walked back to my house, my mind racing and my jaw set. Nothing strange going on, my ass. Coincidences like that didn't just happen.

But no one wanted to admit it. I was either having a complete breakdown, or there was someone who was playing out my sickest fantasies. Maybe the whole town was in on it – and that's why everyone was being so dismissive. Maybe they wanted to keep their sick traditions for themselves.

Don't be ridiculous – that stuff only happens in movies.

According to my numbers, the girl from last night was the eleventh victim, which meant two more people had to go before January. The killer – if there really was one – had two months to kill two more people. And he had already tried to go after Annie once. Had he killed the high schooler because he didn't get Annie? Or had he been planning to kill both of them?

The cold wind blew through my thin jacket. Why had Annie gone walking on that dock? How would the killer have known she would fall through? Had he simply been waiting under the water to grab her? What kind of serial killer does that?

The image of the figure coming up out of the lake a few nights ago flashed through my head. It had been too dark for me to make out many details. It had walked for sure – it left human footprints. But what person could survive in that water? Lie in wait for unfortunate victims? Maybe the killer wasn't a normal human.

My stomach twisted. I wasn't supposed to be thinking about any of this. I was here to make nice, get friends, and prove to my mom I could be normal. None of this was normal.

Why be normal when you can be a hero instead?

A smile curved over my lips. If no one wanted to believe me – fine. I would figure it out by myself, in secret. Once I solved the mystery and exposed the killer, I would be a town hero. The victims' families would be eternally grateful to me for revealing the truth. They would praise me in the newspaper for my bravery and brains. Little kids would stop me in the street to thank me for keeping them safe. My mom would have no choice but to welcome me back with open arms.

This was no longer a test – it was a game.

And I was going to win.

FOUR

I spent all of my free time in the library, researching old newspapers and any possible creatures that could be killing people.

Tredecim had always been a typical, small town. A place people seemed to flee to start over. No one locked their doors. No one stole. No kids ever even ran away from home. People gossiped about nothing.

Dr. Davis had been the town's forensic pathologist ever since he moved here with his wife. Business had apparently been so slow that he became the science teacher on the side while his wife ran the thrift shop. He had never reported anything strange in his findings, which made him my first suspect. He could easily lie on the autopsy reports if he was the one writing them. But to prove it, I would have to catch him in the act

53

and figure out how on Earth he was able to wait underwater for his victims.

Meanwhile, on the off-chance that the killer was some sort of cryptid, I scoured the internet for lake creatures with a tendency to kill humans. The search wasn't promising. There was no shortage of cryptids who had destroyed boats or harassed humans, but they were either of the Nessie variety or something that sounded made-up by a drunk guy.

The legends mostly spun from huge lakes – lakes three times the size of what Tredecim had. Even if there was a Nessie here, there was no way she could physically fit, let alone wrap her fingers around a throat or leave human footprints in the mud.

I left the library each day more and more frustrated. Meanwhile, Jack still fought Henry's rumors that he was the one killing people. Finding a second body hours after telling a murderous ghost story hadn't helped matters. Of course, after sobering up and being interviewed by his dad, he wasn't found guilty of anything other than being a stupid teenager. The girl had been drunk and probably slipped and fallen trying to make her way back home. The whole town showed up to the funeral, and Henry gave Jack dirty looks the entire time.

The closest thing I had to an ally was Annie, who still insisted something had dragged her down. It was too risky to pry for more details – young kids couldn't keep secrets – and I couldn't risk my dad or Marie knowing about my investigation.

In scholarly terms, I was dead in the water. There was nothing for me to do except give the lake a wide berth and stare out my window at night, watching for any other strange creatures to surface.

Time ticked by like dripping tar. The air got colder. We traded our after-school ice cream stops for hot apple cider, and people started making plans for Thanksgiving. Cyan's parents were apparently the best cooks on this side of town, so they invited us and Jack's family to eat with them. The boys just had to survive a few more days of school before their fall break.

I was sitting at my usual spot in the library, trying to concentrate over the sound of a table of high schoolers whining over calculus. The girls were hopelessly lost, and their confusion was starting to grate on my nerves.

"That's not how you're supposed to do that," I commented. The girls jumped in surprise, and I bit my tongue. I probably shouldn't have said anything – I was a stranger to them, and now they probably thought I was a stuck-up, smarter-than-them stranger.

"Well, duh, we have no clue what we're doing!" one of the girls said, tendrils of blonde hair falling out of her messy bun. The other girl grabbed my wrist like I was a safety rope.

"Are you smart? Please tell me you're smart. Can you show us how to do this?" She lifted her math workbook to my face as if holding it directly to my eyeballs would make it make more sense.

Relieved I hadn't offended them, I gently pushed the workbook back down to reading level, and they made room for me at the table. Ten minutes later, you would've thought I saved their souls with how grateful they were.

"My name is Kate, and that's Cailin. Your name is Reece, right? You're just staying here for a few months?"

"That's me," I said. Kate grabbed Cailin's arm, grinning.

"That means she'll be here for the dance! You *have* to come! We're going dress shopping in a few weeks!" Cailin said. "You should totally come with us!" I smiled. This was shockingly similar to an interaction I might've had with my old friends – plans to drive to a mall and sip overpriced coffees while shopping for overpriced dresses. Any offered friendship made me look better in the eyes of my mother.

"Sure," I said.

"Great!"

We exchanged phone numbers before they hurried off to class with the others. *My therapist would be proud of that interaction*, I thought. But that wasn't the first reason I was happy. Going to the thrift shop would be an excellent excuse to spy on Dr. Davis' wife.

...

Thanksgiving Day, I carried over Marie's contribution of cheesy potato casserole and shoved some other dishes aside to make room for it on the kitchen table. As I did so, someone grabbed my arm. A woman with delicate wrinkles framing her sharp blue eyes smiled down at me, her fingers cold on my arm.

"I just wanted to thank you for being such a good friend to our little Cyan," she said, her eyes watery. I could only assume the woman was Cyan's mother. I nodded, wondering what on Earth she had to thank me for. If anything, I should be thanking her for Cyan being my friend. And saving my little sister's life. Was she worried about Cyan not having that many friends? Being bullied by Henry?

"Um . . . no problem," I said. As soon as she let go of my arm, I slipped down the hallway and found Cyan's room.

It looked like a stereotypical teenage boy's room – cluttered and a little smelly. I could hear a shower going behind another door in the corner. The bed was shoved up against the wall, making room for a huge desk littered with papers and art supplies. A frame hung right by the door, displaying a piece of paper.

Adoption Certificate. Jack Cyan Hartzfield.

I guess that wasn't his mother after all, I thought. *Why hadn't he ever mentioned being adopted?* He looked surprisingly similar to his adoptive folks with his pale skin and dark hair. But his name confused me. I had assumed his parents were hippies, naming their son Cyan of all things, but it was apparently his middle name. What were the odds that his best friend would have the same first name?

The walls were painted the same color as the sea and plastered with drawings. They ranged from oil pastels of the lake to cartoons. I plopped down on his bed and found myself flipping through a stray sketchpad. I paused on a stunning drawing of a mermaid. Her long black hair swirled in the water as she laughed, bubbles trailing from her mouth.

The bathroom door opened, Cyan rubbing a towel over his head.

"Reece! I didn't hear you come in." His eyes went wide as he saw me holding his book.

I held up the drawing. "I didn't know you liked to draw. This is beautiful."

He flushed and quickly grabbed it out of my hands, closing it and shoving it under his bed. "I don't like to show off my stuff," he muttered. "I'm not that good yet."

I scoffed, motioning to his walls. "You're a heck of a lot better than me. I can only draw stick figures."

He laughed, attempting to finger-comb his wet curls out of his eyes. "Well, ready to stuff your face?"

I stood up to follow him, but paused as his laptop caught my eye. He paled even more as I walked over to it. I clenched my fingers as he attempted to shut it.

"You're a dirty liar," I grit through my teeth.

"Reece, let me explain –"

"You *did* believe me when I said something weird was going on!"

He rolled his eyes and shut his bedroom door, yanking the laptop out of my hands. "Would you be quiet?" he hissed.

I did not want to be quiet. I wanted to yell and scream at him for lying to me – pretending like he didn't believe me. Was he trying to take the glory for himself?

I was the one who lied. I was the one who had to be a hero. Not him.

"You were looking up death records in Tredecim!" I accused.

He sighed. "Okay, fine. I was doing my own research. I wanted to see if you were right."

"And?"

He ran his fingers through his hair. "You were right. And I saw the bruises on Annie's neck, too," he admitted.

My heart thudded. I poked my finger at his chest, unable to contain my satisfaction despite my fury that he was encroaching on my territory. "I told you! I've been researching every day at the library, but haven't found anything. I've even been watching the lake at night."

His face grew paler the more I talked. "Reece, listen to me, I know you're invested in this now, but please let me handle this. This could be super dangerous. I don't want you getting hurt."

I crossed my arms, the anger settling into my bones. "I'm sorry, but whoever or whatever is doing this went after my little sister! This is most certainly my business!" Whether or not Annie was my little sister was irrelevant. I would be damned if someone else figured this out before I did. This was *my* mystery. My game.

"You don't live here," Cyan said coolly.

"So?"

He sighed. "Look, if it's who I think it is, I want you far away from this. You'll only get hurt."

I blinked, wondering if Cyan's top pick was different from mine. "Who do you think it is?"

Cyan sighed. For a moment, I thought I saw tears welling in his eyes.

"I . . . I don't know. It - it's stupid. There's no way."

I stood solid in front of the door. He wasn't leaving this room until he fessed up. "*Who?*"

"Jack," he whispered, his voice barely audible.

I furrowed my brow. *Interesting.* "That doesn't make sense. He would've had to start doing it at six years old."

"Maybe it's more than one person, and Jack is still learning!" Cyan shot back, his tears suddenly gone. "His dad is a cop. Jack never gets in trouble for anything - not even drinking that night. And he's the one who keeps finding the bodies. It's weird - is all I'm saying. Look - until I know for sure what's going on - I don't want you looking into this anymore. And not a *word* to Jack, understand me?"

I clenched my jaw. I hated people telling me what to do. He grabbed me by the shoulders, his eyes boring into mine. "Reece, promise me. If Jack is dangerous and he suspects we're onto him, we might be next. Annie's already been attacked once."

"I promise," I lied.

He sagged in relief and fixed his hair. "Good. Let's go eat."

I followed him out of his bedroom and into the kitchen. When Jack and his father walked in, Cyan embraced his friend just like he did every day, laughing and joking like his usual self.

I realized two things that day. One: the murders didn't necessarily have to be all from the same person.

Two: Cyan was an excellent liar.

FIVE

After Thanksgiving, the days seemed to pass even more slowly. We transitioned from apple cider to sneaking hot chocolate into the library and drinking it behind the stacks.

My therapist said she was communicating my progress back to my mother, but I had yet to hear her voice since I had arrived. Any probing questions about how long I would be stuck here were met with shrugs and conversation changes.

No matter. I could be patient. I would be whisked away as soon as I figured out who the killer was.

"So, how's homeschool life going?" Cyan asked.

I shrugged. I had resorted to doing most of it at night while watching the lake through my bedroom window. It seemed like whatever creature I had seen crawling out of its depths knew I was doing it – I hadn't seen it since.

"Fine," I said. "How's the world's tiniest public school?"

Both boys groaned. "Awful as always," Cyan said. "But at least we have the winter dance coming up, so that'll be fun."

"Oh yeah, I forgot about that. I was helping some girls with their math homework before Thanksgiving Break, and they invited me to go dress shopping with them," I said.

Jack chortled. "You? Dress shopping? I guess you do wear your private school girl skirt every day, but I just can't picture you in a sparkly one-piece."

I elbowed him, and hid my grin when he nearly spilled his hot chocolate on the carpet.

"Are you going to ask anyone out?" Cyan asked.

"I just figured I would go with you guys," I said.

Jack puffed out his chest. "Nah – I've already got a date. I finally got Clarisse to agree, and I can't wait to see what little sparkly number she wears. Guess you two are stuck going together."

Cyan and I made eye contact across the aisle. Every time I looked at him, I couldn't help but be impressed with his ability to treat Jack like a normal friend despite his suspicions. But I could see it taking a toll on him. The shadows under his eyes grew darker with each passing day. He constantly looked exhausted, and somehow even skinnier than before.

Maybe if Jack tried to murder his date, the mystery could be solved, and Cyan would go back to normal. But I still had a hunch Dr. Davis had something to do with it. My guess made a lot more sense, and if he was a chaperone, I could easily keep an eye on him.

"Sure, we can go together, Cyan," I said. Something flashed behind his eyes, as if he could read my intentions and was dreading another conversation about his worst fears. But he forced his usual smile and wiggled his eyebrows.

"Then it's a date."

. . .

Kate texted me and told me when to meet them at the thrift shop that night. I arrived at six o'clock sharp, slightly apprehensive about wearing people's dirty old clothes and navigating an old minefield. Past me was an expert at talking fashion and being a girl's girl. Current me was going to require a lot of fake squeals and flattery. I needed to pull this off if I wanted these girls to keep being friends with me.

Kate and Cailin smiled and jumped up and down when they saw me. Mrs. Davis grinned when she saw us enter and pointed us towards the back. Several racks of used dresses sparkled along the back wall, and the girls wasted no time in grabbing whatever caught their attention.

As we perused, I tried my best to watch Mrs. Davis out of the corner of my eye, but all she did was sit at the checkout counter with a dog-eared book. She didn't look like a serial killer, but then again, who did? Maybe Dr. Davis was covering for his wife, maybe he wasn't. But unless she tried to murder anyone in the store, I doubted I would glean any new information.

I eventually ended up in a dusty dressing room with my own pile, only to feel my chest tighten as I looked at myself in the first pick: a lime green shimmery thing that would definitely not keep me warm in the colder weather. The fabric felt like it had been worn to this dance by at least three previous generations before me. I swallowed back my revulsion and stepped outside to model it to my new friends.

"Girl, you look like the Princess and the Frog," Cailin said. I couldn't help but agree. I yanked the dress off and put on a black one that looked slightly less used. I came out to *oohs*.

"You look like Morticia Adams," Kate said. "Definitely that one. You look badass."

I helped the other two pick out their gowns, and we paid at the counter. My old friends from Atlanta would've swooned if I told them I got a fancy dress for $5.70.

"So, do either of you have dates?" I asked. They shook their heads.

"Tredecim kids rarely date-date. Being around the same ten people since birth doesn't exactly provide a lot of opportunities," Kate said.

"A lot of people will probably ask you to dance, though," Cailin said. "You're new. And you're pretty."

"Well, I'm technically going with Cyan," I said. "Just as friends, though." They wrinkled their noses and giggled a little.

"He's an . . . interesting guy . . . isn't he?" Cailin said, exchanging a look with her friend. If the comment was a jab, I ignored it. Being with Cyan was a perfect cover. Past me would've been thrilled with the possibility of being bathed in attention. Current me just felt like it would be an inconvenience. The dance would be a perfect time and place to kill someone. Most of the town would be distracted. No one would second-guess another drunk student having an accident.

Cyan would spend his time watching Jack, and I would spend my time watching Dr. Davis.

Very, very closely.

. . .

We actually got to ride in a car for the special occasion. My father and Marie fawned over me in my dress and took about a thousand pictures before letting me leave. Keeping a smile on my face and not flipping off the camera was perhaps my best performance yet. I entered Cyan's house to see his own parents giving him the same treatment mine had given me – except Cyan was being much less gracious about having his photo taken.

His mom cried out when she saw me standing by the door and pulled me over, forcing us to pose for pictures that made us seem much more lovey-dovey than the occasion was supposed to be.

"Okay, Nichole, that's enough," Cyan said, gently lowering her phone. "We're gonna be late."

"Okay, okay, get in the van then," she said. Cyan ran outside, but before I could follow him, she grabbed me by the elbow. When I stopped, she turned me around, holding my hands so hard I thought the bones would snap.

"Thank you," she whispered. "I never thought he would end up going to the dance with a girl – with anyone. Thank you."

I raised my eyebrow. "Um . . . you're welcome?" *Why does this woman insist on thanking me for hanging out with her kid? I wondered.*

She finally let me go, and we rode to the school in awkward silence as she lectured us on not drinking any spiked punch or staying out too late.

The small gym had been transformed. The tables had all been shoved into the corner. Streamers and string lights hung from the ceiling. A disco ball that looked like something Annie would make in art class glittered in the center of the room. A table full of snacks and drinks sat across from the DJ, who was the principal with his laptop hooked up to a portable speaker. The other teachers milled around the room, looking very uncomfortable at seeing their students in less than school-appropriate outfits.

There was already a crowd dancing in front of the speaker. Cyan grinned, wiggling his eyebrows at me. "Please tell me you know how to dance the Cupid Shuffle."

I definitely did, but feigned shyness, shaking my head. He pulled me onto the dance floor anyway, where I might've *accidentally* stomped on his toes a few times as punishment. Meanwhile, I spied Jack dancing with his date on the other side. She was pretty, and her tight dress definitely didn't leave much to the imagination. Jack grinned like an idiot.

After the song ended, Cyan let me escape to the snack table, where I munched on a bag of chips as I watched the others dance. Cyan was definitely the most entertaining one. His movements were fluid and bold, and by the end of the next song, I wasn't the only one staring at him. *He really is beautiful,* I thought. *Why do so many kids give him the cold shoulder? If there had been a guy this hot at my last school, everyone would have been all over him.*

A slow song came on, and most of the students joined me at the snack table. Cyan looked around and offered his hand to a blonde girl. She giggled and ignored him. Cyan shrugged and offered it to another guy, who flushed and awkwardly turned away. Pouting, Cyan walked over to me, extending his hand with a cheesy grin. I rolled my eyes and took it.

He dragged me onto the dance floor and instead of shuffling back and forth, actually made me waltz.

"What are you doing?" I demanded.

"Just do the opposite of what my feet are doing – it's not that hard."

I groaned. This time, stepping on his toes really was an accident.

"You having fun yet?" he asked.

I shrugged. I had kept one eye trained on Dr. Davis the whole time, but he had barely looked up from his phone. "Not as much fun as you seem to be having."

Cyan's eyes suddenly strayed from my face. His grip on my hand tightened. I turned around to see Jack and his date standing by the double doors. They both slipped outside into the cold. I turned back only for Cyan to break formation and walk towards the exit.

"Where are you going?" I whispered, following him.

"Nowhere," he snapped, trying to shoo me away. I ignored him and stayed on his heels as he poked his head outside the door. Jack had disappeared, but his date was still walking across the parking lot and into the woods.

"You're going to follow her, aren't you?" I asked.

Cyan glared at me. "You are not coming with me."

"You're not my mom."

His eye twitched. "Fine. But be quiet."

We stalked after her. I winced every time my heels crackled on the crunchy leaves. Cyan paused at one point to take his shoes off completely, rolling up his dress pants past his ankles. The girl stumbled ahead of us, making enough noise on her own to drown out our footsteps. Her sparkly pink dress snagged on branches and thorns, leaving sequins in her wake.

She eventually emerged in a clearing where the lake bubbled up from the black mud. She hesitated slightly at the edge before stepping into the water, her dress pooling out behind her like a veil. She walked in to her knees. Something rippled around her. It looked like a scene from a horror movie. My stomach clenched, ready to fight whatever monster was about to attack.

Before it could reveal itself, Cyan dove out from the shadows, shouting. "Clarisse, get out of the water!" He jumped in after her, grabbing her around the waist and yanking her backwards. She let him, motionless, face frozen in a flat line.

"It was about to show itself! You scared it off!" I protested, stepping out of the trees.

Cyan snapped his fingers in Clarisse's face. "Clarisse, can you hear me? Why did you come out here?"

Her eyes remained vacant, her head lolling to the side. Cyan swore under his breath and hitched her up over his shoulder. "We need to take her back home, come on."

I yanked up my dress as Cyan jogged through the woods. He was surprisingly fast for such a skinny boy. We emerged in one of the nicer neighborhoods. Cyan pounded on one of the doors, and a very startled man answered it.

"Good evening, sir. Someone spiked the punch at the dance – think she had a little too much. Figured I would bring her home." Cyan practically threw Clarisse at the man before dragging me back down the street. I yanked him to a stop by the lake's edge, panting.

"Where are we going now?" I demanded. "Can we talk about what the hell just happened?"

"We still need to find Jack!" he insisted. "Where the hell could he have gone?"

"Cyan, wait," I panted. "Jack wasn't there. He left her. She walked to that pond by herself." And *Dr. Davis was nowhere to be seen*, I thought. *There goes that idea.* "Something made her walk into that water – and unless Jack has superpowers, then I really don't think he has much to do with this."

Cyan ran his fingers through his hair, breaths shallow. "We just need to find him, okay?" he repeated, his eyes glassy. "I don't have a good feeling about this. Something's wrong, something's wrong." Cyan's nails were digging into his scalp so hard I thought he might draw blood.

Why the fuck is everyone in this town so batshit crazy?

"Cyan, calm down. You need to think about this logically," I said.

"She could've died!" Cyan screamed, his voice so shrill and piercing I winced away. I grabbed his shoulder and pulled him further from the houses, hoping no one had heard him.

"Would you be quiet!" I hissed.

"She could've died," Cyan whimpered, pacing the street. "She could've died and it would be my fault – it would be my fault –"

"Who could've died?"

We snapped our heads around to see Jack standing by the tree line, his body shrouded in shadows. His hair was disheveled and decorated with leaves and twigs. He blinked slowly, like he had just woken up, swaying slightly as he walked towards us.

Cyan stared at his friend like he had seen a ghost. For a moment, I thought he would cry in relief that his friend hadn't been murdered by whatever was rippling in the water, but then his face turned cold.

"What the hell did you do with her?" Cyan demanded, stalking up to his friend and pushing him backwards. Jack stumbled, hitting the ground with wide eyes.

"What are you talking about?" Jack slurred.

"Clarisse! What did you do to her?"

Jack rose to his feet, eyebrows furrowed. "I didn't do anything to her. We were just dancing when she said she had to go home all of a sudden."

"Then why are you out in the middle of the woods at night?"

Jack blinked slowly before shrugging. Cyan's mouth twisted, his hands balling into fists.

"Why are you lying to me?" Cyan whispered.

"Dude, I don't know what you're talking about," Jack protested.

"Yes, you do!" Cyan shoved his friend again, edging him closer to the water. Jack caught himself on the edge of the dock, mouth falling open. He finally looked awake. His mouth opened and closed like a fish.

"What are you talking about, man? Are you . . ." His mouth twisted into a snarl. "You believe the rumors, don't you? You think *I've* been killing people? Dude, you're insane! Why would I do that? How could you believe them?" he shouted.

"Why do you keep getting caught with the bodies? Why do you keep lying to me?" Cyan shoved him again, sending him further back onto the dock. Jack pushed him back, hands balled up into fists.

I watched the display with a furrowed brow. I still doubted it was Jack. He was a foolish teenage boy; he didn't have the resolve to kill a person. But why was Cyan so convinced Jack was lying about something? What did he know that I didn't?

"I need to know. What. Are. You?" Cyan growled, his eyes gleaming in the moonlight.

Jack put his hands up. "What, you think I'm a mermaid or something? That I'm luring people to their deaths?"

Cyan's face drained of color. *Interesting*, I thought.

I hadn't even considered mermaids. They were usually depicted as beautiful maidens, crashing pirate ships with their melodious voices. But they didn't live in lakes. They didn't phase back and forth – except for YA fantasy novels.

My mind flashed back to the drawing of the mermaid from Cyan's room. The drawing he had quickly hid away. Never once had he mentioned doing research on lake cryptids. He had always thought the murderer was a person. Or a group of people.

And he hadn't been afraid to dive into the lake to save Annie.

Damn, Cyan was a good liar. Looks like my second guess was right, after all.

Cyan grabbed Jack, shoving him one last time. With a gasp, Jack flailed backwards. At the last possible second, he reached out and snagged Cyan's tie, dragging him into the black water.

I strolled into the shallows as they struggled in the water. I held my breath as they surfaced, Jack pinned underneath Cyan. Cyan shoved his hand over Jack's mouth before he could scream.

Cyan's irises glowed a startling neon blue. Fins of the same hue grew from his arms, tapering down at his wrists. His waist ended in a bright blue tail, which curled and twisted like a snake. He looked up at me, glowing eyes wide.

"Don't scream," he whispered. His voice still sounded human, as if nothing about his body had changed.

I hadn't been about to scream, but was unsure of what to do as Jack trembled underneath him. Cyan obviously wasn't the killer - he had saved Annie's life and been totally oblivious to the thirteen deaths until I had pointed it out. Was there another mermaid in town?

"Hey, what's going on over there?"

I spun around to see a figure walking down the dark street, flashlight swinging haphazardly. A swear word escaped from Jack's covered mouth. Cyan scrambled out of the water, pulling Jack after him. We all booked it back into the woods, narrowly avoiding the flashlight beam.

We didn't stop running until we were safe in Cyan's room with the door slammed shut. I gasped for breath as Cyan panted against the door. Jack pointed a shaking finger at him, face drained of color.

"You-you're a mermaid," he whispered.

Cyan hung his head. "Merman."

Jack blinked. "What?"

Cyan lifted his head, rolling his eyes. "I'm a mer*man*."

Jack blinked one more time, slowly, before clenching his hands into fists. "I really don't give a shit about your pronouns right now. What the *hell* is going on?"

"You thought Jack was one of you?" I asked. Cyan hesitated before nodding. Jack swiveled to stare at me.

"You *knew* about this?" he demanded.

I explained everything that had happened over the past two months, including my investigation and finding out Cyan had been doing research on his own as well. Jack paced the entire time, shaking his head and occasionally muttering under his breath, dripping lake water on the carpet as he went.

He turned to stare at Cyan after I was done. "So let me get this straight: the real lake monster this whole time has been *you*. And you thought *I* was the one killing people?"

Cyan held up his hands. "I'm not a monster – I'm harmless – I promise," he pleaded.

"You saved Annie," I pointed out.

He nodded. "Look, guys, I'm sorry I lied, but I had to. But I've never hurt anyone. I would never hurt anyone. The legends about merpeople drowning humans aren't true! At least . . . I thought they weren't," Cyan muttered. He moved away from the door and sat on the bed.

"What did you see when you saved Annie?" I asked.

He sighed. "Another merman. But he had a silver tail and red eyes. Annie wasn't lying. He was pulling her under." That's why he didn't want me involved, I thought. He already knew what the creature was. He didn't want me to get hurt. Why is he so nice?

"And you thought it was me?" Jack exploded. "We've been best friends for years! Wouldn't you have noticed if I were a homicidal fish by now?"

Cyan looked down at the floor. "I'm sorry," he whispered. "I was just . . . so nervous. You kept getting caught with the bodies, and I didn't know what to think."

"Well, who is the other mermaid then? Is it another person who lives here?" Jack asked.

"I couldn't see his face well enough to tell. As soon as he saw me, he ran away. Well, swam away."

"How is he getting people to go in the lake?" I asked.

Cyan shrugged. "No idea."

"How do you not know? You're one of those things!" Jack protested.

"Guys . . . listen. Before my parents died . . . they told me some things about our species. But they never once told me that we kill people. They . . . they told me we were the last ones. And when they died . . . I assumed I was it. I had no idea there were any more of us. I'm just as shocked as you are."

Heavy silence draped the room. My mind flashed back to the beautiful mermaid drawing.

"That drawing I saw . . . that's your mom, isn't it?" I asked. Cyan flushed before nodding.

"Either my parents didn't know there were other merpeople, or they lied to me. I don't know what to believe now. And the one thing they did warn me about . . . I haven't seen the other one using. So, I have no clue how he's getting people into the water," he said.

"What did they warn you about?" Jack asked.

Cyan flushed. "You're going to think I'm crazy."

Jack scoffed. "This entire thing is crazy. Try me."

Cyan rolled his eyes and winced like what he was about to say would burn him. "I can control water."

Is he joking?

Cyan being a mythical creature was strange enough, but I was sure some amount of science could explain his body morphing and his glowing blue eyes. But superpowers? That sounded ridiculous – like a kid playing pretend.

Jack reached up to Cyan's desk and came down with a bottle of water. "Prove it."

Cyan crossed his arms. "I use the word *control* very loosely. It's more like water is . . . affected by my emotions. My parents made me swear to never let my emotions get out of control. The results could be . . . bad. I never use my powers. I never will," he added.

That sounds convenient, I thought. *But why would he lie?*

"What about singing?" Jack asked. "Isn't that a mermaid thing?"

"We haven't heard any singing," Cyan said.

"But *can* you sing?" I asked.

He shrugged. "I mean, yeah, but I just think that's because I can sing. There are plenty of humans who can sing, too."

"You're also attractive," I pointed out. Jack raised his eyebrow at me. "It's an objectively true statement," I said. "Mermaids are traditionally pretty."

"Unless the murderer is pretty enough to lure people to their deaths, I don't think my looks apply here," Cyan said. We all froze as adult voices suddenly sounded by the front door. Keys jangled.

"You guys gotta go!" Cyan hissed, shoving us towards his window. "Meet me by the cemetery in the morning." He all but shoved us back out of his window.

Jack and I stood in the trees for a moment. I still felt like I was trying to catch my breath. Jack blinked slowly, his face still twisted.

"You knew that Cyan thought I was killing people, and you didn't say anything? Didn't think to loop me in so I could defend myself?" he asked, his voice unnaturally calm.

Dang it, he's mad at me now, too, I thought. *How can I calm him down?*

"I'm sorry." I hated the way the words tasted on my tongue, but I needed to keep both boys as friends. At this point, we were all involved in my mystery, and I needed them as a resource. "I never thought it was you, but Cyan was acting weird and didn't want me to be involved anyway."

Jack deflated. "I can't believe any of this," he mumbled. "All of this is insane. Someone's been killing people on purpose, Cyan is a freaking mermaid, and . . ." He swallowed. "And I keep finding the bodies," he whispered. "Why the fuck do I keep finding the bodies?"

"I don't know. But we'll figure it out. Try to get some rest. We'll talk in the morning."

We trudged back to our respective houses, the sky rippling with thunder and lightning. I could almost taste the static in the air. I muttered an excuse about being tired to my dad and Marie before escaping into my room and stripping off my muddy dress. I tried my best to scrub off the night's events before collapsing in bed.

I got sent to live in a town with literal lake monsters who are killing people, I thought. *At least I'm living next door to the one who doesn't want to kill me.*

I stayed up, staring out my window. The killer being a mythical creature put a wrench in my plans of being the town hero. Cyan obviously had the upper hand in finding him. But I could help. I had to help. I had to *win.*

Around three in the morning, a now familiar figure oozed out of the darkness. It paused on the dock, turning to stare at me. I offered a tentative wave. It saluted me back before diving off the edge, disappearing.

No one swims here, my ass.

SIX

The next morning, Jack was waiting for me outside. His hands were shoved in his coat pockets, his jaw tense. I wordlessly followed him into the woods. As we walked, he swore as he swiped dewy spiderwebs out of his face and trampled sticks under his feet.

We reached the cemetery. Cyan stood in the center, hands clasped behind his back. He turned, his hair still dripping wet, bags under his eyes. He looked like a soggy raccoon.

Jack crossed his arms, looking his friend up and down. "What, you didn't hear us coming? You don't have like . . . super hearing or whatever to go along with your water abilities?"

Cyan scowled. "No."

We gathered in a circle and sat on the pine straw. Cyan yawned, rubbing his eyes. He looked ready to take a nap on the forest floor.

"Were you seriously planning on keeping this secret your entire life? You thought you could just live your life as a sea monster and no one would notice? What about when you got a girlfriend or boyfriend or whatever? Would you keep it a secret from them, too?" Jack demanded, wasting no time in resuming our conversation from last night.

Cyan deflated. "My parents swore me to secrecy. They told me terrible things would happen if I ever told another human. Believe me, I wanted to tell you so bad, but I just couldn't. You didn't exactly react well," Cyan muttered.

"Well, yeah, no shit. You had a tail and glowing eyes out of nowhere!" Jack pointed out. "Anyone would've panicked."

Cyan frowned and looked at me. "Reece didn't panic."

Jack's mouth snapped shut. For the first time, Cyan's words seemed to sink through his thick skull.

"You know . . . you know I'd never like . . . do anything bad to you, right?" Jack asked.

"No, I don't," Cyan said, his voice thick. "I'm not allowed to trust humans. When I was adopted, I was terrified of anyone finding out. So yeah, I kept it a secret from you, from any future partners, my parents, *everyone*, because that was my real parents' only dying wish. So again, *I'm sorry.*"

Jack sat in stunned silence as Cyan stared at the ground, blinking back tears.

"Hey man, it's okay. *I'm* sorry. I don't know why your parents were so scared of humans, but you can trust me. You can trust *us*, right, Reece?"

I nodded. Cyan wiped his eyes and finally tore his gaze from the forest floor.

"Okay, let's focus," I said. "We're still not much closer to figuring out who the murderer is or how he's killing people. Or why."

"I've been searching the lake for him every night, but no matter where I look, I can't find him. It's like he knows I'm coming," Cyan said.

"Are you sure you haven't seen this guy using your magical water abilities?" Jack asked.

"No. All the victims we've seen seem like they're in a trance of some kind," Cyan said.

"And it seems like they're trying to frame Jack for it," I said. Jack paled.

"Jack, do you remember feeling anything weird at the bonfire? You did spout that prophecy about people drowning that night," Cyan pointed out.

Jack curled in on himself. "I mean, I was pretty drunk. I don't remember much."

"What about last night? You said Clarisse left to go home. Why were you out wandering?" Cyan asked.

"I don't remember," he whispered.

"The killer is messing with people's heads somehow. He's making them walk to their deaths. No one else noticed the bruises until

I said anything. And no one even realized that thirteen people were drowning each year. It's like he's blinded the entire town," I said.

"Except you," Cyan said. "Why hasn't he messed with your head?"

I was pretty sure I knew the answer, but I wasn't about to divulge my secret. I shrugged. "Because I'm from out of town? He might not have the same hold over me as someone who's been here for years."

"What could I have possibly done to merit being framed for murder?" Jack asked, ignoring my comment.

"I thought it was Dr. Davis," I said. "The age fits better, and he would be able to cover it up because he's the town's forensic pathologist. But I didn't see him last night. And I don't know why he would frame Jack."

Cyan tilted his head. "I don't understand why the killer has been doing this for ten years and just now decided to frame Jack."

Maybe he's bored, I thought.

"Are you sure singing isn't what's going on here? Maybe you don't know it works because you've never tried it?" Jack asked.

Cyan furrowed his brow. "What are you suggesting?"

"Just like . . . sing and see if you can make me do anything weird. Just to see. If it works, we'll at least know how the killer is messing with us, and we can like . . . go buy earplugs or something," Jack said.

"You want me to . . . make you do something weird by singing?" Cyan repeated.

"For science!"

Cyan's eye twitched. "Fine, but don't get mad at me if it works." He stood up and started pacing, muttering under his breath.

"Well?" Jack snapped.

"I'm trying to think of a song to sing!" Cyan snapped. "Don't rush me." He paced in several circles before stilling again. He closed his eyes. "*I'll keep you my dirty little secret.*"

Cyan's voice was soft and melodious, like listening to a lullaby. It flowed over the pine straw, echoing off the trees. Cyan narrowed his eyes at Jack and flexed his fingers like he was trying to beckon him closer. Meanwhile, Jack sat on the ground, looking no different. Cyan slowly trailed off. Jack shrugged.

"Did you feel anything?" I asked. He shook his head.

"I mean, your voice is beautiful, man, but I didn't have any sudden urges to go drown myself. Also, really? *That* song?"

Cyan rolled his eyes. "I told you it wouldn't work!"

"We need to narrow down a list of suspects. We need to look at everyone in town and figure out who would have a grudge against Jack," I said. The boys nodded. Jack tentatively wrapped his arm around Cyan's shoulder.

"Are we good?" Jack asked. Cyan hesitated before nodding.

"No more secrets, promise?" Jack asked, looking at me and Cyan in turn.

We nodded. I had no way of knowing if I was the only one lying.

. . .

The next morning, Jack clamored through my window about five minutes before the usual time.

"You're early," I commented, running a brush through my hair.

"Cyan's not here yet, is he?" Jack asked. I shook my head. He let out a deep breath and scratched the back of his head.

"I'm worried," he whispered.

"You would be stupid not to be worried about a psycho killer," I said.

"Not about that! I'm worried about Cyan. There are a lot of things about him you don't know, and now that he's told us what he really is . . ." he trailed off, and I cut my hair-brushing session short.

"You think he's the killer?" I asked, intrigued.

"No! But . . . do you really think he can control water? Or that his emotions control water, whatever he was saying?"

"It sounds ridiculous, but I don't know why he would make that up," I admitted. "Does that worry you?"

Jack swallowed and looked out the window. "Look, there's a reason Cyan has no friends. When he first got here . . . he wasn't doing well. In retrospect – it makes sense because his parents had died and he thought he was the last merman on Earth or whatever – but it was *bad*, Reece."

"Get to the point," I said.

Jack took another deep breath. "He was violent," he whispered. "Like . . . I could hear him screaming and breaking stuff from my house. He had meltdowns at school. Everyone was scared of him."

I tried to imagine skinny Cyan as a little kid being anything more than meek and goofy, and couldn't picture it. Jack seemed like more of the type to be a rowdy kid. Cyan acting like a maniac didn't fit the bill. He was too mellow. Besides, Bryon and Henry definitely didn't act like they were afraid of him.

"No one wanted to be near him. He hurt other kids. He hurt *himself*. Parents were ready to chase him out of town with pitchforks. He was . . . he was *scary*," Jack continued.

"So why did you end up being friends with him?" I asked. Jack looked around again.

"I don't know. I felt bad for him. I knew what it was like to lose a parent. He was calmer around me. But I was still nervous around him until his parents put him on mood stabilizers," he said.

I blinked. "Those are some pretty strong drugs. They usually give mood stabilizers to bipolar people," I said. "Is he?"

"No idea," Jack said. "But they worked. They're still working."

I frowned. "Still?"

Jack nodded. "Like . . . double the dose of a normal person his age."

Aren't doctors not supposed to give kids that young that type of medication? I wondered. His parents are doctors – maybe they pulled some strings.

I shrugged. "I mean . . . if it's working, then why are you worried about it?" I asked.

"This isn't a human on human drugs. This is a *merman* on human drugs. A merman who can apparently move water if he gets too emotional! There's been times where he's . . . relapsed, I guess? Been more depressed or emotional than normal. If he's really got these powers that are influenced by his mood . . . not being on his meds could be . . ."

Disastrous, I thought.

"Do his ups and downs have anything to do with the scars on his arms? Or the eating habits you told me to never comment on?" I asked.

"He's always been anorexic, but he won't admit it," Jack said. "It just gets worse if you try to say anything about it. He freaks out if you bring it up. Same with the cutting. I haven't noticed any new scars for a while, but still."

"He probably does those things to help him feel in control of himself," I said, mostly to myself. I had spent way too much time googling various psychological mishaps before my move here. I knew all the motives for why people starved or hurt themselves. At the end of the day, it was all about control. *Why didn't Cyan feel like he was in control?*

Jack dragged his fingers down his face. "This is fucking insane."

At least if he's hurting himself, it means he's making an effort to tamper his emotions, I thought. *He doesn't want to lose it and hurt people.*

For a brief moment, I wondered what the real Cyan would be like – one without meds and on a full stomach – and if he would be as terrifying as Jack was imagining.

"I've always tried to be sensitive about it. He really is my best friend. And I know he's been through a lot. But no one else but us knows that he's a mythical creature hopped up on an ungodly amount of antipsychotic meds. He's been acting weird and I'm just worried that . . ."

"He's the killer?" I finished. Jack shook his head.

"No. I *really* don't think it's him. But if the killer really can mess with minds . . . Cyan's mind would be a very dangerous one to mess with. What if he . . ." Jack swallowed. "I dunno. Switches sides?"

Then we're fucked, I thought.

"I think if the killer wanted to recruit Cyan, he would've done it by now," I said slowly. "Cyan is obnoxiously nice. He saved my sister. He's been pulling all-nighters hunting for the killer. Besides, he's too young to have been doing this for the past ten years. You're being paranoid."

What if the killer was making *Jack paranoid?*

Jack shifted on his feet. "You sure?" he finally asked. "You don't think he's dangerous? That he *could* be dangerous?"

I knew more about nature versus nurture than the average person. I had stayed up many nights wondering if my accident could be fixed with enough therapy or the right medication.

Maybe Cyan's biological parents really had thought they were the last ones on the planet, or maybe they thought they could save Cyan from their drowning tendencies by nurturing it out of him.

But I knew from experience that no amount of nurture could rewire a brain wired for violence or apathy. If Cyan was born to be a killing machine, the antipsychotics might keep the beast at bay – but for how long? What if he forgot to take his meds one day? What if the killer got his claws into Cyan's head? Would we be his next victims?

Something rapped against the window, and we both jumped and turned to see Cyan grinning at us through the glass. Jack forced a smile on his face like the conversation we had just had never happened, and opened the window.

No more secrets, my ass, I thought.

SEVEN

"We need a plan," Cyan said. "The merman has two more people to kill before the end of the year. We have to stop him."

"And we already know his next target: Clarisse," Jack said.

"How do we know he'll go for her again? She probably doesn't remember what happened. It's not like he needs to attack her again because she knows too much," I said.

"Either way, we should probably go try to talk to her. See if she remembers anything," Cyan said. "And Jack should be the one to do it – you were her date after all."

"Yeah, I'll go over to her place and see what's up," Jack nodded.

"FYI, we did tell her dad that she drank too much spiked punch as we were dropping her off," Cyan said.

"Great," he muttered.

"I want to go back to the place where that other girl died Halloween night," I said. "Maybe I can find something the killer left behind."

"Okay, Nancy Drew," Jack said.

"And I guess I'll keep searching the lake," Cyan said.

"In daylight? Isn't that risky?" Jack asked.

"Nah. I'll go in through one of the streams in the woods. No one will see me," he said.

"Alright, want to meet by the docks in an hour? If we don't show up, we've probably been murdered," I said, the joke coming out humorless. Jack paled but nodded.

I huddled into my jacket and told my parents I was going on a walk as I slipped outside. I strode down the now-familiar path to the cemetery and scanned the woods around me. Everything seemed normal. The trees were quickly becoming bare of their leaves. Birds flew overhead, heading south. It definitely didn't seem like a forest where people were murdered.

I reached the cemetery and headed over to the small lake where the high school girl had drowned. It looked more like a mud puddle to the naked eye, but when I tossed a stone, it splashed and sank, bubbles trailing to the surface. I guess drowning was easier than it looked.

For a moment, I wondered if every little puddle and stream connected to the lake – as if it had underground fingers straining out, reaching out for every life it could grasp. Maybe the lake itself was the monster – some eldritch horror that had become sentient and wanted blood and thought it would be funny to frame Jack.

The closest thing to an eldritch horror here is you, psycho.

I walked around the pond, straining to see if there happened to be a weapon or a strand of hair stuck in the mud around it, but nothing caught my eye. Whoever had cleaned up the girl had done a good job of removing any signs of struggle. If there had even been a struggle.

I sat down on a nearby stone, wondering if I should revisit Dr. Davis as a suspect. He definitely hadn't been at the scene of the attempted murder – but maybe his wife had been lurking in the bushes somewhere unseen. If she were a mythical monster, it would be easy to convince her husband to fib on the autopsy reports. It was the perfect cover. Where had she been last night?

I sighed and stood up to leave, but another figure emerging from the woods made me hesitate. I stayed hidden in the shadows as I watched Henry shuffle through the grass, shoulders hunched and head bent down. He glanced around to see if anyone was watching him before heading towards a specific headstone. Once there, he sighed deeply and sank to his knees, allowing me to read the inscription.

Brian.

Oh my gosh, he was just a friend, get over it, I thought.

That's not a positive thought, my therapist's voice chided.

I rolled my eyes but stayed put, not wanting to interrupt the bully's tender moment. How often did he come here to hang out with his late best friend?

Several minutes ticked by. I was debating trying to sneak through the trees when my phone buzzed.

I winced as Henry jerked his head around, making eye contact through the foliage. I froze, as if he couldn't see me if I didn't move. I waited for him to call me out for spying on him, but he said nothing. Something about the look in his eyes felt off.

It was just like that day at the funeral, where everyone around me had felt like a mannequin. At the time, I had just assumed it was my messed-up brain trying to understand grief, but now I knew I hadn't been misperceiving anything.

Henry's eyes were as glassy as the funeral goers. His chest rose up and down in mechanical motions, as if he were considering each breath he took. Too much time passed between blinks. His head lolled slightly to the side. If real Henry had caught someone spying on him, I'm sure his reaction would've involved a lot of screaming and swearing, but no words escaped his mouth. He was no longer in his body. Something else was holding the reins.

And that something wasn't trying too hard to hide it.

My heart thudded so loud in my chest I was surprised not-Henry could hear it. Why was the creature being so obvious? Was this some sort of display of power? A demonstration? Was I the next victim?

As I was debating whether or not to run, Henry turned and started walking in the opposite direction into the woods, his steps robotic.

Do I follow him? That's definitely how people die in horror movies.

I followed him. As soon as not-Henry noticed I was trailing, he sped up, weaving in and out of the trees with surprising grace.

I broke into a full-fledged run, swiping tree branches and vines out of my way until I landed in a small clearing. Henry was nowhere to be seen. I gasped for breath, turning around and scanning the trees. Was this some kind of trick? What was the point of leading me here?

I rolled my eyes and trudged back towards civilization, only to see Henry walking down the street, heading towards where Cyan and Jack were standing by the dock.

I probably should've been more wary of the six-foot-tall, bulky teenager, but I didn't know how to feel fear anymore. I stepped in front of him, cutting off his path. I scanned his eyes and found they were back to normal. He scowled at me.

"What do you want?" he asked.

"What were you just doing in the woods?" I asked.

"None of your damn business!" he snapped, shoving past me. I frowned as Jack and Cyan jogged up to me.

"What was that about?" Jack asked. I explained what I had just witnessed.

"Red-Eyes knows we're onto him," Cyan said.

"Red-Eyes?" Jack echoed.

"Sorry, the killer. I've been calling him Red-Eyes in my head," Cyan said.

He's toying with us, I thought. I didn't like that. I wanted to be the one controlling the pieces.

Why had Red-Eyes picked Henry as a puppet? We already knew he could manipulate people. Was this a warning? A distraction?

"What happened with Clarisse?" I asked.

"Doesn't remember a thing. And her dad was not very happy to see me. Thought I was the one who spiked the punch," Jack muttered.

"Looks like we're back at square one," Cyan said.

"I think it might be Mrs. Davis," I blurted. I quickly explained why, though my reasons didn't make Jack or Cyan look any less skeptical.

"She's such a sweet lady, though," Jack said, almost sounding sad. "It would suck if it were her." Cyan elbowed him.

"I feel like we can't count anyone out at this point," he said. "Why not? Let's do some spying."

"Some what?" We spun around to see Marie and Annie behind us.

"Some . . . . shopping," Cyan said quickly. "You know, for Christmas presents and such."

Fuck, I thought. *Christmas is coming up.*

Somewhere in the back of my mind, I had noticed Christmas decorations going up around the house, but the reason hadn't really dawned on me until just then. I had no idea how to navigate such a festive holiday around my dad's family. Was I supposed to get them Christmas presents? How on Earth would I know what they wanted?

"Oh, that sounds fun!" Marie said. "Reece, have you thought about what you want from Santa?"

I resisted the urge to roll my eyes. "Oh, um . . . not really," I mumbled. The things I really wanted, catching the murderer and winning back my mom's good graces weren't exactly something you could wrap up in a neat little bow and put under the Christmas tree.

Marie ruffled my hair. "Well, brainstorm and get back to me. It's only a few weeks away!" She turned back to the house with Annie, and I let out a breath.

"I guess that gives us a good excuse to go spy then," Jack said.

. . .

Mrs. Davis had decorated the store with what looked like some donated garland about fifty years old and lights with half the bulbs missing. She smiled from her chair by the front counter.

"Welcome in. Can I help you find anything?" she asked.

"Just doing a little Christmas shopping," Jack said. We headed to the section of the store where shelves were crammed with knick-knacks of every kind.

We spent the next several minutes meandering around the store, watching her out of the corners of our eyes, but it was apparent we wouldn't get much information watching her read a book at the checkout counter.

I gave up and started looking at the items on the dusty shelves, trying to think of what my family would like. Within five minutes, I found an old commemorative cup from the Kentucky Derby and a ceramic unicorn with a broken left hoof.

This is impossible, I thought. But I would look like an asshole if I didn't get them anything.

Meanwhile, Cyan hummed as he investigated. He held up a different unicorn, one that wasn't chipped. "Wouldn't Annie like something like this?" he asked.

"Probably," I said. "Got any clue what my dad or Marie would like?"

"I know Marie really likes gardening. Your dad is more of a reader," Jack said. *How does he know that, and I don't?* I wondered.

By the time we were done, I had found an old crime novel for dad and a book of gardening tips and tricks for Marie. Mrs. Davis checked us out, looking sweet and innocent as always, and we walked back to Cyan's house. As usual, his mom greeted me with untampered enthusiasm even though I was literally just there to use their wrapping paper.

Turns out I sucked at that, too. After my first attempt, Cyan slowly shook his head, tore apart my work, and proceeded to wrap my gifts for me.

. . .

The next few weeks went by in a blur. We all waited for Red-Eyes to strike, but he seemed to be just as busy with the holiday season as everyone else. Christmas morning with a small child was a fiasco. Annie woke the whole house up at the crack of dawn, screaming that Santa had come. I watched through bleary eyes as she tore through her presents, littering the living room with trash. She screamed in delight at every toy, even my crappy one from the thrift shop.

After she was done and occupied, I awkwardly gave my dad and Marie their gifts. They oohed and fawned like I had given them winning lottery tickets, and I pretended to soak up their praise.

"We got you a little something too," Marie said. "But it's outside." Confused, I followed them to the porch. Lying against the siding was a brand-new bike, complete with sparkly red handles, a padded seat, and a bell. My dad pranced beside it.

"We know you have a bike already – but the poor thing looks like it's about to come apart at the hinges. Besides, it's small enough, and Annie has been wanting to learn. She can use the old one." I ran my fingers over the handles. *Damn, this thing must've been expensive,* I thought. *They probably had to go to a real store to get this. How did they know my favorite color was red?*

"Thank you," I said, surprised at how grateful I actually sounded.

Marie ruffled my hair. "You're welcome, Sweetie."

We finished the day with an elaborate Christmas dinner with Jack and Cyan's families. The table looked like it would collapse from the weight of all the food on it – a deep-fried turkey, sweet potato casserole, stuffing, something called sausage balls, and about a dozen other dishes. We loaded up our plates, and I sat on the couch with Jack and Cyan while the adults sat at the dining room table.

"So, what did you get, Reece?" Jack asked.

"A new bike," I said. The boys whistled.

"Fancy," Cyan said.

"I got a new phone!" Jack bragged, waving it in front of our faces. "Oh, that reminds me, I gotta call Clarisse and wish her a Merry Christmas."

"Oh, you two are still talking?" Cyan asked.

Jack winked. "Here and there." He got up to pace as the phone rang.

"What did you get, Cyan?" I asked.

"Just some more drawing stuff, nothing fancy," he said, picking at the food on his plate. Jack returned to the couch, frowning.

"That was fast," Cyan commented.

"She didn't pick up. I'll try again later."

We ended the night by cramming in the living room to watch Christmas movies. The adults nursed glasses of champagne as Annie played with her thrift-store unicorn in front of the TV.

It was radically different from the Christmases with my mom and Brad. Their Christmases were white, pristine, nice dinners with napkins that were ironed. I think I liked this version better.

I slipped into a food coma after the others left, only to be woken up way too early by my phone ringing incessantly. I fumbled to accept the call, dropping it several times before I got a good grasp on it.

"Hell – *ahhhh* – o?" I muttered through a yawn.

"Clarisse is dead."

I woke up immediately. "Say that again?"

"Clarisse is dead. Jack tried visiting her last night and found her in the water by her house," Cyan said.

My knuckles went white. *Damnit.*

"That means . . ." I started.

"That means Red-Eyes has the rest of the week to kill one more person," Cyan finished.

. . .

Instead of a funeral, they held a "celebration of life" at the Baptist church. It was the same as the funeral. Everyone sat with vacant faces, staring at the ceiling or ground as if they were stuck in a boring lecture. Even Clarisse's parents sat stone-faced.

Except this time, Cyan and Jack noticed the mannequins. Cyan stared at the crowd, his eyes big and eyebrows bent. Jack was a slight shade of green and covered his mouth like he was trying not to throw up.

"Are you telling me this is what all the funerals have been like?" Cyan whispered. "Does everyone always look this . . . blank?"

I nodded, and Cyan sank back into the pew as if he was trying to crawl out the other side.

"No one is even crying," Jack mumbled through his hand.

"Why aren't you crying? Didn't you like her?" Cyan asked. Jack blinked as if he had just realized this himself.

"Are you not sad?" I asked.

Jack shrugged. "I mean . . . I'm more disturbed than sad. Holy shit, do you think Red-Eyes is messing with everyone here?"

I flashed back to Henry's vacant expression in the woods.

"He has to be," I said. "Why else would no one care that thirteen people are drowning every year? Red-Eyes is doing something to their heads to make them not care."

I looked across the aisle and found Henry staring directly at me. I furrowed my brow and nudged Cyan.

"What's up with your buddy there?" I asked.

Cyan glanced over and frowned. "Has he been staring at us like that this whole time?"

Jack leaned forward and swallowed. "Why does he look . . . awake?"

We all turned. Henry was, in fact, missing the same glossy mannequin look everyone else had. It was the opposite of the day I had seen him in the woods.

"We need to talk to him," I said.

We ran for the parking lot as soon as the funeral was over, but not quickly enough to track down Henry in the departing crowd.

"Am I the only one who has a bad feeling about this?" Cyan asked, rubbing his arms.

"Red-Eyes can't be controlling him. If he was – he wouldn't be alert," I said.

"So why did Red-Eyes let him wake up?" Jack asked.

"We need to find him," Cyan said, bolting through the crowd. I turned in the opposite direction, scanning. It shouldn't be that hard to find someone who was six feet tall, but it seemed like he had vanished into thin air.

If I were upset and didn't want to be found, where would I go hide? I wondered.

I ran around to the back of the church. Jack had apparently had the same idea as me, and Henry was not happy about being found. He had Jack backed into a corner, who cowered on the ground, his hands clutching his stomach.

"Henry!" I said sharply. He turned around. His eyes were red and swollen, his fists shaking. Cyan appeared behind me, gasping for breath. His eyes widened at the scene in front of him.

"I know," Henry said, his voice cracked. "I *know* you freaks have something to do with his death. I don't know how you're doing it, but it's you three. You're the only ones who were *there* at the funeral." He turned back to Jack. "And I'm going to make sure you never hurt anyone ever again." Henry's fist came crashing down. I wondered how long it would take for someone of Henry's size to beat Jack to death.

My throat suddenly went dry, as if someone had sucked all of the moisture out of the air. Henry's body flew sideways, crashing into the wall but not falling to the ground. A cloud of water held him up.

Cyan slowly came out from my shadow. His eyes were shining the color he was named for. Henry's jaw dropped as Cyan stalked up to him, his lips peeled back from his teeth in a snarl that looked more otherworldly than his tail.

Damn, I guess he wasn't lying after all, I thought.

Jack scrambled up from the ground and all but hid behind me, gasping for breath and shaking.

"Holy . . . shit," he panted. "He does have powers."

It only took a few more seconds for Cyan to realize what he had done. The fury in his eyes fizzled out, and the water broke, sending Henry and a puddle to the dirt. Henry hit the ground with a thud but stayed there, frozen.

Cyan took one step back, then another, digging at his hair. "Oh my god, what did I do?" he whimpered.

Interesting, I thought. *Protecting his best friend was a good enough reason to lose his control.*

"What the hell is going on?" Henry whispered. Cyan turned to look at me, his eyes wide.

"Might as well tell him now," Jack muttered.

About an hour later, Henry was still staring at the ground, hands clasped on his lap, clothes sopping wet. We had gathered around him like we were having an intervention. The explanation came more easily this time. Guess practice makes perfect.

"So . . . yeah," Cyan finished lamely. "That's . . . that's what's going on."

Henry shook his head. "I don't want to believe you. Why . . . why am I just now *realizing* all of this?"

It was a good question. Red-Eyes had had the entire town in a stupor for a decade – too numb to care or notice that thirteen people were drowning, or cry at their funerals. But Red-Eyes had decided to tear the fog from Henry's eyes. Why? I doubted he would let everyone wake up – that would create a panic. I had the feeling he wanted to remain hidden. He had just created another piece for his game. What he was planning on doing with his piece – I had no idea.

"Do you remember anything that might be useful?" I asked. Henry thought for a moment and shook his head.

"I just remember . . . I remember waking up this morning for the funeral and feeling like . . . like everything was fresh. It felt like Brian all over again. And when I got there and saw the looks on everyone's faces . . . it just clicked. I realized that something had been wrong for a while, and you three were the only ones who knew it, too. And Jack showing up around all the bodies . . . something in me just snapped. Sorry, I tried to beat you, man," he said.

"It's understandable," Jack said. "Whoever Red-Eyes is has some sort of vendetta against me. They were probably hoping you would beat me to death."

"If they hate you that much, why don't they just drown you themself?" Cyan muttered.

"They've got one more person before the year is up," I said. "Maybe they're saving you for last." I was met with horrified stares and realized that was probably not a wise thing to say out loud. "Just kidding," I amended.

"What do we do now?" Henry asked.

"You don't have to do anything," Cyan said. "This is our fight."

"You're not leaving me in the dark now," Henry argued. "This . . . Red-eyed whatever killed my best friend!" For a split second, Henry looked like he might burst into tears, but the look vanished as soon as it had appeared.

An idea struck me like lightning.

"Jack, does your dad have a way to look up fingerprints at the police station?" I asked.

"Yes," Henry answered, turning red. "I mean - um - when he booked me after Brian's funeral, he fingerprinted me - so I assume there's some sort of system. Why?"

I knew they weren't going to like the idea, but we were running out of time.

"We have to go look at the body," I whispered.

EIGHT

"I beg your *finest* pardon?" Jack squeaked.

"Clarisse's body wasn't at the celebration – that means it's probably still at the morgue," I said. "If we can get in there, I can check for fingerprints on her throat. We can run them through the database at the police station and see if they match anyone."

"You want to break into a morgue and mess with a dead body?" Cyan echoed.

"You really are a crazy bitch," Henry whispered.

"Do any of you have any other ideas on how we can catch Red-Eyes? We're running out of time," I pointed out. Silence descended like a fog. The boys exchanged glances.

"How would we even get into the morgue?" Jack asked. "I'm positive it's locked. Plus – it's inside the Urgent Care – which is also definitely locked. And probably has cameras. There is no way in hell I'm going to get caught desecrating a corpse."

"Cyan, is there any way you can get a key from your folks?" I asked. All eyes turned to the merman. He fidgeted with his fingers for what felt like an eternity before sighing.

"Fine."

. . .

We lingered in the alleyway beside the morgue, our breath staining the air around us. Christmas lights twinkled on the storefronts that weren't abandoned. Christmas Day seemed like it was eons ago. A person had died since then, and one more would in the next five days unless we could figure out who Red-Eyes was.

"Where the fuck is Cyan?" Henry demanded, pacing. "I still think you sons-of-bitches are crazy for trusting him. If he can control water, what makes you think he can't change the color his eyes glow? What if this is just a scheme to kill all three of –" He stopped abruptly as Cyan appeared from the fog. He jogged up to us, skin shiny with sweat despite the cold.

"Did you get the key?" Jack asked. Cyan nodded, holding up a carabiner. "Good, let's get this over with."

We sidled up to the door. Cyan inserted the key into the lock, and we slipped into the lobby. Only when we were out of view of the front windows did we dare to turn our flashlights on.

"Did you happen to steal a map too?" Jack asked.

"How hard can it be to find a morgue? Let's split up and –"

"No!" Henry said sharply. "Splitting up is how you die in horror movies. We're sticking together."

We tiptoed down the narrow hallway, scanning the doors and rooms as we walked past. Jack sandwiched himself between me and Henry, shaking like a leaf.

"This is a bad idea," he moaned. "This place is probably haunted as hell."

"You willingly went to a Halloween party in a graveyard," I said. "You are fine."

"Found it," Cyan whispered. We gathered around the door. Cold seemed to leak from behind the steel sign labeled MORGUE.

Jack swallowed and nudged me forward. "This was your idea – you go in first."

I tried the handle, but it didn't budge. I frowned and looked for a keyhole.

"There's no keyhole," I said.

"Fuuuuck –" Henry said. "There's a keypad."

I wasn't sure how we missed it before, but right next to the door was a number pad with a blank screen.

"I don't suppose you also stole the code from your parents?" I asked. Cyan groaned and shook his head.

"Oh well, we tried, let's get out of here," Jack said, attempting to pull me away from the door. I brushed him off and crossed my arms.

"Well, any guesses?" I asked.

"We can't guess!" Jack protested. "What if an alarm goes off? Or it's like your phone and it just locks us out for longer?"

Cyan stepped forward and bit his lip before typing in 1111. The screen blinked red and cleared itself.

"Maybe it's one-two-three-four," Henry said, rolling his eyes.

"Well, do you have any other guesses?" Cyan snapped.

"Maybe try one of your parents' birthdays?" I suggested. Cyan tapped in the numbers before shaking his head.

"Maybe it's a number that's significant to Dr. Davis? I mean, he is the one who's probably in here the most," Henry said.

"How are we supposed to know Dr. Davis' favorite numbers?" Jack asked.

"Let me try one more," Cyan said. He typed in another set. After a moment's hesitation, the screen flashed green, and the door popped open with a click. Our jaws dropped.

"How did you do that?" Jack demanded.

Cyan smiled the first genuine smile I had seen in a while. "It was my birthday."

The inside of the room loomed like a cave. The atmosphere went heavy once more. I realized that the others were not going to set toe in that room unless I went in first. I stepped inside, feeling along the wall for a light switch. I flicked it on, wincing at the sudden brightness.

It was a pretty average-looking room. A stainless-steel table stood in the center. A wall of cabinets stood on the back wall. The left wall housed the fridges.

Cyan slowly stepped in after me, taking a deep breath. "Alright, let's find her," he said.

Henry and Jack watched from the doorway as we started opening the fridge doors. They were all empty except for the one on the very end.

"Found her," Cyan said hoarsely. I helped him pull out the door to reveal Clarisse's pale body. Her eyes were still open, her skin milky – almost translucent in places. She looked like a statue carved from marble, and smelled like the cat I had dissected last year in biology.

"Gross," Cyan whispered.

He helped me lift her gurney onto the table. I thought her body would roll around, but it was as stiff as a board.

"I'm going to be sick," Jack moaned, leaning his head against the doorframe. Cyan didn't look much better.

"So am I," he groaned. I resisted the urge to roll my eyes and started unpacking my duffel bag.

"Don't you dare throw up in here. I've got this."

I had taken a forensics class at my private school in my freshman year. The teacher had been a retired crime scene detective and taught us way more than he probably should have about how his old trade worked. Who knew that knowledge would come in handy so soon?

I pulled out my special flashlight and shone it over Clarisse's neck. With my free hand, I took pictures of the prints shining in the orange light. I gently tilted her neck, photographing the other side. I stripped away the gown covering the rest of her, quickly checking before covering her back up.

"Find anything?" Henry asked.

"Yeah. I got pictures of the prints on her neck. I'm checking her hands now." I carefully lifted her stiff wrist. Her nail polish had been scrubbed off, but nothing lay under her nails. She hadn't even struggled.

"I don't see any other prints on her body. Help me lift her back in, and we can get out of here," I said. Cyan reluctantly walked back over as the hallway lights suddenly burst to life.

We all spun to see Dr. Davis standing behind Henry and Jack – eyes wide – his face ashen.

"Dr. Davis! Funny seeing you here," Jack offered weakly.

"Run," Cyan whispered. We dropped the body. Henry pushed Dr. Davis to the ground. I stopped dead in my tracks at the sight of another looming figure in the hallway. Mr. Smith stared at me over the top of his gun.

"You four are in big trouble," he growled.

. . .

Jack huffed against the cell wall as I watched Cyan pace. Henry picked at his nails. They had taken everything upon our arrival at the police station. I could hear Dr. Davis and Mr. Smith whispering in the office down the hallway. My body couldn't think of anything else to do but tap my fingers on the concrete floor. At least they had taken the cuffs off before sticking us in here.

"Dude, pacing isn't going to help us get out of here," Jack pointed out. Cyan shot him the finger before pulling at his hair.

"We are so fucked," he whispered. I winced to think what my father and Marie would think after they received a call stating their daughter had broken into a morgue to mess with a corpse. Maybe if I were lucky, they would punish me before either one of them got a chance to tell my mom. I could hear her whispering to Brad behind closed doors about how much of a *freak* her daughter was. I was definitely failing her test now.

We all looked up as Dr. Davis and Mr. Smith walked in front of our cell. Mr. Smith held out my phone with pictures of the prints.

"You four want to explain yourselves?" he asked. We all exchanged glances.

"Trust me – you won't believe us," Henry laughed.

"Better tell us something before we call your parents," Mr. Smith threatened. I sighed and stood up.

"Someone is killing people in this town – on purpose. I wanted to check the victim for fingerprints," I said. A vein on Mr. Smith's forehead twitched.

"This again? I already told you that you were imagining things!" Dr. Davis hissed.

"So, you were going to break into my office to access my fingerprint database after you were done at the morgue?" Mr. Smith asked, eyes narrowing. *Maybe I explained too much,* I thought.

"Please, Dad, I know we sound crazy, but you have to believe us," Jack pleaded.

"Tredecim is a normal town!" Dr. Davis insisted.

Mr. Smith crossed his arms. "And pray tell, *who* do you think this mystery killer is?"

We lapsed back into silence. There was no way to answer that without outing Cyan. And I doubted blaming a mythical creature would make us look any saner.

"What if we're right?" Cyan asked, each word deliberate. "Because if we are, then someone else is going to die in the next few days. And if you won't believe us, their blood is on your head."

I had never heard Cyan sound so serious before. The temperature in the air seemed to drop several more degrees. Even so, Mr. Smith waved him off.

"I don't want to hear it. Dr. Davis, are you pressing charges?" he asked.

Dr. Davis drummed his fingers on his arms, looking down at the floor. "No. I don't want news of this to spread. I just want their word that they won't ever do something this stupid again."

"Well, I'm not letting you all off that easily. You're going to stay in that cell until your parents come and get you," Mr. Smith said.

Cyan suddenly slammed his hands against the bars. "NO." We all took a step back as his body seemed to warp. He bared his teeth like an animal, and I could swear they had elongated. His eyes turned to glowing blue orbs. He stretched out his hand like it was full of claws, and let out a sound that sent goosebumps down my spine. My mouth went dry.

The stream of water twisting up Cyan's arms was barely noticeable. Cyan must've pulled them straight from the humidity or the sweat from our pores. Henry and Jack winced, covering their ears as the bars groaned, slowly stretching apart. To someone not paying attention, it looked like a skinny teenage boy had just mustered the strength to bend solid metal. Jack looked like he had seen this nightmare a dozen times before.

Mr. Smith and Dr. Davis stared at the display with confusion. With a final screech, Cyan tore the bars of the cell apart. Jack, braver than I was, rushed up and grabbed Cyan from behind as Mr. Smith whipped out his gun. Cyan immediately lunged against his grasp, spitting and growling.

"Cyan, calm down!" Jack shouted, forcing him to turn around and look back at him. He squeezed his friend's face between his hands. I could see his expression reflected in Cyan's glowing eyes.

"You're going to hurt people," Jack whispered. Cyan blinked, and the water around his arms dripped onto the concrete, sinking into the stone. Cyan's eyes flickered back to their normal state, and he stared down at his hands.

In an instant, the monster that had just torn apart metal bars in a fit of rage vanished, leaving the skinny teenager on way too many antipsychotics than he should be. His knees wobbled, and he fell to the ground. Jack caught him on the way down. I wondered how much it drained him to use his powers – whether accidental or not.

"I-I'm so sorry," Cyan whispered.

The police station suddenly plunged into darkness. A cold laugh echoed down the hallway.

"*You should've listened to them.*" The voice was sing-song, half pity and half satisfaction. It crackled over the intercom embedded in the ceiling.

Mr. Smith turned on a flashlight, his face skeletal in the beam. No one breathed. All the color had drained from Dr. Davis' face. Mr. Smith finally turned the gun away from Cyan, scanning up and down the hallway.

"Who's there?" he shouted.

The voice giggled and began to sing. "*Come little children, I'll take thee away . . .*"

"No, no, no, no, this isn't happening, this is not how I die!" Henry shrieked, covering his ears.

Mr. Smith finally looked like the gravity of the situation had dawned on him.

"Stay here," he growled, stalking down the hallway towards the front office. We quickly slipped through the gap in the bars. Dr. Davis didn't bother to get up as we stepped over him.

"Follow sweet children, I'll show thee the way."

"What the fuck are we going to do now?" Jack whispered. Henry wordlessly pointed down the other end of the hallway. I looked to where he was pointing and saw a puddle of red seeping out from underneath a closet door. Jack walked back into me.

"Um, Dad?" Jack squeaked. Mr. Smith turned around, and his eyes landed on where Henry was pointing.

"Weep not, poor children, for life is this way. Murdering beauty and passions."

Everyone else stayed frozen as he walked towards the closet door and opened it. The stench of blood hit me like a brick. The singing stopped.

Cailin hung from a noose, her skin bloated and purple. Stale blood congealed on her lips. The number thirteen had been carved into her forehead.

"Congratulations," the voice gloated. *"You found my thirteenth victim."*

Mr. Smith swore and tore back to the front office.

"You won't find me there."

He returned, dejected, but holding an old-fashioned walkie-talkie.

"Framing your son for the murders was fun at first, but I think it's time for you to wake up. You've been blind for far too long."

"Oh my god," Dr. Davis whimpered, clutching his chest. Behind me, Jack dry heaved before sinking to the floor.

"The real killer is someone in this room," the voice continued. *"Every week, I will provide a hint. The more the suspects reveal, the more merciful I will be. You have until the end of the week to make your first guess."*

"What the hell is going on?" Dr. Davis whimpered. "I don't understand any of this." Mr. Smith turned back towards Cailin's body, stooped down, and picked up a picture lying on the ground beneath her feet. He turned it around, and Henry made a noise like a dying animal.

It was a picture of him. It had been taken at a distance, but it was obvious he was at the cemetery, visiting his late friend. Across his face in red Sharpie was a single word:

Desperate

"I'm a suspect?" Henry whispered.

"Do you believe us now?" Cyan demanded. Mr. Smith dropped the picture and turned his gaze back to Cyan. His grip on his gun tightened. Cyan noticed and took a cautionary step back.

"Perhaps you would like to explain how you broke through those bars," Mr. Smith said carefully. Cyan swallowed, shrinking into himself.

We all knew that Cyan hadn't just pulled those bars apart with brute strength, but had the adults noticed the extra boost his water powers had given him? Jack stepped between his father and his friend.

"Forget about that!" Dr. Davis wheezed. "How could I not have noticed?" He buried his head in his hands, body shaking. I couldn't deny that a big part of me was overjoyed watching the teacher hyperventilate on the floor. *Bet he wishes he listened to me now.*

Mr. Smith stared at us as if he had a thousand questions, but his lips remained sealed.

"What do we do now?" Jack whispered.

"According to that note, the killer is apparently one of us," I said, turning to look at the group. "And Henry is our first suspect."

"It's not me!" he croaked.

"I don't understand the whole secret thing," Jack said. "The killer said the more we reveal, the more mercy he shows? What the hell does that mean?"

"I don't have any secrets!" Henry protested.

"We will not be playing this little game!" Mr. Smith snapped suddenly. "Like Reece said, this killer is only doing this to mess with our heads. I will not have any of you going around, playing detective. Especially you, Jack."

Jack shrank back. Mr. Smith turned to glare at each of us in turn. "Here's what's going to happen. You are going to go home to your families. You will speak of nothing that happened here tonight. And you will let *me* handle this. You are children. This is not your job. I don't want any of you getting hurt, do you understand me?" he growled. We all nodded, even though I knew I was definitely lying.

"Good. Now, go home."

My head spun as I trudged back to my house and tried in vain to sleep. Every time I closed my eyes, I saw the photo of Henry. *Desperate*, I thought. *What was Henry desperate for? What on Earth would make him desperate enough to murder people?*

Why does the killer want us to catch him?

NINE

I was awoken the next morning by Cyan tapping at my window, his hair still dripping with lake water. Jack stood behind him, looking like he hadn't slept a wink.

"So . . . I'm assuming you were lying about not investigating, too?" Cyan asked. I nodded.

"Cool. Us too." Moments later, we sat in a circle on my bedroom carpet. Questions started flying.

"Dude, I know you were mad last night, but you used your powers! What if my dad or Mr. Smith noticed?" Jack accused. Cyan's eye twitched, and the cup of water on my nightstand tilted dangerously.

"Don't you dare spill water on my carpet," I warned. Cyan took a deep breath.

"I don't know what came over me yesterday, okay? I was just really upset and . . ." he swallowed. "And it didn't even matter. Thirteen people still died. I couldn't stop him. Besides, they *didn't* notice. Your dad just asked how I tore the bars apart – he didn't see the water."

"Mr. Smith probably thinks you're the killer," I said. Cyan paled.

"But he's not!" Jack protested. "We can all agree that none of us here is the murderer, right?" *Cyan can't be*, I thought. And Jack definitely can't be. So that leaves us with Henry, Mr. Smith, or Dr. Davis.

Henry was an asshole for sure, but I had a hard time believing he would kill Brian. Besides, Red-Eyes had created this game to play with us. He wouldn't give away the answer so easily.

That left Mr. Smith or Dr. Davis. I had been suspicious of Dr. Davis all along, but if he was the killer, he was an excellent liar. And unless Jack was adopted, too, Mr. Smith couldn't be a merman.

"I think I'm beginning to side with Reece. It's probably Dr. Davis," Cyan said. "I don't see how it could be anyone else."

"Why do you think Henry's picture said *desperate?*" Jack asked. "What does he have to be desperate about?"

"I mean . . . he's really into football. Maybe he's desperate to succeed?" Cyan mused.

"What does being good at football have to do with him being a murder suspect?" Jack asked. "Red-Eyes made it seem like we all have dirty little secrets, and that the more we spill, the better off we are."

"Maybe he's just trying to divide us. Cause chaos, so we don't trust each other, so it's easier to pick us off. I bet Henry's dead by the end of the week if he's not the killer," Cyan said.

"Here's an idea, why don't we talk to him?" I asked.

We arrived at his doorstep half an hour later. He opened the door a crack and squinted at us as if we were roaches.

"Go away."

"We need to talk about your picture," Jack said.

"Look – I don't know what kind of game this psycho is playing, but I'm not a part of it! You heard the Sheriff. We need to let the adults handle it and stay out of their way. As far as we know, the whole thing is made up, and none of us are the killer!" Henry said.

"Red-Eyes said bad things would happen if you weren't honest," I said.

"Fuck off." The door slammed shut in our faces.

"We tried," Cyan sighed.

We walked off the front porch and ambled through the neighborhood.

"So, Henry's basically dead, right? I mean, that's what we're all thinking?" Jack said.

"Probably," Cyan said. "Our best bet is just to follow Henry around all week until Red-Eyes decides to kick his bucket."

"Something tells me Henry won't like us spying on him," I said.

"Then we'll do it in shifts," Jack said. "So, it's less suspicious. Watch him from a distance. Keep the others posted. And when Red-Eyes arrives, boom, we catch him, and this whole nightmare is over."

"I'll take night shifts," Cyan said through a yawn.

I ended up with the morning shift since I woke up early anyway. The most I could do was follow Henry to school and lurk in the library like I always did until the day was over. I would inconspicuously follow him home, where I would trade places with Jack until the night, when Cyan would take over.

Spying was even more boring than it sounded. All week, nothing happened. I couldn't help but feel that Red-Eyes was lurking in the background somewhere, laughing at our futile efforts.

Something no one had addressed yet was what we would do with Red-Eyes once we found him. It wasn't like we could get him arrested. Even if he did end up in a jail cell, he could just use his freaky mind powers to break back out. Something more drastic needed to be done. And I had the feeling I would be the only one up to the task.

After one of my shifts, I found myself wandering through downtown until I arrived at a munitions store. The small building reeked of metal. The old geezer manning the front counter stared down his glasses at me as I walked in.

"You have to be eighteen to buy a gun, Sweetheart," he said. His voice sounded like he gargled rocks every night after brushing his teeth.

I turned on a fake smile and nodded. "I know, sir. My dad just asked me to pick up something he wanted. Is that okay?" I held up a piece of paper with a few items written on it in my dad's handwriting.

"I guess so," the man grumbled. I handed him the list, thankful for a split second this was a town where everyone knew each other and didn't care much about gun laws. He shuffled off to gather the materials. I paid with a pile of emergency cash I had saved up before my exodus here and hurried out of the store with my new goods before the old man could change his mind. Hopefully, he wouldn't go to my father and ask about his new pistol.

I locked my bedroom door behind me and carefully slid the weapon out of its packaging. I had never even held a gun before, let alone shot one, but I had watched a dozen YouTube videos about how to operate and aim the thing. When the time came, I would be ready.

I spent the rest of the night tearing apart an old pair of jeans and stitching them back together to make a holster. Upon examining myself in the mirror, there was no trace of the weapon shoved up underneath my pleated skirt, inches away from my hand.

I grinned in victory as my cell phone vibrated on the bed. I shoved the trash out of the way and frowned when I looked at the text message from Cyan.

It's Henry come to the church its his dad

I slipped out the window and jogged to the prestigious white building in the dark, figuring I would arrive at some grisly scene with Henry's organs splattered across the pews.

It wasn't Henry who was dead. He stood on the stone steps of his father's church as flames soared up into the sky. Through the flames, I could barely make out a bloody corpse slumped against the pulpit. It would be reduced to cinders long before any firemen showed up.

Henry's face was frozen in horror, fingers tearing at his scalp. Cyan made a feeble attempt to lean down and comfort him, but was shoved away.

So, this is what the killer meant, I thought. *He won't kill us. He'll kill those closest to us. We'd followed Henry around for nothing.*

Photos littered the steps, the reflection of the flames glittering against the gloss. Jack walked forward and grabbed a handful.

The pictures showed Henry with Brian. At school, eating ice cream downtown, talking at football games. *Why would the killer put these pictures here?* I wondered. Jack wordlessly turned and showed the pictures to Cyan, who nodded, seeing something I couldn't.

"You were in love with him. That was your secret, wasn't it?" Cyan whispered. Henry drew several shuddering breaths before nodding.

Homophobic Henry was gay. He had been in love with Brian.

TEN

The next morning, Henry was with the boys when they tapped on my bedroom window. They crawled into my room without the normal chatter, staring at me.

"What?" I asked. Jack held up a photo.

"Found this on your front porch," he said. My mouth went dry. It was my yearbook picture from my previous year at private school. The girl in the box looked like a stranger, her hair perfectly curled, her teeth blinding white through her smile. Across her face was a single word written in red Sharpie:

Psycho

"Feel like explaining?" Cyan asked. I swallowed. *No, there's no way,* I thought. *That's too personal. How would Red-Eyes even know about that?*

"You guys know it's not me. I'm the one who noticed the pattern. I've only lived here for a few months. You *know* it's not me!" I protested.

"*We* know," Henry said. "But you better spill. You saw what happened." *Fuck.* I thought back to Annie almost drowning. Would Red-Eyes go after her again, or would he target a different member of my family this time?

I could go Henry's route and keep my mouth shut. It's not like I would particularly miss many people in this godforsaken town. But I was tired of Red-Eyes winning. I wanted a point in my court. Red-Eyes was expecting me to lie.

"Reece, come on. Why would he write *psycho* on your picture?" Jack pressed. I sighed.

"Because it's technically true."

Back in Atlanta, I had signed up for a rock-climbing course at the gym. The instructor had been a gangly teenage boy with pitted acne marks. He had stumbled across the explanation of how the ropes and pullies worked, but assured me the whole system was safe. But halfway up the forty-foot wall, one of the metal buckles on my harness snapped, the sound like a gunshot.

The only thing I remembered clearly was sitting on the floor and feeling the blood between my fingers, wondering why everyone was screaming, wondering why I wasn't screaming. I hated blood, after all. I was a typical squeamish teenage girl who couldn't even stomach a nosebleed. An ambulance came and whisked me to the hospital. My mom and stepdad thought the doctor's diagnosis of a concussion wasn't a big deal.

It wasn't until a month later that they realized the concussion was worse than they thought.

I hadn't broken down in the typical way teenage girls do – with high-pitched screaming or tears. I had broken quietly, not even noticing until my mom told me in no uncertain terms that I was *scaring* her.

"I have a brain injury," I said. I remembered my friends whispering about me when they thought I couldn't hear them. The text messages and invites to hang out dwindling to nothing. Remembering wanting to be bothered, but not being able to care.

"I was in an accident. I hit my head really hard. And I have brain damage. The doctor said there's not really a formal diagnosis, but my amygdala doesn't work the way it used to."

"What does the amygdala do?" Jack asked.

"It helps a person understand and interpret emotions. It's how you feel, have empathy, get upset, that sort of thing."

"And yours is . . . broken? So, what, you don't have any feelings?" Henry asked.

I hesitated a beat. There would be no coming back after this. People treat you differently after you tell them you can't care about them.

"Not really, no." The silence felt like it stretched on for hours.

"I guess that explains your resting bitch face," Jack finally said.

Cyan slapped his arm. "Dude!"

"What, I'm right!" Jack insisted. "You even said the first day we met her that she seemed off!"

I stiffened. So they had noticed something. They were just too polite to bring it up.

"But . . . you care about us?" Cyan asked. "I mean, you're nice. You stood up for me. You can't just have like . . . no feelings whatsoever?"

I shrugged, my mask slipping away. "I really don't care that much about any of you. But I know it's important to act like I do. The only thing I really care about right now is beating Red-Eyes at his own game. And that involves making sure all of you don't die."

Cyan turned away from me, his eyes glistening.

"Jeez, man, that's . . . harsh," Henry said.

"I'm just being honest," I said. "I know I should feel bad that I'm hurting your feelings, but I don't."

"Well, you don't have to worry about lying to us anymore," Cyan muttered, wiping his eyes.

"Why are you even pretending?" Jack asked. "I mean, I get that you want to beat Red-Eyes or whatever, but why were you nice when you first got here?"

"My mom made me come here. She said if I could keep up normal relationships, make some friends, then she would bring me back and treat me like a normal kid. But if I couldn't – then she was going to institutionalize me."

Cyan covered his mouth, his tears gone. "That's horrible. She would just abandon her kid after a brain injury? Is her amygdala broken, too?"

"It was the only threat that worked on me," I admitted.

After the accident, I hadn't cared about faking my emotions. How other people responded to me wasn't my problem. Empathy was a weakness that left you vulnerable to manipulation. My broken amygdala had freed me from that burden.

Threatening to take away my freedom was the only thing that motivated me to wear the mask. My mom had turned being a normal person into a test, and I would be damned if I didn't pass.

I wondered if my mom would feel guilty if I got brutally murdered. Maybe she was a sociopath, too.

But even as the thought passed through my head, I knew that couldn't be true. My accident had brought out all sorts of emotions from her. She was the most mom-like she had ever been in that hospital room, hovering and caring for my every need, wiping away tears of relief. But there was one emotion that was stronger than love: fear. And my mom was terrified of me.

"Is that it?" Henry asked. "No other dirty secrets you're hiding?" I shook my head, hoping I had spilled enough to convince Red-Eyes I was honest. Surely, I would feel *something* if someone in my family died because of me? How broken was my brain exactly? I wasn't sure I wanted to know.

"The hard part is . . . I remember what it feels like to care. To love people. I just can't do it anymore," I said. "If it weren't for my mom threatening me, I wouldn't even be faking it."

Henry suddenly slammed his hands down on the floor. "Oh my god, wait." We all stared at him in silence.

"Want to share with the class?" Jack asked.

Henry pointed at me. "You have brain damage!"

"We've established that," I said.

"Red-Eyes fucks with people by messing with their brains!"

Cyan's eyes went wide. "Ohhh . . . that makes perfect sense. Reece, you're immune to whatever weird mind-powers Red-Eyes has because you have brain damage. It's not because you're new in town or whatever. He can't mess with your emotions because you don't *have* any."

I blinked.

"That's actually badass," Jack said.

"I'm the only one here he can't manipulate," I realized.

"It means you're safe," Henry said. "Safer than us, at least."

It also makes me very similar to the killer, I thought. *Two psychopaths playing a game, trying to outwit each other.*

My mother had told me that confessing my injury would result in disaster. She had told me in no uncertain words that I would be cast out by whoever found out my secret. People don't trust sociopaths, after all.

But that hadn't happened. And my so-called secret was apparently the only thing protecting me from getting brutally murdered by a mythical serial killer.

That wasn't even the best news. I could quit masking, quit pretending like having friends mattered, quit smiling and laughing at appropriate times. I didn't have to pretend anymore.

And *that* made me feel something.

The constant tension of putting on a show vanished from my body. My shoulders stopped hurting. My stomach stopped twisting. Relief had never felt so sweet before.

"Okay. So, we're back to square one," Jack said.

We spent the rest of the morning talking in circles before the boys had to leave for school. Before Cyan slid out the window, he turned to face me.

"Thank you for being honest earlier," he said.

I scoffed. "Wasn't like I had much of a choice."

He nodded. "At least no one will die this week," he said.

. . .

Not having another potential death looming over our heads almost made the week seem jovial. I gave myself a break for the first time in months, taking strolls around the lake to relax instead of spying or thinking about ways to outsmart Red-Eyes. Putting on the mask around my temporary family became much easier when I wasn't forced to wear it all the time. For the first time in months, I felt like I could finally breathe.

Until Red-Eyes changed the game again.

I didn't recognize the body. It was an older person, probably someone on the brink of retirement. I was heading home from my daily walk in the woods when I found him lying in the middle of the trail, his throat marred with black bruises.

Apparently, Red-Eyes' definition of mercy was murdering someone not related to you.

The victim had a sticky note on his shirt. I reached down to grab it and scowled.

Good job, Reece.

ELEVEN

I left the body for someone else to find and crammed the sticky note in my pocket. He was found a few days later. We didn't go to the funeral. When Mr. Smith demanded whether any of us knew anything about the victim, we lied through our teeth.

That Monday, I awoke to a message from Cyan telling me to meet him in the woods. When I arrived, he was sitting crisscross on the pine straw, his hands balanced on his knees. A small sphere of water hovered in the air at eye level. It slowly shifted, changing from a sphere to a cube, then a pyramid.

"That's impressive," I said. Cyan kept his eyes trained on the ball as it suddenly grew spikes.

"It is," he admitted. He looked up at me, and the ball fell back into the pine straw with a gentle plop. He suddenly looked very tired, the bags beneath his eyes darker than they were five seconds ago.

"I've been practicing," he said, like he was admitting to cheating on a test.

"Isn't that a good thing?" I asked.

He shook his head. "I promised my parents I would never use my powers. Let alone practice. But I've already lost control twice, and I don't know how to shoot a gun or protect myself or you guys otherwise, so . . ." He motioned towards the wet patch of ground. It was then that I noticed a picture lying beside him. It showed him as a blurry figure walking home from the dock, trailing wet footprints. Across the back of his head was the word *dangerous*.

Cyan noticed me looking and took the picture in his hands.

"This was on my doorstep this morning," he said.

"We already know you're dangerous," I said. "What else is there?"

Cyan's hands trembled on the photo. "I stopped taking my meds," he whispered.

At this, I paused, my chest suddenly growing tight. Jack's private conversation with me flashed through my head.

"What meds?" I asked, reminding myself I wasn't supposed to know about the pills to begin with.

Cyan opened and closed his mouth several times before words came out. "I um . . . I've been on mood stabilizers for a long time. They help me stay calm, numb, grounded. And that's great normally, but it's really hard to use my powers when I'm on them. I stopped taking them when you and Jack found out what I am."

"Why feel so bad about it then? Like you said, you can use your powers to protect us," I said.

"It's like the lake is whispering to me, trying to convince me to set her free. I'm trying to keep myself grounded, but . . . it's hard. I don't know what will happen if I mess up. I don't want anyone to get hurt," he whispered. "I thought you would understand more than Jack," he said. *Because I have psycho problems too,* I thought.

"Are you asking me not to tell Jack?" I asked. He hesitated and shook his head.

"I'll have to tell the others before the week is up if I don't want a family member to die," he said. "But I just . . . I need a day or two first. I don't want Jack to be scared of me," he said.

"He's already scared of you," I said, ignoring the way Cyan winced as if my words had cut him. "Look at me," I said. He did so, and I made sure I was staring right into those luminescent blue eyes of his. The cold steel of my pistol pressed against my thigh.

"Can you control yourself, yes or no?" I asked.

Cyan nodded hurriedly. "I promise. I can handle it," he said quickly.

"Respectfully . . . I will put you down if you can't," I said. Cyan swallowed and nodded. At that moment, Jack and Henry came crashing through the woods.

"Sup, guys." Jack's eyes narrowed on the photo. "Dangerous? What does Red-Eyes mean by *dangerous?*"

Cyan opened his mouth to talk, but stopped suddenly, clutching his head.

"What's wrong?" Henry asked. Cyan winced, rubbing the bridge of his nose.

"I don't know. My head . . ." His arm suddenly dropped, and he wavered on his feet. He stared vacantly into the woods, mouth hanging slightly agape. He bolted into the trees, leaving us in his dust.

"Where the fuck does he think he's going?" Jack demanded. I sprinted after him, and after a moment of hesitation, heard the others trailing me.

Cyan was surprisingly fast. He ripped vines out of his way and managed not to trip on the countless weeds blanketing the forest floor. I ignored the swipe of thorns and sting of branches whipping me in the face as I chased after him.

You better not be leading me towards my death, I thought.

He suddenly skidded to a halt, and I wasn't able to stop myself in time to keep from bowling him over. He yelped as I tackled him to the forest floor.

"Get off me!"

Jack and Henry reached us, panting and sweating.

"What the hell, man? Why'd you run off like that?" Henry demanded. Cyan blinked and then seemed to realize where he was. He stared at the foliage around him, eyebrows puckered.

"I don't . . . I don't know." His eyes suddenly narrowed on something in the trees. "Um . . . do you guys see that?"

I squinted through the branches and strode forward. I pulled away a fistful of foliage. Hiding in the vegetation was an old shed. The wood drooped down into the dirt. The vines seemed to be the cement preventing it from mildewing into dust.

Cyan and the others helped me clear away the brush. The shed wasn't very large, maybe five feet by five feet. Cyan tried the rusted handle and pried open the door.

The inside was clean. A broom lay in the corner. There was a small metal trash can filled with food wrappers. Papers covered the walls. In the center of the room lay a manila folder. Scribbled in red Sharpie was a short and unsurprisingly creepy message:

For you.

"Did Red-Eyes just make you run into the woods to find this place?" Jack whispered. "Cyan, why did you come here?"

"I don't know. I was feeling perfectly fine, but then had the overwhelming urge to just . . . run here. I couldn't help myself. God, my head hurts."

Goosebumps rose on my arms. Jack shoved Cyan towards the folder. "I think that's for you."

Cyan cautiously strode forward and opened the folder. He sat down and sifted through a handful of papers, frowning as he looked them over.

"Well?" Henry asked. "What is it?"

Cyan's fingers clenched the papers. Thunder rumbled above.

"This is the police report from the car accident."

"What car accident?" Henry asked.

"The one that killed my parents."

I frowned. Cyan had never mentioned that his parents were killed in an accident. How would Red-Eyes have gotten a copy of that? Even if he could read our minds, he knew information about us that even we didn't even know.

Cyan slowly stood up, white-knuckling the papers.

"What's wrong?" Jack asked.

"They died because someone ran a red light. They never found the guy, but it was still an *accident*." He held up the papers. Someone had scribbled over them in red marker.

IT WASN'T AN ACCIDENT

"I mean . . . it's totally possible that Red-Eyes is lying just to get a rise out of you," Jack said. "Why would someone want to hurt your parents?" Cyan stared down at the papers, refusing to answer.

"Um, guys? Have you looked at the walls?" Henry asked. I looked up. Perfectly pinned to the walls were pictures of our group. The only ones that were missing were Henry's, Cyan's, and mine.

"I think we just found Red-Eyes' base of operations," Jack said.

"Why would he want us to find these?" I muttered, staring at the remaining pictures.

Jack was next in the lineup. His photo said *fool*. Dr. Davis was next to him. His photo said *blind*. Mr. Smith was last. His said *liar*.

"Okay, this is terrifying," Jack said. "What the actual *fuck* is going on?"

The killer just changed the game again, I thought. *He left all of those pictures up for us. Why is he giving us more clues than the adults?*

We stepped back outside the cabin. Jack paced as Cyan kept staring at the papers.

"Why does Red-Eyes think my dad is a liar? What does he mean by calling Dr. Davis blind?" Jack rambled.

I sighed. Jack's voice was starting to get more and more annoying, and I wouldn't be surprised if Cyan burst into tears at any moment. I looked around the clearing, trying to block out their voices. Something about the area looked familiar. I frowned and walked around to the back of the shed.

I ended up in the same clearing that I had followed Henry to the other week. Only this time, there was a rusty shovel sticking out of the dirt in the center.

Cyan and Jack came up behind me.

"Oh, I don't have a good feeling about this," Henry said, clutching his stomach.

"This is where I followed you to that day I saw you in the cemetery," I said. "But there wasn't a shovel last time." I stepped forward and grabbed the handle. I guess I hadn't gotten Red-Eyes' hint the first go-around, and he wanted to give me another chance.

I stabbed at the dirt. The others watched in silence as I dug. The ground was soft.

Ten minutes later, my shovel hit something hard. I sank to my knees and started pulling the dirt away with my hands. My fingers got tangled in a strand of white hair.

I wasn't sure how long it took bodies to decompose in the dirt during winter. I could tell it was an old woman in spite of the mushy skin. I had accidentally split her skull with the shovel.

Above me was the familiar sound of Jack dry heaving. I stood up and looked at Cyan, whose face was paler than normal.

"You know her?" I asked.

"Kinda. I didn't know she was missing, though. She was a shut-in," Cyan said.

"Why would Red-Eyes bury her all the way out here and leave her for us to find?" Jack called out from a distance.

"I don't know, but we need to call Dr. Davis. He needs to do an autopsy on the body," I said.

Henry whistled. "He's not going to like that we're messing around after they told us to stay out of it."

"That's fine with me. I want them to answer for what their pictures say," I said.

. . .

True to Henry's prediction, the adults were not happy. Mr. Smith spent at least ten minutes berating us for getting involved as Dr.

Davis poked and prodded the old woman's body, sighing over and over again as if he could make us all disappear.

"Respectfully, sir, yelling at us isn't going to fix the problem," Cyan said. "We just found the killer's hideout. I'm sure there's something in there that can tell us who he is."

They followed us around the back of the building and inside, where Mr. Smith tsked at the pictures on the wall. Cyan held up the folder with the papers.

"This was left for me. It has the police report from my parents' car accident in here, but he scribbled all over it. Do you know . . . do you know if these look normal? I mean . . . my parents did die in a car accident, right?" Cyan rambled, looking up at Mr. Smith with giant eyes.

Mr. Smith casually flipped through the documents before handing the folder back. "I'd say this is the killer trying to mess with all of you like I told you he would do."

Of course he is, I thought. *That's his entire game. But he had yet to lie.*

"Yours is the one that says liar," I pointed out.

Mr. Smith's eye twitched, but he shrugged. "Cops lie to get their jobs done. And the killer probably wrote *blind* on Dr. Davis' because he missed the bruises on those bodies all those years. Case closed." He pointed his finger at all of us.

"Here's what's going to happen now. You three are going to go home and stay there. We will take it from here," Mr. Smith said, his eyes dark. "And I don't want to hear any more arguments about it. Are we clear?"

I pictured taking the gun out from under my skirt and evening the playing field.

"Yes, sir," Jack muttered. Mr. Smith stepped forward and snatched the papers out of Cyan's hands.

"I'll need those, too. We can dust them for fingerprints."

We followed Jack out of the shack and trudged back home.

"We can agree that made your dad hella suspicious, right?" Henry pointed out.

Jack rolled his eyes. "You guys seriously think my dad, the cop, is Red-Eyes? He's *human*."

"I mean, you saw how quickly he dismissed us at the police station. No follow up questions about how I broke the bars or how we figured everything out. You would think that he would've grilled us for hours about everything we knew," Cyan grumbled. "I'm just saying. It's a little suspicious."

Jack suddenly stopped in his tracks, his jaw clenched. "My dad is not a serial killer!" he snapped. "He's a *cop*. He's spent his entire life helping people and raising me by himself. So don't go throwing around accusations."

Cyan's jaw dropped. I crossed my arms as Henry cast uneasy glances between the two of them.

"Well, *forgive* me for being suspicious of everyone right now," Cyan finally said, clenching his fists.

"Yeah? Don't forget that *you're* the one who lied to me for years," Jack shot back. "And you seemed really hesitant to explain why your picture says *dangerous* on it. My dad doesn't exactly seem like the liar here."

Lightning flashed across the sky. Cyan suddenly looked venomous. Tiny water droplets rose into the air by his feet. I imagined them forming into spikes like they did earlier, hurdling through the air and into Jack's forehead.

But killing each other now wouldn't help the situation. Red-Eyes was obviously trying to divide us, like Mr. Smith had pointed out. Cyan and Jack were being pulled along like fish on hooks.

"Jack is human," I said. "So, his dad has to be too. Unless he's secretly adopted."

"I'm not the adopted one," Jack grit through his teeth.

"Guys, this isn't helping," Henry said.

"Well, I'm out of ideas!" Jack shouted. "People are still dying, and even though Cyan swears up and down that he's scouring the lake every night, he can't seem to find anything."

"At least I'm trying!" Cyan shouted. "What have you done? Oh, right – *nothing*. Even Red-Eyes knows you're useless."

"I'd rather be a fool than some dangerous mythical freak!" Jack spat. My hand strayed further to where my gun was strapped underneath my skirt. Henry stepped between Jack and Cyan like that would help dispel the tension.

"Fine. If you don't want my help, then I won't bother." Cyan pushed past me and ran down the path, disappearing.

"Yeah, run away and hide like you always do!" Jack spat after him. "I'm done with this shit." He stomped off towards his house, leaving Henry and me in awkward silence.

"Whelp, that didn't go well," Henry muttered. "Let me try to go talk to him." He jogged after Jack. I trudged back to my house alone, wishing I were the creature that could make people do whatever I wanted. The boys were so irrational. If they would quit acting so emotionally, we could get this mystery solved once and for all.

I stepped through the front door to find my dad and Marie hunched over a pile of papers at the kitchen table. They jerked to attention when they saw me. Their faces were gaunt and pale.

I frowned. In the brief time I had known them, their faces never looked like that. My gut twisted in the same way it had when I had realized the drownings weren't happening by accident.

"What's going on?" I asked.

My dad swallowed, mashing his fingers together under the table. "We just got off the phone with your mother."

For a moment, I was too startled to speak. My mom hadn't bothered to call or check on me once. All attempts to ask about her had been gently squashed by my therapist. Had she finally decided that I was normal enough – that I was ready to come home? Why else would she be calling? My heart soared with hope.

"Is she letting me come home?" I asked, barely able to contain my smile.

Marie patted the kitchen chair next to her and held my hand as I sat down. Why were they acting like someone had just died?

My dad opened and closed his mouth several times before words came out. "I'm sorry, Sweetie. I – we've tried to convince them to give it more time – but she wouldn't listen –" His words started to blend in my head.

My fleeting sensation of hope vanished out from under me.

"Spit it out," I demanded. My dad winced and grabbed my hand.

"Your mother is giving us full custody of you. You're not going home."

TWELVE

The details of how I reacted were fuzzy. Based on how raw my throat was, it must've been loud. And my dad and Marie had done nothing but listen as I threw a tantrum like little Annie. My brain processed pieces of information between breaths.

She keeps insisting that she'll never feel safe around you.

We can appeal this. The battle's not over yet.

I know this isn't what you wanted, Sweetie, but you're always welcome here.

The fragments ran through my head on a loop as I lay in bed, staring at the ceiling, my throat burning and my head pounding.

My mom didn't want me anymore. Looking back, this had probably been her plan all along: dump me with my dad, placate me with false hopes of being able to come back home, and vanish. All the work I had done to make friends and smile when I didn't feel like it was wasted.

The game I had been playing had never mattered.

She was never going to let me come home.

At some point in my self-pity, I fell asleep. As usual, I was woken up by familiar tapping. I opened the window only to see Jack by himself.

"Have you seen Cyan? His parents said he never came home last night," he said.

I wanted to scream. Who gave a shit where Cyan was?

"No, I haven't seen him," I muttered.

Jack stiffened. "Jeez, are you mad at me, too? You would be upset too if someone accused your dad of being a serial killer," he snapped.

My eye twitched.

"Jack, no one gives a shit about your feelings," I spat. He took a step back as if my words had stung him.

"What's your problem?" he snapped.

"My problem? No – *this* isn't my problem anymore. I'm done trying to save a town full of ungrateful, dramatic, stupid people like you. You can figure this out alone." I slammed my window shut, the glass rattling. Jack stared at me open-mouthed for a few seconds before flipping me the middle finger.

"Fine!" he shouted, his voice muffled. "I'll figure this out by myself." *Good fucking riddance*, I thought, slinking back to bed and burying myself under the covers.

Fuck Red-Eyes and his stupid game. This wasn't my town; these weren't my people. What was the point of saving everyone if I couldn't be the hero who would get me back home?

This entire town could drown for all I cared.

. . .

I spent the rest of the day wrapped in blankets. I was occasionally woken from my sleep by my phone buzzing. A glance revealed Henry had been texting me.

Reese have you seen cyan? No one can find him. His folks reported him missing

You need to call me ive got news

Reese???

I ignored his messages. I, of course, knew exactly where Cyan was – hiding down in the bottom of the lake, brooding over his stupid fight with his best friend instead of being worried about what he should be worried about. God, teenage boys were so stupid.

Normally, I would assume Cyan would be too nice not to appease Red-Eyes and save his family. But he was off his meds and clearly not managing his emotions as well as he claimed. Maybe he would sacrifice one of his family members instead of admitting he was just as dangerous as Jack feared he was. Either way, this was no longer my fight. If Cyan wanted to disappear and make one of his family members pay the price for his cowardice, that wasn't my problem.

My dreams were littered with nightmares. I saw Cyan being swallowed by mud at the bottom of the lake, sludge silencing his screams. I saw Jack dead in the cemetery, his throat decorated with bruises. Henry swung from a noose he had tied himself.

A soft knock on the door was the next thing that woke me up. Marie poked her head in.

"Can we talk?" she asked.

"No."

She came in anyway, shutting the door behind her and sitting next to me on my bed. I ignored her, scrolling through my phone. Henry had tried to call me a dozen times. Why the fuck was he bothering me so much?

"I know this didn't go the way you wanted," she started. "And I know that's very disappointing for you, whether you can feel it or not."

I scoffed. "There's no point using your psycho-babble on me."

"I know," she said softly. "There's no changing people like you. You have brain damage, and while the brain is adaptable . . . it's not that adaptable. Your mother was a fool to ever think otherwise."

I put my phone down. I had barely had a conversation with this woman, and now she was telling me my mom's insistence that I be normal was never going to be possible?

"You *knew* I wasn't going to get better?" I repeated, almost too stunned for the words to process.

"That's the thing, Reece. You *have* gotten better. You've learned to make friends, keep them, and show yourself the way you want the world to see you. You might not be doing it for the same reason most people do, but the effect is still the same. Unless you confessed, no one else would know the difference."

I guess she had a point. What was the difference between being normal and appearing normal?

"What's the point of being better if I can't go home?" I muttered.

"It's not like you're banned from Atlanta forever. In a few years, you'll be off to college, and you're smart enough to get in just about anywhere. You've got your whole life ahead of you with parents that actually give a shit about you."

I raised my eyebrow. Before now, I couldn't have imagined sweet Marie swearing.

"You don't think my mom gives a shit about me?" I asked.

She sighed. "I can't imagine ever sending my baby away. No matter who she turned out to be."

I frowned. I had been living here for only a few months, and Marie already seemed willing to go with me through hell or high water. It wasn't like I had been a perfect angel here either. I had gotten them shitty gifts for Christmas, stirred up trouble by nagging them about the thirteen deaths. I had barely spoken to either of them. Why did she care about me?

"I just don't get how you feel that way," I said.

She smiled. "It's just how my brain is wired. You don't have to understand it. We'll be here for you no matter what. And if I could give you some advice . . ." She clutched my hand. "Don't burn your bridges with your friends here. I know you can't care about them the same way others can, but I know they care about you. They'll remember you when you leave. Keep treating them well and maybe one day they'll return the favor."

Return the favor.

Maybe I shouldn't let them get murdered by Red-Eyes, I mused.

"Thank you," I said, surprised at how much I meant it.

She smiled and stood up, hesitating once she reached the door.

"Keep playing the game," she said.

I furrowed my brow. No one knew that I had thought of my act as playing a game.

"I'm sorry?" I said.

Marie turned back around, but something was off. Her head tilted to the side, her lips slightly drooping. Her eyes focused on some invisible point in the distance.

"Play the game," she repeated, blinking slowly. "Finish the game."

Red-Eyes is here, I thought, stealing a glance out the window. As soon as I turned back around, Marie was back to normal, blinking as if she had just woken up from a nap.

"I feel like I was going to say something else, but now I can't remember," she said.

I forced a laugh, already reaching for my phone. "Oh well."

She finally left, and I scrambled to call Henry back.

"Oh my god, where the fuck have you been?" he shouted from the other end. I winced, holding the phone away from my ear.

"Long story. What's going on?"

"I went to talk to Dr. Davis and made him tell me what he found in that old woman's autopsy."

I wondered how exactly Henry had made Dr. Davis talk, and decided it was better I didn't know the details.

"Okay, and?"

"That old woman died last year," Henry said. "And she was definitely murdered. Her spine was broken in several places. Either she fell down multiple flights of stairs or someone took a baseball bat to her. And her house didn't have any stairs."

It took my brain a few moments to comprehend what he was saying.

"Fourteen people died last year," I realized. "Not thirteen."

"Yeah." Henry kept talking, but his words faded to background noise. I frowned, trying to make sense of it all. Why would Red-Eyes go out of his way to hide one body in particular? Why kill an extra person? Why reveal her?

He was changing the game *again*.

Or was he? Why did he want us to figure out who he was so badly?

My heart fell to my feet. *The killer wasn't one of us. It never was.*

"Oh my god," I whispered.

"What? What?" Henry demanded.

I shook my head. That was . . . *that* was crazy. There was no way I was right.

But what if I was?

I grit my teeth. It didn't matter how I felt about this stupid town or my mother. Red-Eyes thought he was smarter than me, a more talented psycho than me. I would be damned if he thought he could win now. This wasn't about winning my mother's favor anymore. It was about my pride.

"Never mind. Have you told Jack yet?" I asked, making sure my gun was strapped to my inner thigh.

"No! I've been calling him all day, too, but he hasn't picked up. I thought both of you were dead in a ditch somewhere," Henry said.

Jack's last words echoed through my head.

Fine, I'll figure this out by myself.

Knowing him, he had done something stupid. The killer had been using him like a puppet for months. I shouldn't have let him go off searching alone. I swore as I pulled on my shoes and clambered out of my window.

"Meet me at Jack's house right now."

I bolted through the dying grass to see Henry already banging on the door. I joined him, and moments later, a very disgruntled Mr. Smith yanked it open, staring down at me like I was a roach.

"Fourteen people died last year," I gasped. "Not thirteen – my whole theory is –" I stopped when I saw Jack standing back behind his father.

Black bruises covered his neck like a collar. His normally bright eyes were dark and hollow. He shied away as we stared at him, as if he had been caught in his underwear.

"Jack," Henry whispered. "What happened?"

Mr. Smith actually laughed. For the first time, I noticed he was soaking wet. "You want to know what *happened*?" He pulled us inside and shut the door, motioning at his son. "He was attacked by that . . . that *thing*! I found him in the nick of time!"

"Jack, what do you remember?" I pressed. He shrugged, curling in further on himself.

"It doesn't matter what he remembers," Mr. Smith said. "I just solved this entire little mystery for all of you. It's –"

The door suddenly blew back open. Cyan stood in the foyer, dripping lake water and gasping for breath.

"Jack – I'm so sorry," he blubbered. "I never should've accused your dad, and you're right, I stopped taking my meds so I could use my powers and –" He stopped short. Somewhere in his rant, Mr. Smith had revealed a gun. Jack cowered in the corner as Henry and I exchanged a look.

"Do you want to explain to me why I found your fingerprints all over my son's throat?" Mr. Smith asked.

Cyan's face drained of color. Jack refused to look at us, but I could see tears dripping onto the floor.

"What?" Cyan whispered.

Mr. Smith took a step forward. "Do you want to explain why I found your fingerprints all over my son's throat?" His voice was a shout by the end. His knuckles were white on the gun.

Those weren't Cyan's fingerprints, I thought.

"I-I have no idea what you're talking about!" Cyan sputtered. "I've never laid a hand on Jack. I saw those pictures for the first time the same day you did!"

"The evidence doesn't lie. I know what you are." Mr. Smith pointed the gun at Cyan. Cyan took a slow step back, raising his hands.

"Y-you can't be serious," he whispered. "It's not me. Jack, come on, back me up."

Jack shook his head. "I don't remember what happened. It – it could've been you."

"Jack!" Cyan protested.

Henry suddenly spun to face the door again, his eyes wide. "What the –"

A sharp pain exploded in the back of my skull, and everything went black.

THIRTEEN

The light in the room seemed intent on causing me as much pain as possible. I heard groaning. I forced myself to open my eyes and tried to blink away the sudden brightness. Someone had tied me to a chair in the police station. Sitting at my feet like it was circle time were Cyan, Jack, and Henry, all staring off into space, eyes glassy.

Mr. Smith lay beside the desk, bleeding and broken in several places. His arms were bound behind his back. Tears oozed from a black eye. A ghost of a figure sat in the rolling chair, his feet propped up on the table.

The stranger looked up at me, his once blonde hair now streaked with algae and hanging in tangles over his red eyes. I couldn't help but smile.

"I was right," I said.

Brian laughed. The same Brian Henry had secretly been in love with. The same Brian who had been an ass to Cyan the day before Jack told him to go drown. The same Brian whose funeral I went to. The same boy sat five feet away from me, just as alive as the day I last saw him.

"You faked your own death after Jack told you to go drown," I said.

"Ding, ding, ding!" Brian put down the knife on the desk, stretching. He spun in the chair, letting his feet rest on top of Mr. Smith's head. He snapped his fingers, and the boys suddenly jerked to attention. Cyan immediately tried to get up, only to stop as Brian pointed the knife at his chest.

"Please, don't get up on my behalf."

Cyan slowly sank back down. The air in the room seemed to grow heavier. Brian leaned back in the office chair, grinning at us. I was only interested in knowing the answer to one question.

"Why did you say the murderer was one of us?" I asked.

Brian's grin grew bigger, and he leaned down to Mr. Smith, who shifted feebly. "I believe Mr. *Falcon* can answer that for you," he whispered.

His real name wasn't Smith?

"That's not our name," Jack protested.

"It used to be," Brian drawled.

Mr. Smith – or Mr. Falcon now – muttered something that was lost to the carpet. Brian rolled his eyes. "Fine. I'll say it. Cyan, you're a siren." Brian giggled. "It almost rhymes."

Cyan blinked. "Um . . . I know."

"No, you don't. You think you're a *mermaid*, not a siren. See, mermaids are . . . harmless, shy little things. Sirens, on the other hand . . . we're special. *You* especially. You have no clue how excited I was when I figured out exactly what you were that night you saved Annie," Brian grinned.

"Cut the riddles, man. *Why* have you been killing people?" Jack demanded. Brian narrowed his eyes at Jack, who suddenly fell silent and docile once more. He picked a piece of carpet as if it were the most fascinating thing in the world. Brian grinned again.

"See, Cyan, I'm like most sirens. Almost all of us can control how others feel . . . make them extremely interested in a stitch of carpet. Make them curious enough to drown. Make them sad enough to shoot themselves."

"I'm not like you," Cyan said, his voice hollow.

"Of course not! I already said . . . you're *special*." Bryon picked at his dirty nails with a blood-stained knife. "Killing people all by yourself, all anonymously for so many years . . . it got boring," he continued. "So, I decided to have some fun, frame Jack, make him squirm. Making both of you paranoid and suspicious of each other was the best part! But when I realized who you were that night you saved Annie . . . oh . . . things got much more interesting."

"Why did you say one of us was the killer?" I interrupted. "Why did you lie?"

Brian switched his glare to me. "Be patient now, Reece. I didn't *lie*." Brian lifted his feet off of Mr. Falcon and pulled him into a sitting position. He yanked his head up to the ceiling by his hair, pressing his knife into his Adam's apple. Jack finally looked up from the carpet, going pale.

"This one has murdered plenty," Brian sneered. "Falcon, you're going to tell him this part, or I'll slit your throat right now," he hissed.

Mr. Falcon struggled weakly. A thin line of red trickled onto his uniform. "Cyan, you're the last siren who can control water. We thought all of you were already gone," Mr. Falcon finally croaked.

Cyan blinked. "How did you know I'm a siren? Who is *we*?"

"The Siren Slayers. We've been tracking sirens down for decades. To keep humans safe." Mr. Falcon almost sounded proud as the words passed his lips. He cried out as Brian dug the knife in deeper.

"Admit what you did. Admit what you stole from him. From me!" Brian hissed.

"Stole what?" Cyan shouted.

"I killed Brian's parents. And I killed yours, too," Mr. Falcon cried.

The oxygen was sucked from the room. Cyan froze. Jack let out a sob. Henry covered his mouth. Brian grinned, releasing Mr. Falcon to fall back to the floor, twirling the knife. My heart pounded in my chest. Mr. Falcon's inscription in the photo suddenly made perfect sense.

Liar.

Red-Eyes had been telling the truth. We had just been looking for a different murderer.

"The Slayers have been picking off our kind for years. I had no clue I lived in town with one until I realized Cyan was supposed to be dead.

"You see, Falcon here tried to kill me, too. He thought he got the job done, but I survived. He stabbed my mother six times and my father seven times before they finally stopped fighting. But just for good measure, he set the house on fire with me locked inside." Brian slammed the heel of his foot down on Mr. Falcon's nose. Mr. Falcon's scream echoed through the office.

"Thirteen people dead for the thirteen stabs!" he laughed. "And after I'm done killing Reece and Henry, you're going to watch me kill your son. It'll be the last thing you ever see. And you'll rot in your guilt until you're a grease stain on the carpet." Brian looked up at Cyan. "And I want you to join me."

Cyan recoiled. "Why would I do that?"

"This son of a bitch murdered your parents! He *lied* and said it was your fingerprints on Jack's neck and photos to *frame* you! He's been trying to figure out how to kill you ever since you revealed your powers. And even when he's dead, there will be others. We will never be left alone until all of the humans are gone!" Brian shouted.

So Falcon had noticed Cyan using his powers at the police station, I realized. He didn't say anything because he didn't want to talk about his knowledge of sirens.

"Not all humans are bad," Cyan whispered. "My friends would never hurt me."

"Are you sure?" he drawled, pointing his knife at me and Jack in turn. Cyan swallowed. Brian got out of the chair and stalked towards us, tracing Cyan's cheekbones with the curve of his knife. "Reece is no more sane than I am. And your supposed best friend has been terrified of your little outbursts since day one. Don't you know what people do when they're afraid?" he whispered. Cyan looked at Jack, who I was very surprised hadn't thrown up yet.

"If you join me, I'll let you avenge your parents," Brian promised.

Will he take the bait? I wondered.

Cyan slammed his foot down on Brian's, swiping the knife out of his hands. Cyan sliced through my bonds as Brian stumbled backwards. I grabbed Jack and Henry and made sure they followed us as we bolted out of the police station, booking it down the street. People stopped in their window shopping and stared.

"Reece, get everyone out of the way. I'm finishing this!" Cyan pushed me away and turned around as Brian oozed out of the police station, walking like he was on a peaceful stroll.

"What about Mr. Falcon?" I demanded.

"I'll worry about him later." Cyan white knuckled the knife as Brian clapped his hands together.

"You're making a big mistake, Cyan," Brian warned. Cyan dropped the knife. He reached his hands out, and water rose from the street, pooling around his hands. The townspeople screamed. Jack whimpered.

"GET INSIDE NOW!" I screamed. I shoved Jack away from me, and he leapt into action. He grabbed an older couple and pushed them towards the Thrift Shop. He barricaded the doors behind them, and I stood in the street, watching Brian and Cyan tear at each other like wolves. Streams of water cut through the air like knives, but Brian didn't seem to feel them as he clawed at any part of Cyan he could reach. I felt under my skirt and smiled when I felt the gun still secured in its holster. I would be damned if Brian didn't die today. I pulled it out and clicked off the safety. Brian had Cyan in a headlock. His face was turning purple.

"Drop the gun or I'll kill him," Brian threatened.

"You should know that threat won't work on me," I said, slowly stepping forward. Brian smiled.

"Fine." He trained his gaze on Jack, whose head lolled to the side. He wrapped his fingers around his bruised throat and started to squeeze. The older couple gasped and tried to pry his hands away, but he was too strong. Brian was too strong.

"STOP IT!" Cyan screamed, thrashing in Brian's grip. "Reece, I'll kill you if you let Jack die." I rolled my eyes and lowered my gun. Jack let go, gasping for breath, slumping against the glass. Brian let Cyan fall to the ground.

"I think I'll kill you next, Reece. The old-fashioned way," he breathed.

Out of the corner of my eye, I saw Henry inch his way across the pavement, his finger to his lips. *Stall him*, he mouthed.

"Good luck." I raised my arm, aiming and pulling the trigger. Brian clutched his arm, blood pushing through his fingers. He giggled. Did he ever stop giggling?

"Never used one of those things before, huh? Your parents would never be stupid enough to give you a weapon after what you turned into," he jeered. I pulled the trigger again, the kickback pushing the gun back into my chest. The second shot went wide, as did the next three. I stopped breathing as the gun clicked, nothing left in the chamber.

Brian giggled. "It's a shame you weren't born a siren. You would be excellent."

I backed away, clutching the empty gun like a baseball bat. "Yeah, too bad."

Brian scooped his fallen knife off the pavement and ran towards me. I stayed still, hoping my reflexes would be fast enough to block the knife with my empty gun. I told myself that even if he did stab me, it wouldn't hurt that bad, and I could keep fighting.

One second passed. Then another one. At the end of the third, I blinked to make sure my eyes were still working right.

Brian had stopped running towards me. Henry stood behind him, the tail end of a metal pipe still clutched in his hands. The other end poked out from Brian's chest. He stared at it, slowly reaching up to touch it with a dirty fingernail.

Well shit.

Henry let go, stumbling backwards, blood smeared on his hands. Cyan ran up to me, yanking me out of the way as Brian collapsed to his knees. He tried in vain to push the pipe back out the way it came, but it wouldn't budge. Tears poured from Henry's face as Brian's blood gushed onto the concrete.

Brian looked back up at Cyan, that stupid grin still plastered to his face. He reached out and grabbed Cyan's ankle. "You're going to regret this. I'm not done yet," he whispered. His body went limp. His glowing red eyes faded to a glassy sheen. Blood trickled out of his mouth. His impaled chest stopped rising and falling.

I gingerly reached out and kicked Brian's hand off of Cyan, who looked dangerously close to throwing up.

People slowly started trickling out of the shops, pointing and whispering. I looked down at my own body to make sure it was still whole. Jack staggered out of the thrift shop.

"Is he dead?" he croaked.

Cyan stood up and nodded. "It's over." Jack made it two more steps before another shot sounded. Cyan ducked, letting out a scream. We looked down the street to see Mr. Falcon aiming his pistol at us.

"Get out of the way," he said.

I narrowed my eyes as I stepped in front of Cyan. "Fuck you. This entire mess is your fault." Even though I couldn't make myself care about Cyan, I could definitely care that Mr. Falcon was an asshole who had created Red-Eyes to begin with. I had every excuse in the book to kill without reservation, but I didn't. What gave him the right?

For a moment, I thought Mr. Falcon would mow me down with his gun.

"Jack, you need to get away from him right now," Mr. Falcon said. "He's dangerous. You have no idea what he's capable of. There's a *reason* his parents had to be disposed of."

Jack's face was the color of glue. He stood frozen by the thrift shop, eyes dancing between his father and his best friend.

Come on, Jack, don't be a fool, I thought.

"I-I-I don't know who to believe," Jack whispered, taking a step back.

Idiot, I thought. Behind me, Cyan's face was streaked with tears. The crowd around us was growing, and they didn't look like they knew who to believe either. Mr. Falcon was approaching slowly. If he could convince everyone he was right – things would not end well for Cyan.

And I was not going to let the real killer win this game.

"Cyan, run," I said.

"Where?" he whispered.

"Somewhere they'll never find you."

The crowd advanced. Cyan whimpered.

"I'll come back."

"GO!" I shouted. I flung my empty gun at Mr. Falcon. It startled him enough for his next shot to go rouge.

And then the sky dropped.

It hadn't so much as sprinkled since I had been here despite the sky always being heavy and gray. The drops stung as they whipped against my skin. The smell of blood and petrichor filled my nostrils. My clothes were soaked, the gutters choked, and I couldn't see or hear a thing other than shouting and howling wind. The crowd fled in search of drier places, leaving Mr. Falcon standing in the torrent, face twisted.

I looked behind me and squinted through the downpour. I couldn't help but smile.

Cyan was gone.

CYAN

On my first day of kindergarten, another student stole my water bottle. He did it right in front of me, snatching it off my desk on the way to lunch. When I asked for it back, he stuck his tongue out and ran away, giggling. I tried to tell the teacher, but when she went to talk to the boy, he had written his name on it already. I had no clue how to write or even what the alphabet was. The teacher reprimanded me for trying to claim something that wasn't mine.

That water bottle had been one of the first things my parents bought me. It was green, my new favorite color after the move. Our old home in the sea didn't have any grass or flowers. As much as I missed the ocean, I couldn't deny how beautiful my new surroundings were. Losing that bottle felt like losing a limb. I had to get it back, but it never left the other kid's sight the rest of the day. On the walk to the car rider line, I saw it in his backpack. My vision went hazy, my little hands curled into fists, and I thought about how much I wanted the boy to suffer for his sin.

The bottle exploded.

The metal twisted and tore, sending sharp fragments flying through the air. Water ballooned out of it like a small hurricane had been unleashed. An innocent passerby caught his cheek in the crossfire, the wound deep enough to bleed. The pop sounded like a gunshot.

The kid stood there, mouth hanging open, not a sound reaching past his lips until his mom thundered towards him. She pushed me out of the way as her little boy burst into tears. Others whispered and avoided the shards like they were radioactive as a teacher attempted to mutter an explanation.

The more upset the boy became, the faster a grin spread across my face. Satisfaction made my fists relax. If I couldn't have my green water bottle, no one could. Fair was fair, right?

"*What is wrong with you?*" My dad's voice was a growl, a noise I had never heard before. He yanked me from the sidewalk into the car and sped away so fast I didn't have time to put on my seatbelt. My heart hammered in my chest, my body frozen solid in the backseat of the car. My mother had her arms crossed, jaw clenched, knuckles white as she gripped her arms.

I tried to speak, tried to say that I hadn't done it on purpose. *Or had I?*

"He took it and wouldn't give it back." My childish voice came out as a whisper.

"It doesn't matter," my mom hissed. "We brought you to land to keep you *safe*. What you did was dangerous." The traffic light turned red, and my dad slammed on the brakes. I flung my arms out to keep myself from hurdling into the driver's seat. My dad faced me, his eyes dark like a storm.

"We've talked about this. Only bad mermen use their powers," he said. "You don't want to be a bad merman, do you?"

Tears flooded my eyes as I shook my head. "I promise. I won't use them ever again," I said. The light turned green.

That's when the other car hit us.

ONE

My parents were murdered.

The stolen minivan sped down the road, my knuckles white on the steering wheel. Occasionally, the repetitive white lines would be interrupted by the events of the past twenty-four hours. Mr. Smith's, wait, no, Mr. *Falcon's* gun staring at me. Brian's blood pouring onto the pavement. The horrified looks of the townspeople as they saw me for who I really was. Mysteries I hadn't known existed were solved.

My parents were murdered.

I clenched my teeth, almost hitting the other car sneaking up in my blind spot. I had never driven a car before, but I couldn't stay in that town for another second. I had broken the two rules I had sworn to my dead parents I would keep, and everything was ruined now. I was either cursed or the curse to begin with. I couldn't keep hurting people – lying, breaking my promises.

How was I ever supposed to look Jack in the face after knowing what his father had done? It wasn't like he had bothered to stand up for me in my final moments. The only people who were confidently on my side were my childhood bully and a bonified psychopath who couldn't care about me if she tried.

The rest of the townspeople had been gawking with their jaws hanging to the floor, like I was a freak who belonged in a horror movie. God knew what Nichole and Robert would think when they heard the news. I couldn't bear to see their faces. I couldn't bear to watch Jack's decision on who to trust.

So, I listened to the psychopath. I took advantage of the chaos (*had I caused that storm on purpose?*), bolted from the scene of my crimes, stole my adoptive parents' car, and peaced out.

My head hurt too much to think any further ahead.

The sky was turning black quickly. A new light popped up on the dashboard, indicating that the ancient car was almost out of gas.

I snapped out of my stupor. I hadn't bothered to think of a single logical thing before I had skipped town. I was missing my phone, my wallet, anything that would have proven useful. And my clothes were still soaking wet.

At least I could fix that problem. I snapped my fingers and suddenly I was bone dry – the water relocated to a plastic bottle rolling around in the backseat.

Trying not to swerve off the road, I dug around the center console, sighing in relief as my fingers closed around the stash of emergency cash Robert kept in the car. A glance showed I was seventy bucks richer. Now I just had to find gas.

I pulled off at the first sign of civilization and drove up to a decrepit station. The air was cold and sliced through my thin t-shirt as I fumbled with the gas pump. I had never pumped gas before, and when I finally figured it out, the pump demanded $58.17 of my seventy dollars. I climbed back in the car, shivering and drained.

This was a terrible idea.

I could barely remember my life outside Tredecim. I had no clue where I was going. I had no phone to Google directions. Robert and Nichole were probably frantic. They hadn't seen me in days. What story would they hear? What story would they *believe?*

I couldn't help but white knuckle the steering wheel again. My best friend's father had murdered my parents. My best friend's father had tried to kill *me.* My best friend's father had framed *me* for attempting to kill his son.

And my best friend acted like he didn't know who he could trust.

My stomach lurched. I threw open the car door and dry heaved onto the pavement, clutching my stomach as waves of pain passed through my gut.

By the time I could sit back up, the attendant from inside had moved to stand by the door and was narrowing his beady eyes at me. I suddenly worried if my parents had already noticed I was gone. What if they had put out an alert for me, and people all over the country were searching for a kid with long black hair in a rusty minivan?

I turned the car on and sped down the road, sweating in spite of the cold. I almost pulled over to yank off the license plate, but surely that would look more suspicious? If I got pulled over without an ID, it would all be over.

Where the fuck was I even going?

Where had Mr. Falcon gone? Was he still in Tredecim? Was he searching for me? Was he planning on finishing the job?

I can never go back, I realized. That's what he would expect. I had to find somewhere to hide. Change my name – dye my hair – something so he would never find me again. My last words to Reece could never come true.

The night continued. The few cars left on the road glared at me as if they wanted to hit me on purpose. My stomach growled, but I shoved it down, ignoring the pangs. The heater gave out around four in the morning. Cold air leeched into the car as the sun began to peek above the horizon.

I tried not to scream as I banged my head against the steering wheel. *I should just go back home,* I thought. I'm never going to make it out here.

I'd rather die in the car than be murdered.

The needle was drifting dangerously toward zero as the sun rose high enough to shine into my eyes. There was no way I could afford to fill up the entire car again, and my vision was starting to blur. I needed to find a place to pull over and think of an actual plan before I wasted any more gas.

I pulled off on the next exit and coasted until I saw a building. Through my tilted vision, it looked like an abandoned barn. No cars lingered by.

I drove around the back and made sure the doors were locked before climbing into the backseat. I barely had time to close my eyes before I succumbed to sleep.

When I woke up, the world was black. My head swam as I tried to sit up. I stumbled out of the car. My breath pooled in a cloud at my feet. I forced myself to shuffle along, my head wobbling on my neck as I walked. By the time I was able to hold it up straight, a familiar figure haunted my sight.

Brian stood in front of me, his hands folded politely behind his back. He looked like he had when he was alive – neat, combed blond hair, thin freckled face, sharp smile.

"*You've made a grave mistake,*" he whispered. Blood spurted from a hole in his chest, drenching his clothes. His hair grew into tangles over his gleaming red eyes. I stumbled backwards as he laughed – the noise echoing through the trees. My head began to throb, like a worm was chewing through my brain.

"You're dead," I insisted.

"*So?*" His grimy hands traced my cheeks. His blood splattered my shoes as it hit the ground. I pressed my hands over my heart, trying to search for a beat. I felt nothing. My body was cold like a stone. *Am I dead, too?*

"*Aren't you angry?*" Brian whispered. I tried to push him away, but he barely moved.

"Get away from me," I rasped. Brian disappeared, and the pain in my head faded. I collapsed to my knees, gasping for breath. *How am I breathing if I'm dead?* I pressed my hands against my heart, against my throat, against anything, trying to feel a flutter. My insides were silent.

Oh god.

I looked around the forest, trembling, my fingers clawing at the dirt. *Am I stuck here? Am I damned? I wasn't the psychopath!* I didn't realize I had shouted the words out loud until they echoed around me.

"*Aren't you angry?*"

I froze and turned around to see Brian once more. Blood oozed from his eyes. He grinned through his yellow teeth. "*I want my revenge.*" His hands shot out, grabbing my hair and dragging me towards him. "*And you're going to give it to me,*" he whispered. My skull exploded in pain.

I screamed as I woke up, nearly hitting my head on the car's roof. Sweat poured down my back. A quick look around reminded me I was still in my parents' stolen van. *I could've gone my whole life without a nightmare like that*, I thought, wiping my forehead with my shirt.

I rubbed a circle in the fogged-up windows and looked outside. The sky was fading to dusk, and other cars were parked around me. Country music and soft lights flickered from the barn.

My back smarted – sleeping in a van was not nearly as comfortable as movies made it out to be. My head still throbbed. An aspirin sounded like heaven.

Fuck, I don't have any of my meds, I realized. I mean, I had quit taking them a while ago . . . I would probably be fine.

I risked opening the door and stepping outside. Dust curled out from under my feet, and I held my arms as I walked to the front of the building. A fading neon light proclaimed they were open, and the smell made me realize someone had converted the old barn into a dive bar. A group of heavily tattooed men hung by the front door, laughing through clouds of cigarette smoke. One wore a literal eyepatch. Who does that?

One of them caught a glimpse of me and smirked. "Glory hole's out back, freak," he sneered.

Fucking kill him. Make his lungs so dry that the next puff of that cigarette makes him explode.

Whoa, calm down, I thought, shaking the disturbing image from my head.

I considered my options. I had less than twenty bucks, an almost-empty car, and no clue where I was going. I hadn't eaten in several days, as my stomach kept politely reminding me. I needed a meal and some directions. Hanging out at a sketchy dive bar seemed like one of the least dangerous things I had done in a while.

I walked towards the door. The men around it stopped laughing and stared at me. The one missing an eye looked like he wanted to eat me. He might've scared me if I hadn't just had a nightmare about a homicidal supervillain with bleeding red eyes. I ignored them and pushed past the doors. Country music played softly in the background. The barn was empty save for a bartender and a cook in the back.

I shuffled up to the bar and sat down, wincing as the stool made an ungodly screeching noise on the wood floor. The bartender raised his eyebrow at me and slung a rag over his shoulder.

"Boy, I know you're not old enough to be drinkin' at this bar," he said, his accent thick and slow.

"Do you have any food?" I asked. He rolled his eyes and shoved a menu that looked about fifty years old across the counter. I scanned the options, searching for the cheapest thing. I settled on a chicken-finger basket and a cup of water for $7.99 and grudgingly gave up the bills to pay for it. I scarfed it down, barely pausing to breathe between bites. I had to resist the urge to lick the grease off the wax paper.

After the bartender took the basket back, I sat with my elbows on the bar, wondering what the hell I was going to do. If I couldn't go back home, where else was I supposed to go? How was I supposed to get more gas, more food, a phone, or a freaking map?

I could steal. Surely it wouldn't be that hard to pickpocket a drunk guy? But if I got caught and the police were called, it would all be over. I couldn't do anything risky.

At least going to the bathroom is free, I thought, getting up. As I reached for the door, the cook from the back opened it. We locked eyes. He had floppy red hair and stubble to match. He wasn't my type; I never understood the appeal of beards.

But based on the look in his eyes, I could be his type. He hadn't moved from the doorframe yet. Maybe it was the hazy lighting, but I swore his cheeks were pink.

"What's your name, Stranger?" he asked, his accent low and slow.

"Cy – I mean . . . Jack," I said. *Better to go by my human name.* "Can you tell me where we are?"

"Few hours from the coast," he said. *The coast. The ocean.*

Possibilities suddenly swarmed my mind. Brian said we weren't the only sirens – that the Slayers were hunting the ones of us that were left. Was it possible they lived by the Atlantic? Maybe I could find some others – finally get my questions answered. I wanted to know what else my parents had lied to me about.

"About how far of a drive is that?" I asked.

"Two more hours," he said. *That's not much more gas money,* I thought. But I would still need more for food, a phone, clothes, probably – *no, definitely* – deodorant.

"Would you let me help you wash dishes for some money?" I asked. He beckoned me to follow him as he walked down the hallway and through the employees-only door. It smelled like fries and oil that hadn't been changed since the 80s. The bartender from before crossed his arms and eyed me up and down.

"Fella wants a job," the redhead said.

"No," the bartender said flatly. "I barely got enough customers to justify paying you, let alone whatever riff-raff you decide to bring back here." The redhead deflated but nodded, giving me a sympathetic look.

"Sorry, man."

I spent the rest of the night sitting in the minivan, trying to will my headache and remaining hunger pangs away. My one opportunity to earn money the god-honoring way had dissolved to dust under the glare of the bartender. I wouldn't feel that bad stealing from him, but then I risked getting the cops called on me. Maybe I could beg on the street, but I had barely seen any other cars drive by. Besides, couldn't I get in trouble for panhandling, too?

Maybe I should walk to the ocean.

Maybe you should use your powers.

I frowned as the thought crossed my mind. Using my water powers to earn money didn't make any sense – unless I could convince people it was a magic show.

No, idiot. Your other powers.

The way the redhead had blushed in the bathroom flashed through my head. *Okay, so he thought I was cute,* I thought. That's not a superpower. I tried to seduce Jack, and it didn't work. The myth that mermen could lure others to their deaths was only that – a myth.

You're not a merman. You're a siren.

As if by fate, the back door of the bar opened. The redhead carried a bag of trash over his shoulder, his breath white in the cold air. I watched him as he threw it in the dumpster, and almost yelped when he suddenly looked over at me, his eyes boring into mine.

He glanced back behind him, and then at me, and then behind him again before scurrying over to the van. I opened the door, tense as he slowed to a stop.

His cheeks were flushed again – or maybe it was just the cold. He fiddled with his thumbs.

"Sorry to disturb you," he finally said. "It's just – my dad said he was gonna call the cops on you if you didn't leave by morning. Just thought you'd want to know," he mumbled, looking down at the ground.

Jeez, this kid's got it bad, I thought. How come no one I ever flirted with at Tredecim acted like this?

Seduce him.

"Thank you," I said. "Do you want to sit in here for a minute? It's not much warmer, but you look cold." He looked back at the bar and hesitated. "You don't have to stay long," I said. He finally worked up the courage and crawled into the backseat with me.

"Have you been living in here?" he asked.

"Kinda," I admitted, pulling at my hair.

"You in some kinda trouble?" the redhead asked. *You could definitely say that*, I thought.

"Long story. What's your name?" I asked.

"Devin."

"What are you doing being a line cook for a dive bar, Devin?"

He was putty in my hands. It was like he had never been asked a personal question in his life. He rambled and rambled about how it was just him and his dad. They lived in a mobile home a mile up the road, but had fallen on hard times. He would much rather spend his days doing anything else – he loved horses – but his dad had him working so much he didn't have any time to do anything fun. The bikers always hanging around out front but never buying anything didn't exactly help business either.

I soaked up his words, keeping my eyes trained on him as he talked. At some point, he relaxed, leaning against the seat with his ankle on his knee.

"Wow," I finally said. "Sounds like your dad is a real pain in the ass."

He laughed. "Yeah. I mean, he's doing the best he can. I'm sorry again about not being able to get you a job. Looks like you're in more need than we are."

I shrugged, my palms sweating. *Make him give you what you want.*

"Maybe there is a way you can help me," I said, my voice velvet, my hand moving slightly closer to his. His body immediately went tense again. I could smell his sweat.

"What do you need?" he asked.

"To get to the coast without being found."

I still didn't have a clear plan in place, but something in my gut told me that I would find my purpose once I got back to the ocean. I just needed a way to get there without being caught or running out of money.

Devin nodded, looking determined. "I'll be back before morning. Lay low. I'll get you what you need."

Hours later, I was awoken by a tapping on the windshield. I opened the door and let Devin clamor into the backseat. The sun was barely starting to peek out behind him. At least this nap hadn't involved any horrible nightmares.

"This was all I could get," he said, panting. He handed me a tattered book bag. I opened it, grinning.

Devin had managed to scrounge up everything I didn't know I needed – a new license plate, a burner phone, and enough cash to fuel up the car. He had even gotten me a stick of deodorant.

"Where did you get a license plate?" I asked.

"Don't worry about it."

I sniggered. "Thank you. Now, what can I do for you?" I asked.

Devin flushed again, looking down at the floor and mashing his thumbs together. "You don't got to do anything for me, man," he said. "I mean, you listened to me talk last night." *Dang, that's really sad,* I thought.

"You don't have any friends? A girlfriend?" I asked.

He shook his head. "All the folks at my school think I'm white trash," he muttered. "And they're probably right. But one day I'm gonna get out of this dump and make something of myself."

My hand was holding his before I realized it. "There's nothing wrong with you," I said. "Anybody would be lucky to have you. You're hardworking and kind – that's more than most people out there right now." *Some people are murderers.*

He smiled. Our eyes landed on our joined pair of hands. I wondered if it was too late to remove mine without making it awkward.

"I appreciate that more than you know," Devin said, squeezing my hand before opening the car door. "I've got to get back before my dad notices I'm gone."

I leaned out after him. "Are you sure there's nothing I can do to repay you?" I asked.

He turned around and smiled, tipping his cowboy hat. "You already have."

Half an hour later, my license plate was switched, the car was full of gas, the sun was firmly in the sky. I programmed one number into my cell phone and labeled it IN CASE OF EMERGENCY. I liked to think that somehow, having Reece as a secret last-resort would keep me safe – a good luck charm of sorts. As I started driving, I replayed every word that had been exchanged between me and the redheaded cowboy.

I hadn't *actually* seduced him, right? I might've been a little flirty, but I was always flirty. He hadn't thrown himself at me or anything; he had just done me a few favors. He was just a nice guy, right? I hadn't *made* him do anything. I couldn't – that wasn't something I could do. I wasn't dangerous. I wasn't like Brian.

On the way back to the highway, I passed the dive bar a final time. I slowed to a crawl, wondering if I would see my savior one last time.

I didn't – but I did see the same group of bikers loitering by the front. I frowned, and suddenly I had parked the minivan and was walking towards them. The bikers stopped and stared. I flexed my fingers, feeling the moisture trapped in the dirt. I could feel it vibrating under my feet, eager to follow my demands.

"You guys believe in mermaids?" I asked. A clump of water rose from the ground and congealed in the air, hovering like a UFO. A glass bottle crashed to the ground as Blackbeard's body went slack with shock.

From an outsider's perspective, it probably looked like telekinesis. But there wasn't anything I could do to control the water. It knew what I wanted and was happy to serve.

The blob hurled towards Blackbeard's face, wrapping around his nose and mouth like a blanket. He pawed at his face, screams garbled, and eyes bulging as his friends tried to peel it away. As his skin started to turn purple, I relaxed. The water returned to the ground. Blackbeard fell to his knees, sputtering for breath.

I knelt on his level. "If I were you, I would leave this establishment. Do you understand me?"

Blackbeard nodded, wheezing. The others watched in shocked silence as I walked back to my car. I sped off into the distance. A few hours later, the air started to smell like salt. Spanish moss draped itself over the trees. A seagull cried overhead.

Welcome home.

. . .

I thought diving into the ocean for the first time in years would be a magical, nostalgic experience. I had vague memories of laughing and giggling as I chased my parents through the waves, the taste of salt on my lips, the colorful fish.

It was not magical or nostalgic.

The salt burned my chapped lips, and the waves tried their best to throw me back onto shore. As I dug my fingers into the ground and attempted to drag myself back underwater, something buried in the sand pinched one of my fingers.

I almost turned around and went back to sleep in my car, but I forced myself forward until I was in open water. It was freezing. The lake got plenty cold in winter, but this felt like taking an ice bath. The water was clear, and I suddenly felt very nervous being in the open. The lake had offered plenty of places to hide. I was used to algae, not seaweed or crabs. The small lake fish typically left me alone, but what about ocean fish? Was I predator or prey out here?

At least I'll be able to see if any sharks or god knows what else tries to eat me, I thought, swiveling around.

I swam forward, shivering. I could swim across the lake back home in five minutes. I swam for five minutes and stopped, wondering how deep I should go. I wanted to find other sirens, but I had no clue where to start. Who's to say there were even any here? Were they pretending to be humans on land, or did they live in the ocean?

Thanks to my lying parents, I literally had nothing to go on. Brian hadn't specified where his family was from before being murdered. Maybe they were pretending to be human like my parents, or maybe they lived in a cave somewhere in the ocean.

I stayed close to the coast and eventually swam back up to the surface. I scanned the shore to make sure no one was there before pulling myself to the surface. I walked back to my car, my stomach growling. I had $27.16 left of the money after filling up the car enough to get here. I could afford another meal.

I wandered around town until I found a gas station still open. I purchased a suspicious-looking hot dog on the rollers and ate it back in my car. *I need to get better at not eating again,* I thought. Especially since I no longer had any of my meds. I couldn't risk any water accidents. Yesterday at the bar was the last time. I had to stop.

I left the hotdog wrapper balled up in the passenger seat and lay down in the back in an attempt to sleep. I would figure out what to do in the morning.

Not wearing a seatbelt that day saved my life – or doomed me – either interpretation would fit. My small body went right through the window, leaving my parents trapped inside as the car flipped like a pancake.

It took me precious seconds to pick my head up off the asphalt. I followed the trail of skin and blood back to the car. It had landed upside down. My parents swung from their seatbelts. Blood dripped from a gash on my dad's forehead. My mom's mouth hung open. Both of their eyes were closed. Other cars screeched to a halt. One person jumped out and ran to my parents, shouting. Another was talking on their phone. I scanned the area but didn't see another injured car. Whoever had hit us was already gone.

The stench of what I would later realize was gasoline filled my nose. It was puddling under the car. I fought to lift the rest of my body. My parents had lectured me a thousand times about how we were never supposed to go to a hospital or call the police for anything. I had to stop whoever was calling for help and get my parents out of the car. I could fix them up at home. Maybe then they would forgive me for using my powers.

The puddle under the car ignited. The humans who had gathered around to help screamed and jumped backwards as car parts went flying. Heat scorched my face, the force of the explosion rolling me further away from the accident.

When I opened my eyes again, I was looking at the beach. Waves lapped up on the golden shore, unaware of the catastrophe happening yards away.

I could save them. Coax the seawater across the street and extinguish the flames. But there was a small crowd of humans who would see every move I made. They would report me. Even if my parents survived, we would be damned to whatever nightmares humans would have in store for freaks like us.

You don't want to be evil, do you?

Sirens wailed in the distance as smoke billowed up in the sky. Someone finally noticed me and ran over, shaking me, shouting in my face to see if I was responsive.

But all I could hear was the crackle and pop of my life burning away.

TWO

The room in the front office was stuffy. The secretary handed me my schedule like she had been expecting me to show up. "Mrs. Wellborne will be your homeroom teacher. Need help finding the room?"

I shook my head and shouldered the run-down bookbag Devin had given me as I ventured into the main hallway. The number of other teenagers around me was instantly overwhelming. People who looked like bodybuilders shoved me, and smaller kids squeezed through the gaps. Everyone was talking, gossiping about their friends or panicking about a test. The noise was enough to make my skull vibrate.

The bell blared, nearly making me jump out of my shoes, and the hallway suddenly emptied. I took a deep breath and started checking my schedule against the numbers on the doors. I finally found my first period and cautiously poked my head in.

Most of the other kids were already seated, looking bored as they doodled on their papers. Two other kids who looked as awkward as I did stood by the front wall as the teacher angrily muttered to herself. She looked up at me over her glasses, and I swore I saw a vein on her forehead twitch.

"Don't tell me. You're in my class too?" she asked. I debated turning back down the hallway and running for it, but I held up my schedule with a shaking hand instead. "Yes?"

She rolled her eyes. "Thank god this is my last year," she muttered. "Three new kids in one day. I was supposed to have small classes." The other two kids glanced up at me. One of them had curly golden hair and a jawline that could cut glass. The other was a short girl wearing a t-shirt that said *Team Oxford Comma* tucked into a button-up skirt and red Converse to top it all off. I wiggled my eyebrow at both of them, but quickly remembered I wasn't here to flirt or gain attention. I was here to find the other sirens. I had no clue if any were here, but it wouldn't hurt to look.

Turns out, it was pretty easy to walk into a school and pretend you were a student. The front office already had a schedule for me.

"Well, might as well introduce yourselves and find a seat," the teacher said, pushing her glasses up her nose. "We have a lot to get done today." The blond boy cleared his throat.

"My name is Hamen," he said, his voice deep and rich, almost like he was a newscaster in a previous life.

"I'm Abigail," the girl said, her voice delicate and squeaky.

"Jack," I said. The name tasted bitter on my lips, but I didn't want to attract any unnecessary attention.

"Very well. You three go sit in that back corner. I'll catch up with you guys in a minute." We shuffled to the back and sat down at a table. *At least I'm not the only new kid,* I thought. Abigail glanced between the two of us, picking at her cuticles. Hamen stared down at the table, barely blinking or moving. *Might as well start here,* I thought.

"Sooo, where are you guys from? What brings you here?" I asked.

"My family just moved here from Ohio," Abigail said. "You?"

"California," Hamen said.

I nodded. "Well, I've always lived here, but I've been homeschooled," I lied.

"Why'd you switch?" Abigail asked.

"Just wanted to try something different before college," I said. I didn't know why I hadn't thought of looking for sirens at a school before – the idea was brilliant. It was the perfect disguise, and unlike my first day of kindergarten, I knew how to handle my emotions. There would be no exploding water bottles today.

Mrs. Wellborne walked over to our group, dropping a stack of papers between us.

"So, the others have been working on a group project for the past few days. I'll extend the due date for you all since you're new, of course, but you'll have a lot more homework to do."

Hamen picked up a packet and frowned. "Can I work by myself?" he asked.

Mrs. Wellborne raised a tired eyebrow. "You realize it'll be a lot more work for you, right?" Hamen nodded. "Very well." Mrs. Wellborne turned to face me and Abigail. "What about you two?"

"We'll work together," Abigail said quickly, shooting me a sideways glance. *I guess I'm working with her*, I thought.

Mrs. Wellborne walked away, and Hamen promptly tuned us out by shoving in a pair of earbuds. I grabbed a paper and started to skim, but few of the words processed through my brain. In the background, Abigail made suggestions about what we could study. I blindly agreed to it, too busy wondering who could secretly be a siren to pay much attention.

The bell finally rang, and I hurried through the hallway to my next class. By some miracle, I had ended up in chorus. *At least that's something I'll enjoy.*

The teacher was a young blonde white woman wearing a pencil skirt and a ruffled red blouse that matched her red lipstick. I introduced myself to the class, grabbed a copy of the sheet music, and took a spot in the front row. Another student sitting at the piano cleared his throat and began to play. I started singing along, and by the time the first verse was done, half the class was staring at me, including the teacher. She stopped everyone in the middle of the next verse and walked over to me.

"What did you say your name was again?" she asked. I swallowed, wondering if I had done something wrong.

"Jack, ma'am."

"You have a beautiful voice, Jack. Why don't you come to the front?"

I had no choice but to follow her and face the room. "Would you mind singing the second verse for us?" she asked. Flushed beneath the lights, I swallowed and began to sing. By the time I was done, several mouths were hanging open.

Crap, I'm not supposed to be getting this much attention, I thought.

"I think we just found our new soloist," the teacher said. "That's how I want all of you to sound!" The rest of the class applauded, except for the kid at the piano, who looked like he wanted to squish me under his shoe. *What's his problem?* I wondered.

By the end of class, I had an inkling of what it felt like to be popular. Out of the corner of my eye, I saw several girls giggling and blushing as they pointed at me. The teacher showered me with compliments to the point of embarrassment.

I didn't understand. I had sung in front of other kids at Tredecim too, but they had never reacted like this. Had Brian just put everyone under a spell to hate me, no matter what I did? If I ever went back, would everyone like me?

No, they would be terrified of you. You're a monster.

The bell rang, and I started to filter out with the others when one of the giggling girls pulled at my shirt. She had her dark hair shaved in a pixie cut and almost too many piercings to count.

"Hey, Sweetie, want to help me put all the sheet music back into the closet real quick?" she purred. I nodded without thinking about it and followed her despite not collecting any of the folders strewn on the bleachers.

She held the door open for me and shut it behind us. Only then did my brain register the lack of collected materials.

"Hey, don't we need the –" I turned around to see her cheery smile replaced with a scowl.

"Do you want to explain what the hell you were doing out there?" she demanded, her eyes flashing red.

They had to sedate me at the hospital. Every time I wandered close to consciousness, I clawed needles and bandages off my body and flung them at whoever happened to be closest. I responded to a psychologist's attempts to talk with spitting and demanding to see my parents.

When the doctors finally convinced me they were dead, I stopped fighting. Stopped talking. Stopped eating. I might as well have been dead, too.

A social worker arrived with my parents' remains in a cardboard box. She asked me where I wanted to scatter their ashes, and I ignored her. I didn't deserve a goodbye, or closure, or the medication they gave me that made the raw spots of missing skin not hurt as much.

It was my fault that my parents were cinders.

THREE

I almost fainted. I almost screamed. I almost took every molecule of water out of the air and flung it at her face.

But all I actually did was stand there, frozen as memories of Brian replayed themselves from my head.

Why does this one have red eyes, too?

And how the fuck did she know I was a siren?

A knock sounded, and the girl wordlessly opened it. The piano kid walked in, looking no happier. His arms looked like he spent all of his free time weight-lifting and getting tattoos.

This is how it ends, I thought. *I'm going to get murdered in a music room closet.*

"I already texted Claire; she's gonna wanna see this," piano kid said, crossing his arms. "You want to explain yourself? Why were you charming everyone?"

His words swum around in my head, none of them quite registering. It was all I could do to stay on my feet. I desperately wanted to siphon all the water in the air around me and use it as a battering ram to escape, but I had just promised myself I was done using my powers. I would either escape the old-fashioned way or die.

The pair exchanged a look, their harsh gazes slightly softening.

"Sweetheart, you do know you're a siren, right?" the girl asked.

I laughed so hard it sounded like a bark. They both jumped back, nearly upsetting a music stand. "How–how could I not know I'm a siren?" I cackled, ignoring the irony that I definitely didn't know I was a siren until a few days ago. They let my laughter wind down.

"Let's start over," the girl said slowly. "My name is Victoria. That's Roger. What's your name again?"

"Cyan," I said. "Wait, fuck, I mean Jack." Victoria and Roger exchanged another look. I ran my fingers through my hair, praying I would melt into the floor.

"Jack is my human name. You know, because . . . Cyan sounds so weird? Never mind. You guys are sirens, too? I've never . . . I've never met other sirens." It was only a half-lie.

"Ohhh, that's why you're so clueless," Roger said. The bell rang again, making us all jump again.

"Jeez, we don't have time for this whole conversation right now," Victoria said. "Meet us on the beach later tonight, by the old lifeguard tower. And for the love of god, no more singing around the humans until then!"

I could only nod as they ushered me out of the closet. I fumbled with my schedule and somehow found myself in gym running laps and losing very badly at dodgeball. I went through the rest of the day in a fog, my heart pounding, my hands trembling.

I'd found them.

Later that night, I stumbled upon the old lifeguard tower after wandering down the beach. Three figures sat atop the sagging structure, whispering in the darkness. Why are we meeting on land? Shouldn't a siren get-together be underwater? I wondered.

I climbed the steps and offered a wave as the group looked up at me. Victoria and Roger leaned against the railing as a younger blonde kid barely looked up from her phone to scan me over.

"Sup, Newbie. I'm Claire," she said, tapping the floor next to her. "Heard you don't even know what charming is."

I sat down, feeling like it was my first day of kindergarten all over again. "No . . . afraid not."

Claire clicked her tongue. "Let me guess – parents killed by Slayers, too, huh? That's why you're out here all by yourself, not knowing your tail from your asshole?"

"You know about the Slayers?" I whispered.

"How do you know about the Slayers but not charming?" Roger demanded. Victoria elbowed him.

"Be nice!" she hissed. She turned a softer gaze to me, as if I were a wild animal she was trying to coax into a cage. "How old were you when your parents died?"

I swallowed. "Five. I was adopted by humans, but . . . I ran away trying to find others."

"So, both of your biological parents were sirens? They were both killed by the Slayers?" Roger clarified.

"Of course. It's not like sirens and humans can have kids," I said, chuckling. I was met with silence.

"Um . . . . yes, they can. My father is a siren, and my mom is human," Victoria said. "It's quite common."

My head spun. My parents had constantly lectured me about how sirens and humans were forbidden from falling in love. I had spent my whole life bracing myself for loneliness.

My eye twitched. "Really?"

She nodded. "Yeah. They didn't even tell me I was a siren until I was older."

"How could you not notice having a tail?" I laughed.

"Cyan, we get our tails from our mothers and our powers from our fathers. Victoria didn't have a siren mom, so she just has the powers," Roger explained. "She can't even charm people – that's why she can sing in chorus. Both of my parents were sirens, so that's why I only play the piano."

My laugh quickly faded. Did my parents lie to me about *everything?*

"So . . . what's the difference between charming someone and using your powers?" I asked.

"Charming is a fancy word for making someone horny," Claire said.

Victoria rolled her eyes. "Crudely put, but yes."

My gut twisted. Devin's flushed face appeared in my memory.

"But it's not like I can *make* people do whatever I want by . . . charming them, right?" I protested, thinking back to Jack and Reece. I had tried to lure them into the water the stereotypical-siren way, only to be met with blank stares.

"You can only charm people who bat for your team," Roger said. "And no, it's not quite that simple."

Clarie's eyes flashed red. "That's what your powers are for," she grinned.

"So, what can you three do?" I asked, ignoring the shiver traveling down my spine.

"Same thing as you. There were two types of sirens. We're all part of what's called the Red Powerline well because . . . our eyes are red. We are blessed, cursed, whatever you prefer, to fuck with people's emotions," Claire said.

Just like Brian, I thought, wrapping my arms around myself. *Wait, what do they mean by same as you?*

Roger crossed his arms. "Just because we have them doesn't mean we have the right to use them," he said, sounding borderline parental.

Claire rolled her eyes. "I only mess with people sometimes," she whined.

"Do you not use your powers at all?" I asked Roger.

He shook his head. "I don't think it's right to mess with people's heads without their consent. And getting consent is basically impossible, so . . ."

"I try to use mine to make people feel better," Victoria said. "Like if I know someone's really stressed about a test, I'll help them relax."

"And I only use mine to mess with people who bother me," Claire said, shooting me a look. "So *don't* bother me."

I swallowed and gave her a thumbs-up. *Okay, so not* just *like Brian*, I thought. These all seemed like relatively level-headed people . . . certainly not serial killers out for revenge.

"What's the other kind of siren?" I asked, sure, I knew the answer already.

All three took a deep breath, like they were about to relive a complicated memory.

"Fucking psychos," Roger muttered under his breath. "The goddamn reason the Slayers started hunting us to begin with."

"The good thing is – they're all gone now," Victoria said. "The Slayers killed all of them a while ago. Rumor has it there's a few Slayers still hunting the Red Powerline on the west coast, but they'll never find us over here."

My blood ran cold. Something squirmed in my gut.

"They were the Blue Powerline," Claire said. "My parents told me they were created by the ancient sea gods to punish the humans for sailing their waters. They terrorized the seas for hundreds of years, luring humans to their deaths, crashing their ships. The seas did whatever they wanted, and what they wanted was destruction."

Oh no, don't say it.

"Hence, why the Siren Slayers were organized. They went after the Blue Powerline first. They spared any member of the Red Powerline who helped the Slayers track them down. Once they were all dead, most of the Slayers retired, but there's those few stubborn ones left who think we all deserve to kick the bucket," she finished, picking up her phone again.

My heart forgot to beat. I was sure I would scream if I dared open my mouth. *There's no way,* I thought. *She has to be making that up. A whole line of sirens responsible for all the myths? That's insane.*

"It's true," Victoria said, as if she could see the doubt on my face.

"Why-why just the . . . I mean, it's not like we aren't dangerous too," I said, trying not to let my voice wobble. "We can make people do whatever we want."

Roger shrugged. "I mean, we *can* be dangerous if we want to be, I guess. But that goes for any organism. We get to *choose* when we want to use our powers, and most of us barely use them, if at all. The Blue Powerline never had a choice. That's just what they were. Dangerous."

You don't want to be a bad siren, do you?

"So, there's only one Powerline now? The red one?" I asked.

"Not if the third one actually exists," Roger grinned. Victoria and Claire rolled their eyes.

"Roger is convinced there's a third powerline of sirens that can only feel emotions from other people," Victoria said.

"Not sirens – mermaids," Rodger argued. "My grandmother told me stories about them for years! And I swear I've seen them since moving here. They're all blue – have these weird extra fins on their backs. Super skittish."

Brian's words echoed through my head. *You think you're a mermaid. Harmless, shy little things.*

"Yeah, yeah, mermaids exist," Claire mocked. "So do vampires and werewolves." Roger crossed his arms.

"Maybe they do! Who's to say we're not the only mythical creatures out there?" he countered. *Wait until he finds out the Blue Powerline isn't dead,* I thought. I stood up, trying not to vomit. I had originally wanted to tell them everything about Brian and Tredecim, but there was no way to do that without revealing what I really was.

I muttered an excuse about having homework to do and stumbled down the stairs back to the sand. I bolted as soon as I was out of sight. I didn't stop until I was back in my car with the door shut.

And then I screamed.

Oh my god.

I slammed my fists against the steering wheel, my eyes gleaming. Their words replayed in my head on a loop.

Happens all the time.

Humans and sirens could fall in love. There had been no reason for me to try to hide my identity and repress every crush I had ever had.

It only works on people who bat for your team.

Now it made sense why my singing hadn't worked on Jack or Reece. Jack was your average straight boy, and Reece . . . well, Reece was just Reece with her broken amygdala. Powers were immune on her. But I had apparently charmed all the straight girls and gay guys in my chorus class, including the teacher . . . which was gross now that I was thinking about it.

The Slayers killed all of them a while ago.

No, they didn't.

The seas did whatever they wanted, and what they wanted was destruction.

The nail in the coffin. I was the monster of monsters. A subsection of a species that murdered humans for fun. It made too much sense. No wonder Brian was enamored with me. No wonder my parents and the Slayers were terrified of me. I was the perfect killing machine and had no idea.

This is why my parents lied to me, I thought. They knew they were being hunted. They knew they were the last ones. That's why we came to land and fled to the East Coast. They were trying to escape. They were trying to keep me safe.

But it hadn't worked. The Slayers had found us anyway. Except they missed one. Me.

My stomach lurched again, and I sucked in a deep breath to keep myself from throwing up.

Mr. Falcon had realized exactly what I was the moment I had used my powers in the jail cell. That's why he wanted to get rid of me so bad. But his plan hadn't worked.

All the oxygen seemed to disappear from the car. I could scarcely breathe.

Victoria said there were still Slayers left. With my luck, every Slayer on the planet probably now knew I was alive – that they hadn't extinguished the Blue Powerline after all. They were going to stop at nothing to put me six feet underground. It was only a matter of time until they found me.

All because of Mr. Falcon.

I curled my knees up to my chest, breathing hard. *What the hell am I supposed to do now?* I thought. I couldn't go back home. I couldn't stay here and put the others in danger. Where was I supposed to go?

You should kill Falcon.

I hated Nichole and Robert. The social worker who placed me with them told me how lucky I was that I was being adopted at the ripe old age of five after only having been in the system for a moment, but I didn't feel lucky. My skin itched like the scales underneath were trying to claw their way out – a constant reminder that these strangers would never know who I really was. I no longer had breaks where I didn't have to pretend to be human.

I was furious. Furious that my parents had died, furious I wasn't allowed to save them, furious they had left me here without another soul in the world I could be honest with, furious I had to live with strangers.

But I couldn't exactly tell anyone that without exposing everything I had sworn to keep secret. Nichole and Robert's home was soon peppered with holes in the drywall, claw marks in the floor, and broken furniture. Every attempt to demonstrate kindness was met with cruelty on my part. I wanted my new guardians to hate me as much as I hated them.

FOUR

I lay awake in the backseat of my car, unable to sleep. If my parents were watching me from beyond the grave, they would see their worst nightmare coming true. They had risked everything trying to keep me safe, trying to keep me from becoming the monster from the myths.

It hadn't worked. My violent tendencies as a kid made too much sense. I had never grown out of it – just smothered it with medication and starvation.

And now I couldn't stop thinking about murdering my best friend's father. I really was a monster.

A monster who had just started in another high school. Was it too early to drop out? What would the other sirens think if I disappeared? Would they read between the lines and help the Slayers find me themselves?

Kill Falcon.

I shook my head and begrudgingly began the walk to school. Pretending like everything was normal seemed like the safest choice until I figured out what to do next.

That proved more difficult than I thought. As soon as I stepped into chorus, Roger and Victoria cornered me.

"Dude, where did you disappear to yesterday?" Roger demanded, his arms crossed.

"Leave him alone," Victoria crooned. "We probably overwhelmed him yesterday – right, Cyan? Or Jack, I mean."

I nodded, unsure of what else to say. How long would it take for them to realize I was one of the creatures that was supposed to be extinct?

"Yeah, sorry. It was just . . . a lot," I said, running my fingers through my hair.

"My dad said you were welcome to stay with us," Victoria said, placing a manicured hand on my arm. "I told him you were a runaway, and he totally understands."

"Thanks, I'll . . . I'll think about it," I said as the teacher shouted for our attention. Shivers traveled down my spine as she winked at me before guiding us through the first song. I lip-sang, careful not to let a single note past my lips.

The bell rang after an agonizing forty-five minutes. I shuffled to my next class, trying to figure out what to do between impulsive thoughts of hiding in the sea for the rest of my life and murdering my best friend's dad.

Part of me rationalized it was the only logical thing to do. Killing the guy who wants to kill you was a perfectly reasonable thing, right? It was self-defense. But there were several logistical issues. What if another Slayer found me first? What if Falcon's death just made the other Slayers even angrier? How would I do it and get away with it? I wasn't a criminal mastermind.

Just drown him, cut apart his body, and feed him to the sharks.

An involuntary shiver traveled down my spine. I'm not killing anyone, I thought. That'll just make me the monster they think I am. But maybe . . . maybe there was another way to get Mr. Falcon out of the picture.

My parents' death had been staged to look like an accident, a hit-and-run where the driver was never found. If I could prove the driver was Mr. Falcon, he would be arrested. He would definitely have a hard time killing me in prison. It wasn't like he would be able to justify himself by saying that his victims were mythical creatures. Maybe it would still piss off the Slayers, but it would be one less person to worry about. Maybe I could disappear again, go into witness protection so they couldn't find me.

But how on Earth would I go about proving it? I wondered.

"Um . . . hello? Earth to . . . what was your name again? Jack?"

I jerked my head up to see the new girl from yesterday standing in front of me. She was wearing another t-shirt and ruffled skirt combination. "Oh yeah, sorry. What's up?" I said.

"We're supposed to be working on this project together, remember?" she said. She dragged a desk over beside mine. "So, did you actually read over the directions at all, or am I gonna have to explain everything again?" she asked.

I smiled sheepishly. I couldn't even remember what class I was in to save my soul. "Sorry, I've been . . . distracted . . . what's your name again?"

"Abigail," she said, rolling her eyes. "If you want, you can come over to my place after school to work on it. It's gonna be a long project. Maybe you'll be less *distracted* there."

I nodded halfheartedly. *Great, now you have to keep going to school if you don't want to dump this entire project on her*, I thought. I definitely didn't want to spend my free time doing homework. But maybe going to her house would help me appear normal.

"Give me your phone number so I can text you the address," she said.

I rattled it off. Before school ended, I used a library computer to Google the directions to her house and scribbled down a crude map.

Wait, I'm on a computer.

I looked around to make sure no one was watching over my shoulder and quickly typed in the first burning question in my mind.

How are hit-and-runs investigated?

A million results popped up, and I clicked on the first website I saw. I scrolled through the page. *Police tape off the scene . . . bystanders interviewed . . . security footage reviewed . . .*

Had any of that been done? I wondered. My memories from that day were pretty sketchy, other than my parents calling me evil before bursting into flames. Maybe I could go to the police station and ask.

I almost laughed aloud. Mr. Falcon had been a cop. Maybe a fake cop, but still. For all I knew, all Slayers were masquerading as police officers. If Mr. Falcon had actually reported me, showing up at a police station asking for details about my parents' deaths would be a dead giveaway. I wouldn't make it that easy for them.

Besides, if the whole thing had been orchestrated by the Slayers, then maybe there was no actual investigation. Brian had printed out a police report and scribbled the truth over it, after all. The report said nothing about possible suspects or foul play.

I sighed. *This is pointless,* I thought. *There's no way I could ever find proof that Mr. Falcon actually did it.*

Unless you find him and torture a confession out of him.

After school, I followed my crude map to Abigail's house. Her address led me downtown first, where I was shocked to realize I recognized some buildings.

There was a little ice cream shop on the corner. I still remembered the first time my parents had cautiously walked up to the counter and ordered me something after seeing other kids enjoy it so much. We all fell in love with ice cream that day. We went back every day, working our way through every flavor on the menu. And then my dad would put me on his shoulders and carry me home as ice cream dripped onto his dark hair.

Home.

My chest seized. Without thinking, I let my feet carry me down the familiar streets until I was looking up at the dirt-stained trailer. My first human home.

A little boy playing basketball across the street noticed me staring. "I wouldn't go in there if I were you. Place is totally haunted."

"Anyone live there?" I asked. The boy shook his head. I wanted to point out that if my parents were haunting anything, they'd probably haunt the car they died in instead of the house, but I didn't. I waited for the boy to go back inside his house. I walked up to the front door. The porch sank beneath my feet. I lifted my hand to knock as if anyone would answer.

Why is the house still sitting here? I wondered. Why would no one buy it and fix it up?

My hand strayed closer to the doorknob. It turned easily in my hand.

I jumped backwards as if I had been burned. What was the point of going inside? It wasn't like the answer to my problems would be hiding under the floorboards. I had a perfectly normal study session to attend. Exploring an abandoned house wouldn't help me stay under the radar.

I tore myself away from the house and booked it down the street. I didn't stop running until it and the damned ice cream ship were out of sight.

Fuck, why did I ever want to come back here?

I eventually slowed down, gasping for breath and wiping the sweat off my brow. I pulled my map from my pocket and started back towards Abigail's place. An hour later, I found it after triple-checking the address was correct.

I was standing in front of no mere house – more like a castle. Stone pillars with lions on top guarded the cobblestone walkway to the front door. A bright turquoise pool glistened in the sunlight off to the right. Not a blade of grass was out of place on the lawn.

As I stood there staring at the stone-encrusted walls, Abigail opened the front door. "You gonna come in or just stand there?" she called. I made my legs move and headed inside. I whistled as I stepped into the living room – no, not living room – it was fancier – like a *foyer*. An entire jeweled chandelier hung from the vaulted ceiling. The walls were painted rich-person beige that matched the couches and chairs. Abigail looked out of place in her leggings and crop top.

"Are you sure that your parents won't mind me being here?" I asked, checking the bottoms of my shoes to make sure I wasn't tracking in any dirt.

"I live with my aunt, and no, she won't mind. She's hardly ever here, anyway."

I followed her through a set of French glass doors into a gigantic indoor pool. Abigail tossed her bookbag on a chair by the edge and stretched.

"I like to do my homework in here if that's okay," she said. "I like listening to the water. Let me grab you another chair." She vanished through the doors, leaving me feeling another level of inadequacy as I stared at the pool. *Her aunt is either a drug dealer or Jeff Bezos*, I thought. *Maybe she'll let me take a shower.* You could fit a whole school bus of homeless kids on the top floor, and she would probably never notice.

I accidentally kicked her chair as I strolled around the pool. Her bookbag slid to the floor, spilling its contents over the stone. I dove for the papers before they fluttered into the water and placed them on the chair before moving her bag to a safe spot. It was decorated with a dozen colorful pins. I chuckled as I looked over them. There was one with the dog on fire meme, and one that proclaimed *fries before guys*. Abigail chose that particular moment to walk back in as I was giggling.

"Having fun there?" she asked, her tone amused.

"Totally." I paused as I traced over a dinosaur pin with pink, blue, and white stripes. Most people would've missed it, but I knew what those colors meant.

"Are you trans?" I asked.

The color drained from her face. Her mouth opened and closed several times before words came out. "None of your damn business," she muttered, stomping up and yanking her bag away from me.

"Oh, sorry, I didn't mean to be nosy. I – I'm totally cool if you are!" I said quickly, putting my hands up.

She took a deep breath, turning her back to me. "I think you should go," she said coldly.

My hands fell back down to my sides. I stepped towards her, guilt burning a hole through my insides. "I-I'm sorry – I didn't mean to offend you. I'm not homophobic or anything if that's what you're afraid of –"

"Just go!" she snapped, turning. Her elbow hit me in the ribs, and I stumbled sideways. My worn-down shoes failed to find their grip on the slick stone floor.

Fuck.

I yelped as my legs gave out on me, falling backwards into the pool very much like the time Jack had pushed me off the dock. Only this time – I didn't drag anyone else in with me.

Warm water enveloped me – holy shit, the pool is *heated?* – and I watched in vain as my legs condensed into my tail.

Fuck fuck fuck how is this happening again?

I debated staying underwater forever. She would eventually have to leave, and I could make my escape then, right? Run to the ocean and hide there forever.

But what if she called someone? What if she posted about it online and the Slayers saw it?

I clawed my way back to the surface. I gasped for breath for several seconds before gathering up the courage to look at Abigail. She stared at me, her mouth hanging open. She remained that way for several very long seconds before screaming.

I winced at the shrill noise, retreating from the edge as she pointed at me, grabbing a textbook from her bookbag and holding it over her head like she was going to chuck it at me.

"What the fuck?" she screamed.

Just stay calm. You survived this process with two other humans already, I told myself.

"I guess we both have secrets about our bodies?" I chuckled weakly. She stopped screaming long enough to glare at me.

"You have a *tail*. We are not the same," she seethed. I put my hands up. "I promise I'm not dangerous." *Liar*. "Can we please just talk?"

She stared at me, the book wavering in her hands. "I thought you were a vampire," she finally whispered.

I blinked several times before her words sank into my head. "I'm sorry?"

"I thought you looked like a stereotypical vampire kid when I saw you at school the first time. You know . . . like if you had to be any mythical creature . . . you would be a vampire. You know . . . because you're kinda goth."

I burst out laughing. That was the same thing Reece had said when we ran into her in the woods. The book slowly lowered as my howls bounced off the ceiling.

"Why are you laughing?" she demanded.

I wiped tears from my eyes as I tried to compose myself. "Do you normally try to guess what mythical creatures your classmates are, or is this just ironic?"

She let the book drop to the ground as she sighed. "If you promise not to eat me or do any weird mermaid things, you can come out of the water."

I could hurt you just fine from a distance.

I carefully made my way to the edge. I took my time pulling myself up out of the pool and phasing, as if I were showing her that there were no weapons on me. She sat down hard in her chair as I shook the water out of my hair.

"Talk," she demanded.

"Hold on now, you have secrets too. Why are you so scared of being out of the closet? I mean, I'm bi, so I get it. I mean, I don't *get it*, but –"

She leaned forward in her chair, white knuckling the armrests. "You don't get shit!" she hissed. "First of all, I barely know you. Second of all, I didn't tell you or anyone else here because moving was supposed to be my chance to start over without any of the crap I had to deal with at my last school!"

I squirmed under her glare. "If it makes you feel better, you pass really well," I offered sheepishly.

She crossed her arms. "It doesn't! You have no clue what it's like to live in a world where you have to keep secrets just to be considered normal!"

I crossed my arms back. "Yes, I do actually," I said. Her glare finally softened. I cleared my throat. "Okay, ask me questions. But I also get to ask you questions – sound fair? I don't tell anyone, you don't tell anyone?" She hesitated a moment before nodding. "You can go first," I said.

"What the fuck are you?"

"A siren." *Fuck, why didn't I say merman?*

"Like those creatures from the legends?"

I winced and slowly gave her the same half-truth explanation I had given Reece and Jack – leaving out the part about the superpowers, group of murderers out for my head, and my newly-discovered sketchy family history.

"You said you're not out to anyone here? What about your aunt?" I asked.

She looked down at her lap. "Of course she knows. She raised me. She's been supportive of me the whole time. But the town I originally lived in, which watched me transition . . . they were more or less supportive. Nothing terrible happened, but I just wanted a chance to live as . . . normal a life as I could. And I thought moving to a new place where no one knew me from before would help."

I nodded. "So, when did you transition?"

"One question at a time. It's my turn." She wrung her hands together. "What are you doing here?"

I winced. "I'm . . ." There was no way I could tell her why I was really here. She didn't deserve to be dragged into this mess any more than Victoria and the others. I racked my brain for an excuse that would sound plausible. "Sirens are . . . migratory."

She raised her eyebrow. "Migratory?"

"Yes. We like to travel around a lot. Visit new places. The East Coast is warmer this time of year compared to the West." I had no clue if that statement was true or not, and I found myself praying that Abigail wasn't too much of a science nerd to see past my lame explanation. Thankfully, she seemed to buy it.

"And this migration includes going to random high schools?"

"One question at a time, remember?"

She pursed her lips.

"So, when did you transition?" I asked.

"Well . . . I kinda started when I was really little. One day, I told my aunt I wanted my name to be Abigail, and she went along with it. When I got older, she noticed it wasn't going away and took me to a psychologist. I started transitioning officially when I was ten. Started HRT when I was fifteen."

"Wow, I thought you had to be eighteen to start that?"

"My aunt and I were . . . very convincing. I'm lucky, I guess."

"Good for you."

"So, why are you going to high school? Where are your parents? Where do you live?"

I tried not to let the flash of anger show on my face. "My parents actually live . . . in the ocean. But most siren parents let their kids live on land for a few years to experience human life, which is why I go to school."

Abigail's eyes grew round. "Wow, that's incredible. So, you grew up in the ocean as a kid? And started living on land by yourself as a teenager? Just to experience everything?"

". . . yes." Technically, the first part wasn't a lie.

"Do you want to stay here on land or go back to live in the ocean with your folks?"

I forced down the lump that formed in my throat. "Not sure yet," I said quietly. We tapered off into silence. *This so isn't fair,* I thought. Abigail had just spilled her guts to me, and here I was, lying through my teeth. But there was no way in hell I was going to tell her what I had just come from. It was easier this way. Whenever I chose to leave, I could just tell her that I had decided to rejoin my parents and be done with it. She would go on for the rest of her life remembering me as a strange visitor – nothing more.

"Thank you for being honest with me. I'm sure it's difficult to be so open with humans," Abigail said. The knot of guilt in my stomach promptly tripled in size.

"Of course. I appreciate your understanding and not . . . freaking out. At least, not freaking out the entire time."

She chuckled. "And I appreciate you not being transphobic," she said.

I smiled, and my heart gave an unexpected lurch in my chest.

I sat on the steps outside, fumbling with a toy car and listening to the lake waves lap at the grass. Nichole and Robert remained inside, hopefully talking about how horrible I was. My knuckles were bruised and swollen from my latest tantrum. It had been a week of trying to make them regret bringing me into their home, but they weren't budging.

They weren't like my real parents. Never once had they yelled at me or whispered threats that could make the sun shiver. Every hateful word or broken thing was met with a gentle word, an attempted hug, a band-aid, a pitying look in their eyes.

It made me hate them more. They had no right to be kind to me when my real parents knew what I really deserved.

"Hi."

I looked up and saw another boy standing in the grass. He had messy brown hair and dark, tanned skin.

"Hi," I said. The boy took a step closer.

"You're my new neighbor," he said. "I live next door. Whatcha got there?" I shrugged and held up the battered toy car. "Can I play with it?" the boy asked. I nodded, and he joined me on the steps, plucking the car from my hands.

"My dad said that your parents died in a car accident, and that I should be nice to you," he said, twirling the car around in the air. "My mom died too."

For the first time since my arrival, my shoulders softened. "How did your mom die?" I asked.

"Giving birth to me," he said. "I never met her."

"I'm sorry."

"It's okay."

We sat and played in silence as I stared out at the lake. The water looked dark and gross, and didn't smell great either. I missed the ocean. I hadn't even taken a shower for fear of accidentally revealing myself.

The gentle waves suddenly swelled, and I dug my fingers into my arms. *Stop it calm down.* The waves quieted. I sighed. The boy noticed me staring out at the water.

"You can't go swimming here," he said. "Lake's too dangerous."

I frowned. "Wait . . . you're saying no one ever swims in there? Like . . . ever?" I asked.

The boy shook his head. "Nope."

Desperate thoughts filled my head. Maybe if I snuck out at night to swim, no one would see me. I could still be a merman in the dead of night when no one was watching. It wasn't ocean swims with my parents, but it was something.

No, I thought. *It's too dangerous. I can't risk it. If Nichole or Robert caught me sneaking out, it would be over. I can't reveal my secret. I can't be evil.*

FIVE

If I had a nickel for each time I had accidentally exposed myself by falling into a body of water, I would have two nickels. Which wasn't a lot, but it was weird that it had happened twice.

I couldn't help but compare Abigail's reaction to Reece and Jack. Both had started loud and asked a million questions, but I had felt safer leaving Abigail's house than I had after shoving Reece and Jack out my bedroom window. For some reason, I knew Abigail would keep my secret safe. I could trust her. She knew what it was like to hide.

I couldn't help but deliver an awkward smile when I saw her the next day at school. She grinned back as I settled next to her. We started working on our project since we hadn't exactly gotten to it the night before. Part of me was sad when the bell rang and we had to go our separate ways.

As soon as she was out of sight, I went right back to worrying about the Slayers. I was no closer to answers than I was the day before.

I couldn't stop thinking about my parents' house.

Part of me itched to go back. Maybe if it were really haunted, I could finally get some answers out of their spirits. Maybe they would apologize for lying to me.

They were just trying to protect you. Don't be selfish.

I swallowed a sudden lump in my throat. I had never had the opportunity to mourn at a headstone. Maybe going back there would be a way to get some closure. Maybe they left some things behind that would show that they really did love me more than they feared me.

Was it selfish and unnecessary? Probably. But the little boy who had let his parents burn alive wanted to say goodbye for the first and final time.

I waited until it was dark to make the journey. The door opened without hesitation, and I stepped inside.

For an abandoned house, it didn't look that bad. I guess thieves hadn't bothered to break in or steal because we had nothing of value. There was a thick layer of dust covering everything, but the paint wasn't peeling, and I couldn't smell any mold. I closed the door behind me and took a deep breath. I was five years old the last time I was here. Random memories revealed themselves as I walked through the empty house.

The kitchen still had a tablecloth with yellow flowers on it. My mom had been so excited when she found it at Walmart. She thought it was fascinating that humans decorated so much. Out in the sea – we hadn't had anything of the sort – just the ever-changing landscape.

The floor creaked under my weight. My throat closed up as I walked into my old bedroom. My one and only stuffed animal still lay on the bed – a green sea turtle I had nicknamed Jelly. I had cried and begged my parents to buy her, and they relented – if only to get me to shut up and quit drawing attention. At the time, she had been the only thing that reminded me of home.

My parents' room was painted yellow – another personal touch my mom had added. The mattress lay bare. They hadn't quite understood the point of covering a soft surface with more soft surfaces just for sleeping. A fly buzzed around the ceiling fan. I swallowed a sob as I sat on the edge of their bed, tracing the details in the padding.

My parents might not have been the most lovey-dovey people ever, but there's no way they were murderers, I thought. Maybe it was their parents or their parents' parents that were the crazy ones, but not them. Not me. *Right?*

The air in the room grew heavy, and I took a deep breath, digging my nails into my palm. I searched the rest of the house, but found nothing. We had had very little time to accumulate knick-knacks or make personal touches. All that was left of our second life was the dusty yellow paint and Jelly, whom I grabbed before sneaking out the front door.

I hesitated on the front porch, the Moon shining overhead. The trailer didn't look haunted anymore, just sad and lonely.

"Bye, Mom. Bye, Dad," I whispered under my breath. The house did nothing in return. I bit my lip, feeling guilty and angry all at once. "I know you're probably disappointed in me," I muttered. "But I promise – I'm getting justice for you. I won't let us fade into nothing."

I began my walk back to the van, ignoring the pangs of hunger in my stomach and clutching the musty stuffie to my chest. Newfound determination bloomed in my chest. I didn't know if spirits were real or not, but if they were, I was going to make my parents' ghosts proud of me if it was the last thing I did. It was the least I could do after failing them so many times.

Footsteps sounded behind me. I paused and spun around. The sidewalk was empty. The streetlights shone yellow on the pavement. The wind was salty. I turned and kept walking, but heard the noise again.

Shit, what if the house really was haunted? Was I being followed by my parents' ghosts?

I looked down at Jelly. Her black plastic eyes stared back at me, providing no answers. I sighed and squeezed her to my chest, only to feel a hard lump on her underbelly. I flipped her over and could barely make out a blinking light shining under her shell in the darkness. Dread curdled in my stomach.

Fuckfuckfuck

I forgot to breathe. What *were* the odds that my parents' house had *really* stayed abandoned for all those years? People bought houses from dead people all the time - and it was a decent house, too valuable to sit there for years.

Jelly fell out of my hands as someone grabbed me from behind. I twisted from their grasp and locked eyes with my assailant, fists clenched, adrenaline pounding through my veins. I was expecting Mr. Falcon - an adult armed with a gun, probably dressed up in a common work uniform. What I actually saw was creepier - someone much shorter and skinnier wearing a black hockey mask that covered their whole head.

"What do you want from me?" I snarled, even though I was sure I knew the answer. God, why did I have to stick my nose around in my past? I should've known the Slayers would've kept tabs on my parents' home. They had been lying in wait for me to come back, and I fell right into their trap. I was so stupid.

The Slayer didn't say anything as they pulled a silver knife from their right boot. Wait - a knife? What was this - the 1800s? Why were they attacking me with a knife and not something that could get rid of me from a distance?

The knife sailed through the air, heading right towards my chest. A shield of water instantaneously formed from the damp air, catching the knife inches before it sank into my flesh. *I guess you can use a knife to attack someone from a distance.* I jumped backwards and the water splashed to the ground, the weapon clattering to the concrete.

Shit, I used my powers, I thought. I just removed all doubt. I was the monster they were looking for.

"Who are you?" I demanded, trying to steady my shaking voice.

The Slayer rushed toward me. It occurred to me that it probably would've been smart to grab the knife and use it to defend myself, but by then, I was bolting to the ocean as fast as my legs could move. I couldn't even beat Brian in a fight – and he wasn't a trained assassin. There was no way I stood a chance against Hockey Mask.

I yelped as they tackled me from behind, sending us rolling across the sand. They ended up on top of me, the knife back in their hands. As the blade careened towards my chest, a wave of water crashed into us. For a moment, I had no clue which way was up or down as the water surged around me and up my nose.

I found land and gasped for breath as the water finally receded. Water streamed from my clothes and hair. It was a miracle I hadn't phased. Running away would be a lot harder without legs.

The Slayer was in a similar state a few yards away, coughing up seawater and dripping wet. They looked up and were back on their feet in an instant. My heart dropped as they ran at me, knife still brandished in their fist.

"Leave me alone!" I shouted, flinging my arms towards him. The ocean responded accordingly. A wave hit the Slayer with the force of a train, throwing him all the way back up towards the sidewalk. The Slayer's body collided with a street lamp pole before sinking motionless to the ground. Relief made my knees weak, and I sank to the sand, suddenly very grateful that my heart was still beating.

Wait, shit, are they dead?

My relief vanished as I scrambled back to my feet. I stood frozen, my heart hammering in my chest. Had I just killed someone? Goddamnit, why did I stop taking my meds? Why couldn't I just stop using my powers?

Evil.

After a few more moments of the stranger lying still, I inched over. I knelt and pressed my fingers against their throat. A pulse fluttered under my fingertips. Oh, thank god, I didn't kill them.

But you could. Drag him back to your van and torture them for information. Use that knife to carve a pretty design on their skin.

I shook my head, nearly jumping out of my skin as the Slayer groaned and stirred. I skittered away. I most certainly did not want to be there when they woke up or if they had backup on the way. I turned tail and bolted for the sea.

I never went back to my car. I had been *this close* to being caught. Who knew how much information the Slayers already had about me? Maybe they had just been biding their time to strike when I was alone and there were no other people around. Or maybe they hadn't known I was here until I had triggered the device in Jelly. Maybe they had put an alarm on my car, too. I wasn't about to risk walking into another trap.

I lingered in the sea until morning. I walked faster than normal to school. They couldn't kill me in the middle of a public school day, could they?

I breathed a sigh of relief as I settled into my first period. Abigail sat next to me.

I so do not have time for a stupid school project. What if she were secretly a Slayer and just biding her time to kill me?

I scanned her, as if I could see if she was harboring any weapons or hateful morals based on vibes alone. She didn't seem the murderous type in her skirt and baggy t-shirt.

Mrs. Wellborne rapped on the board to get our attention, and I spent the rest of the day debating whether I should ghost her or not. If the Slayers knew I was here, they might consider her another obstacle to get rid of. On the other hand, being around her might keep me safe. They couldn't expose themselves by murdering me in front of a normal person.

Goddamnit, why didn't I lift the mask of my attacker? Why was I so stupid?

I almost debated asking Roger and Victoria in chorus, but decided to keep my mouth shut. If they knew Slayers had found me, they would wonder why. I wasn't sure if I could explain my way out of that one. They thought they were safe here, and I didn't want to be the one to break the news that I had ruined that. Hopefully, the Slayers were just after me – not them. I didn't need more innocent people dying because of me.

I avoided Rodger and Victoria, certain they would be able to tell what I had done, and hurried to P.E. as soon as the bell rang. Gym was getting harder and harder to muscle through. Swimming for miles was easy compared to running laps with the sun beating down on my head.

The only meal I was getting was the free school lunch, and that wasn't enough calories to deal with the insufferable coach.

After we ran our laps, he herded us back inside for a game of dodgeball. Everyone groaned except for the handful of boys who had more muscles than brains.

Less than a minute in, a ball landed squarely on my nose, and I flailed backwards, smacking my head on the waxed floor. A sharp pain traveled down my spine, and everything flickered.

My first meeting with Brian was burned into my memory. He was one of those people who never seemed to age. Back then, he still had the same bony face, stringy blond hair, and smile sharp enough to cut glass. Of course, back then, I didn't know he was a member of my species I was so desperate to have contact with. Or a serial killer.

But it didn't take me long to figure out he was an asshole.

I had stepped outside to sit by the lake when I saw Jack and Brian arguing. Brian was clutching a tattered baseball in his hands, dodging and side-stepping as Jack tried to get it back.

"Aw, you gonna cry about it?" Brian jeered. I barely knew Jack from Adam, but Brian reminded me of the jerk who had stolen my green water bottle.

"Give it back," I shouted. They both paused in their fight. Brian's gaze sliced through me like a knife. An involuntary shiver traveled down my spine.

"Ew, Jack, you know the new kid?" Brian grinned. "I heard my parents calling him a psycho."

I didn't know anything about being a psycho other than that being one was bad. And I wasn't a bad person. I hadn't used my powers or exposed my secret since my arrival.

"I'm not a psycho," I growled. "Give him the ball back."

Brian stalked forward, icy eyes floating over me. "My parents told me to stay away from you cuz you're crazy! You probably killed your real parents, and that's why you're stuck here now."

My breath was stuck in my throat. Jack's jaw dropped. Brian smiled.

The shock of his statement only lasted a few seconds before I saw red. I raised my fist, unsure if I was planning on punching him or ripping his heart out of his skinny chest.

Before I had the chance to do either, someone else caught my hand and held it back. I was crushed against my adoptive father's chest, and for the first time, I heard his words turn cold.

"Don't you ever talk to my boy like that again," he hissed at Brian.

I was whisked away from the situation and carried back into the house. Nichole closed the door behind us, her delicate eyes full of concern as Robert plopped me down on the couch in the living room.

"Jack, are you okay?" he asked.

Usually, this would be the time when I would start screaming and throwing things, but my body felt frozen as Brian's words replayed through my head.

You killed your real parents.

Tears rolled down my cheeks. Robert held my hand as I cried for the first time since my parents' accident.

I didn't stop for hours. I sobbed until my chest hurt and my head throbbed, through lunch and dinner, and was still sniffling by the time they were tucking me into bed. The whole time, they didn't breathe a word of comfort or tell me to ignore what Brian said. They just held on to me like I was a balloon trying to float away.

The next morning, I felt like a different person. I shuffled down the hallway to see them sitting at the kitchen table, sipping cups of coffee. I stood in silence at the entryway, trying to think of something meaningful to say, but all that came out was a small, "I'm sorry."

They bid me sit with them and offered their first and last words of comfort. "We know you didn't kill your parents. And we know you miss them. We know we can't replace them, and we won't try. You don't ever have to call us mom or dad. But we do want to give you a nice home to stay in. We want to help you."

Help you.

My real parents had never offered to help me. When they announced we were moving to land to live amongst the creatures I had been taught to be terrified of, they never offered a comforting word or a reassuring hug. They expected me to toughen up, get over it, adapt, or die. That was their love, their protection.

A part of me wished they had loved me more like these new parents.

SIX

"Hey . . . are you still coming over tonight?" Abigail asked, rocking back and forth on her heels.

I blinked, realizing I was at school for perhaps the first time that day. I didn't even remember showing up that morning. I looked around, trying to figure out where I was. We were standing outside the gym. My hair was wet from my recent shower. My nose hurt, but I couldn't remember why.

"Oh yeah, totally!" I said. She smiled.

"Cool!" She skipped away - literally skipped - *who does that? That's adorable* - and I found myself mirroring her smile.

As soon as school was over, I started the long walk to her house. I knocked on her door, and she opened it almost immediately, awkwardly gesturing inside the house. I stepped in with just as much grace, running my fingers through my hair. I followed her to the pool once more, and we emptied our bookbags onto the tile. We locked eyes. Hers were really pretty – green ringed with gold. I wondered if she was straight or gay.

"Sorry for staring. I just have so many questions still," she laughed, looking down at the ground. I chuckled. Reece and Jack had interrogated me like I had committed a crime. Abigail was asking me questions like I was a celebrity. The change in tone was nice. It felt nice to be appreciated instead of feared.

"It's okay. You can ask more . . . if you want," I offered.

She shook her head. "If I start now, I'll never stop, and we need to get work done."

We spent the next few hours digging into the project. I took special care not to look too knowledgeable. I was just *migrating* after all. If I looked too smart, it might be suspicious. We took breaks to grab snacks from her aunt's massive – I mean *massive* – pantry. The kitchen was all granite and hardwood cabinets. I had to stop myself from gobbling everything I saw.

It was dark by the time we wrapped up. The weather was starting to warm up, and we ended up sitting by the outside pool, our feet dangling in the water.

"Does it feel weird to have water on your human feet?" she asked.

I giggled. "No. You know I can take showers and stuff without growing a tail – right? I have to be totally submerged to phase."

"No, I *don't* know," she grinned with a playful shove. "That's why I keep asking questions!"

"Well, ask then," I said. "We've been productive enough today."

She pursed her lips, head tilting in thought. "What's it like being a siren?" she asked after a moment.

"Lonely," I blurted without thinking. "It's kinda nice being around other humans."

She nodded. "Guess you could say the same thing about being trans," she muttered, kicking her feet in the water.

"Did it hurt your feelings when I said that you passed?" I asked.

She sighed. "I mean . . . yes and no. I want to pass. It feels like taking the coward's way out, but it's so much easier. No one yells at me when I go to the bathroom or use the girls' locker room. Guys are more likely to give me the time of day." *So she is straight.* "But a part of me wishes I didn't feel like I *have* to pass – you know?"

I nodded, even though I really didn't know.

"I mean, growing boobs and growing my hair out helps out my dysphoria, but it doesn't make me feel any more like a girl. I've always been a girl. Nothing changes that. But that's not how people see it." She brushed her foot against my leg. "I mean, I'm sure you still feel like a siren when you have legs instead of a tail, right? Transforming doesn't make you feel *more* siren."

I nodded. "No, it doesn't."

"Exactly. If you told people you were a siren looking like this, they'd all laugh at you. But if you had your tail, everyone would believe you. I'm a girl regardless of whether I have boobs or not. But a lot more people believe I'm a girl when I look like one," Abigail said.

"Makes sense," I said through a yawn.

"I should let you get going. How long of a drive is it to where you're staying?" she asked.

"Um . . . I actually walked here," I said.

She frowned. "From where?"

"The school. It's only like . . . three miles. No big deal."

Her eyes went huge. "Only three miles? Do sirens have super endurance or something?"

I laughed and shook my head. "Nah, it's fine, really."

She didn't look convinced. "Where are you living?"

Ugh, I really didn't want to admit this part out loud, but I had the feeling Abigail wouldn't rest until I told the truth. She seemed like the type who could smell lies.

"An abandoned car I found," I said. "Can't exactly afford a hotel or apartment without a job or . . . you know . . . human ID."

She shook her head. "No way. You're staying here."

I held my hands up, horrible scenarios crawling through my head. The last thing I needed was the Slayers tracking me to this nice girl's house.

"No, really, you don't have to worry about me," I said. "I'm fine where I'm at."

She narrowed her eyes. "So, how are you showering and getting food?"

I shrank under her stare. ". . . at school."

"Yeah, you're staying with me."

My mind raced as I tried to think of a way out of this. She must've seen the panicked look on my face because her intense stare softened.

"Look, at least move your car and park over here, okay? I won't make you stay inside if you really don't want to. But please don't let yourself go hungry or without hygiene. I don't know what sirens typically do in the wild – but brushing teeth is very important for humans." She suddenly smacked her forehead. "Duh! I totally forgot! My aunt has this fancy houseboat she keeps at our dock. You can stay there!"

"Oh, that actually sounds . . . really nice," I said, the words escaping my lips before I could stop them. She scrambled to her feet, and a few minutes later, we were walking down to the beach to their private dock.

The boat was indeed very nice. The door led to a massive living room and kitchen combo. The coaches were upholstered with real leather, and the TV didn't have so much as a speck of dust on the screen.

I whistled. "Dang. You sure I'm allowed to stay here? What about your aunt? I might get mud on the carpet."

Abigail grinned. "Of course. My aunt's a pilot – she's practically never here – so she'll never know. Anything you need at all – just let me know. I got you." I flushed and turned my head before she could notice.

"There's got to be something I can do to pay you back."

"You're already letting me be nosy as hell. That's payment as far as I'm concerned."

This girl is probably a Slayer, and I'm totally falling for her trap, I thought. *But hey, to get this whole boat to myself might be worth the risk. I'm going to get to sleep in a real bed!*

"You know what – you're here to experience human life – so let me be your tour guide. There's a state fair in town this weekend. I can show you all the exhibits – the rides – all the junk food. It's a peak human experience. C'mon, please?" she begged, sticking out her lower lip.

I laughed and found myself nodding. She looked adorable like that.

"Sure, that would be fun."

I snuck out for the first time. My heart was hammering so loud I thought for sure my parents would hear it through the walls. It took me ten minutes to coax my bedroom window open, and another ten to brave the entire four-foot drop to the pine straw below.

As soon as my bare feet touched the ground, I raced to the lake's edge, skidding to a stop right before my toes touched the water. I looked around at the other houses, squinting to make sure no lights were gleaming or faces staring through the windows. Thank god there were no street lamps here. The only light that could expose me was the Moon.

I looked back down at the dirty water and waded in, careful not to make a sound. The water was surprisingly warm. Mud squished between my toes. I wrinkled my nose but pressed forward until I was underwater. My body shivered in relief as my legs twisted together.

I half swam, half felt my way forward through the murky water, occasionally bumping into lake fish or slimy plants that felt like tentacles. I finally found a sandy spot not covered in muck and curled up, running my fingers over my blue scales, reminding myself I was real.

Then the tears started again.

You would think it would be difficult to tell if you're crying underwater, but your eyes still get hot and your chest still heaves like it does above the surface. I sank my nails into the sand and let out a silent scream, the only evidence a trail of bubbles floating towards the surface.

Part of me wished I had died in that car accident. Part of me was angry I had been dragged away from the ocean. Part of me regretted not using my powers to save them.

The biggest part felt guilty for starting to like my new guardians. They were human, after all. No matter how nice they were, I could never reveal my secret. I could never be perfectly honest with them. My parents' ghosts would probably rise from the grave if I ever dared to break their rules.

Your new parents don't think you're evil.

I curled my tail around myself. I wanted to repay the kindness of these strangers who had taken me in while honoring my first parents. And maybe make myself a little happy along the way as well.

I could start being nice to the new parents. Stop destroying their home, stop making their lives difficult on purpose. But I would never reveal my secret or use my powers. I owed my first parents that much.

And I would sneak out at night to swim – the only luxury I would allow myself. Maybe the lying would be easier, and I would hate myself a little less.

I realized very shortly after sneaking back in that nothing except soap was going to get rid of the smell of lake water. I showered for the first time since my arrival and put on clean clothes before heading downstairs. Seeing Nichole and Robert at the kitchen table still filled me with disgust, but I shoved it down.

There was an extra person at the table, too, Jack, the neighbor.

"Good morning. How did you sleep, Jack?" my dad asked.

"Good," we both said. Neighbor Jack giggled.

"Isn't it funny how you two have the same name?" my mom laughed. "What are the odds?" I faked a laugh as I dug my fingers into my palm. The only reason I was called Jack was because my parents had Googled basic human names and given me the first one they found. Jack was not my name any more than I was human.

"Do you have a nickname or something?" Neighbor Jack asked. "I mean, since I was here first, it's only fair that I be the original Jack."

"My middle name is Cyan." The words escaped my mouth without permission. My first parents had begrudgingly let me keep that small part of my identity when we had moved to land, but they had made me swear to never use it.

"Cyan? That's a weird name," Neighbor Jack said.

"It's another word for blue – like his eyes," my dad explained. Jack shrugged, shoveling another spoonful of cereal into his mouth.

"Okay, then your name is Cyan now."

My breath caught in my throat as my parents looked at me.

"Is that okay with you?" my dad asked.

My parents' ghosts screamed at me from the grave. *Cyan isn't a normal human name. You're risking everything.*

Be quiet, I told them.

"Yes," I said. "Cyan can be my name."

SEVEN

True to Abigail's word, she knocked on the boat door as the sun was rising that Saturday morning, already smelling of bug spray. She ordered an Uber and sprayed me with the sunscreen, making unnecessary comments about how pale I was as she rubbed it into my skin. Her hands were warm. She smelled like cherries.

Once we arrived at the fair, she lit up like the lights flashing on the rides. She grabbed my hand and spent the next two hours dragging me onto every ride that looked like a death trap assembled out of toothpicks. I had never actually been to a fair before, so it wasn't hard to act fascinated at all the carnival games and food. I quickly learned that roller coasters were not my thing, but I plastered a brave smile on my face and tried to convince myself the chances of me perishing were way greater outside the park than on the rides.

After nearly dying a handful of times, she pulled me over to the source of fried food. Rows of tents filled the field.

"Anything look good?" Abigail asked. My stomach growled, and I buried the sensation without a second thought.

"Um . . . I'm not super hungry, but you get whatever you want!" I said. She stared at me for a second before skipping off to a booth that sold cheese and bacon sprinkled with French fries. She carried the small bucket over to an empty table and shoved a fork in my hand.

"At least try it," she implored. "Have you ever had French fries? They're delicious." I speared a chunk and let myself eat it. *Holy shit, it's so good.* The fries were crispy and salty, covered in that melty, plastic cheese I had loved as a kid. But I had to keep myself under control. I couldn't risk another slip with my powers. I swallowed and put my fork back on the table.

Abigail frowned. "Do you not like it?" she asked.

"Huh? Oh – no, it's really good," I said.

She narrowed her eyes at me. "So . . . why aren't you eating?"

I shrugged. "Just not a big eater. Why?"

She pursed her lips. "Not to sound body-shamy or anything, it's just that you're skinny. Like . . . really skinny. It looks like I could snap your wrist like a toothpick."

I flushed, subconsciously lowering my hands under the table. I had already had this lecture with Jack several times, and I had the feeling I was going to have it again with Abigail.

Except she knew what I was. I didn't have to lie to her.

But of *course* I should lie to her. She didn't suspect that I was dangerous, and I certainly didn't want to give her any reason to think I could be. But something about being around her just made me want to spill my guts. Even about things that were difficult to admit to myself.

"I have trouble eating," I admitted. "And it's not because I have body-image issues or whatever . . . it's a . . . control thing. It makes me feel safer."

"Soo . . . you have an eating disorder."

I groaned. I hated that word. It was just another way I was broken. Another problem to be lectured about.

"It used to be worse," I said, somewhat defensively. This did not seem to calm Abigail down.

"Uh-huh. Don't think I haven't noticed your scars either." I shrank into my hoodie, self-consciously pulling my sleeves down.

"Abby, please. It's not a big deal," I whispered, wishing I could go back in time and take back everything I had just said.

"You have an eating disorder and self-harm. People die from those, you know."

"I haven't self-harmed in a long time. And I'm not going to die." *It would be incredibly ironic to die from my eating disorder with the Slayers after me.*

"Like hell you're not. Eat the damn French fries. Who cares if they make you feel out of control or whatever?" *You would definitely care*, I thought.

In true mother fashion, she wouldn't let us get up from the table until I ate at least three more bites. Once satisfied, she dragged me over to the games. She eyed the booths like a falcon circling a mouse, pointing out each one in turn.

"Okay, most of these games are scams. They're made to look easier than they are to get you to play. And they make it seem like you'll get one of those huge prizes, but they really give you the tiny ones that are hidden in the back." She swiveled her finger to one with balloons and water guns. "If you're going to play any game and actually win, that one's your best bet."

I grinned and grabbed her hand. "Well, I challenge you then!" We took our seats at the stand. I aimed my water gun at the bullseye and prayed I would win a toy to impress her.

The buzzer went off, and it was clear Abigail had set me up, because her balloon instantly filled to the brim, the lights around it exploding in rainbows as she cheered. The attendant brought her what looked like a stuffed whale, and she squealed and squished it to her chest while sticking her tongue out at me.

"I win; I win!" she bragged. I flicked her off, and she grabbed her chest in shock. "Now, where did you pick up that kind of language?" she gasped, pretending to swoon. I giggled and used the opportunity to swipe the whale out of her arms. I held it above my head and swerved through the crowd as she chased me.

I ducked into the only building and found myself in a room full of booths. Nicely dressed salespeople immediately turned and locked their eyes on me. Abigail caught up to me and stole her whale back. "Ah, I see you found the infomercial section," she said. "The peak of American capitalism. C'mon, let's go." We descended through the rows of products – from beard oils to mattresses to Tupperware.

Abigail seemed determined to stop at every stand and talk to the vendor before bolting to the next table. She finally slowed down at a stand selling hot sauce and t-shirts. A burly white guy in a ball cap stepped up, grinning at us.

"Welcome, folks! Anything catching your fancy?"

Abigail inspected a bottle of hot sauce. "How much?" she asked.

"Ten per bottle. And all of our proceeds go to help veterans get service dogs," he said, pointing to a sign above his head.

"Aw, that's adorable," she said.

"Yup. Way too many vets kill themselves a day, and getting them a service dog to help with their PTSD can literally save lives." The man looked at me. "What about you, sir? Fancy a t-shirt?" I looked over the wall of shirts – all awash in red, white, and blue patriotic images. One featured a flag spelling out the Second Amendment. Memories of Reece shooting at Brian flashed through my head.

"Definitely a fan of the Second Amendment," I joked.

"Hell yeah, man. They ain't gonna change my rights, that's for sure, just like how you can't change your gender," he said, eyeing my long hair.

Abigail and I both stiffened. *What the fuck?* I thought. *Did he really just say what I thought he did? What was even the point of that? We were talking about veterans needing service dogs.* I could see Abigail's eye twitching, and I put a hand on her shoulder.

"You don't need to buy anything from this guy," I whispered. She forced a smile.

"No, no I will. And I'll even take that t-shirt. But just know –" she leaned over the counter, right into the man's face. "Your sacrifice gives me the right to cut my dick off," she whispered.

The man's mouth opened and closed several times, but no sound came out. Abigail shoved a fifty towards the register, grabbed her hot sauce and t-shirt, and stomped off. I left him with a middle finger before catching up to her.

"That guy was an asshole," I muttered. She rolled her eyes.

"Seriously. And people think that queer people are the ones trying to shove our agenda down everyone else's throat," she said.

We stayed the rest of the day, riding rides and eating junk food until they announced the fair was closing.

"I need to pee so bad," I said. "I'll meet you by the front gate." I slipped inside the building and into the bathroom. It was surprisingly empty, which was good because it smelled terrible. I relieved myself and was scrubbing my hands off with as much soap as possible when a tall figure opened the stall behind me.

I blinked at the mirror. The guy looked familiar – where had I seen him before?

"Oh, hey. You're Hamen, right? I think you're in my science class," I said, rinsing off my hands and turning to face him.

Every muscle in his face looked taut. His mouth was pressed in a thin line, his dark eyebrows furrowed.

"Hello, Cyan," he said.

Whelp, this is awkward, I thought. I nodded and headed for the exit.

Wait.

I froze, my heart jackknifing.

He called me Cyan. I haven't told anyone my real name.

I turned back around, the color draining from my face. It seemed obvious now. He had the same build as Hockey Mask. He had appeared the same day I had at school. He had known exactly who I was from day one.

He took a step closer. I scanned him for weapons, wondering if I was about to have to fight for my life in a carnival bathroom. "What, no quips this time?" he asked.

The fuck? I hadn't remembered making any snarky remarks during our first fight. Why was he confronting me now? Had he assumed I lifted his mask while he was unconscious? *How the fuck did he know my name?*

I took a deep breath, trying to figure out how to respond in a way that would prolong his attack.

"I'm not dangerous," I said.

Hamen's eyebrow lifted. "I passed your message to Mr. Falcon. He told me to tell you *good luck.*"

My breath got stuck in my throat. Mr. Falcon was here in town. He was working with Hamen.

What the fuck, what message was he talking about?

Who cares? Kill him.

I winced, backing away. Hamen didn't move. The corners of his mouth lifted slightly, as if he was laughing at my panic.

My phone buzzed in my pocket, probably Abigail asking where I was. I could not suck her into this mess. There was no way Hamen would try to kill me in public.

I turned tail and bolted out of the bathroom, weaving through the crowd until I almost ran Abigail over by the front gate.

"Whoa, chill out there. You look like you've seen a ghost," she laughed. "C'mon, the Uber's here."

I forced a smile, pretending like my legs weren't shaking. "Yeah, let's go."

An hour later, we crashed on her living room floor beside the pristine white couches.

"So, what did you think of your first human carnival?" she asked.

You mean other than running into someone trying to murder me? I thought.

"I think I would've enjoyed it more if I had won a whale," I joked. She stuck her tongue out at me and clutched it tighter to her chest.

"But I need it to remind me of you," she pouted.

"Are you calling me a whale?" I demanded, pretending to look hurt. She giggled. It was a lovely sound. I could listen to her laugh all day long.

I found myself blushing and looked down at the ground, hoping she hadn't noticed.

"I'm glad you had fun," she said. I smiled up at her, remembering how her hand had felt in mine.

"I'm glad I finally found a human friend," I said. That time, I could've sworn she was the one who blushed.

"Look, I didn't mean to make you feel awkward or bad back there with the whole French fry thing. I just . . . I just don't want you to feel like you have to do stuff like that," she said quietly, avoiding my gaze. "You're a really cool and nice person and you . . . deserve to be healthy, you know?"

My throat suddenly closed up as tears clouded my vision. I quickly wiped them away before she could notice. *Holy shit, why is this girl being so nice to me?* I wondered.

"Um . . . thanks," I whispered. The air turned awkward as we lay in silence. *Change the subject,* I thought. "You know . . . since you took me on a human experience, I could return the favor by taking you on a siren experience."

She raised an eyebrow. "What do you mean?"

"You could go swimming with me," I offered shyly. "I mean, I can't make you breathe underwater or anything, but –"

"I would *love* that!" she interrupted, the air turning cheerful once again.

"Sounds like a date," I said, winking. That time, she definitely flushed.

Why are you flirting with her? This is literally the worst time ever to flirt with someone. People are actively trying to kill you right now.

But she's nice, I protested. *I'll make sure she doesn't get hurt.*

She walked me back to the dock and dropped me off, wishing me a good night before striding away. Too worked up to sleep, I paced throughout the boat, smiling for what felt like the first time in years. I mean, don't get me wrong. Jack had been a wonderful friend. He was the only one in Tredecim who would have anything to do with me for years.

But he had started acting differently since Brian lifted the fog. I wasn't sure if I could ever forget the looks of suspicion he had sent my way. I had left him behind with the news that his father was a murderer without a single comment or consoling word. It wasn't his fault that his dad had killed my parents.

Your parents are dead regardless. Someone has to pay.

Abigail was a friend without baggage. She had no clue what I was running from, what I was trying to accomplish. Cyan was still a secret, and she thought Jack was a great friend. She thought she knew more about me than she really did – and that suited me fine. She was a way to pretend that all was normal – all was fine – all was –

Fuck.

I had almost forgotten that the person trying to murder me was going to be in first period tomorrow.

I debated for most of the night about going to school the next day. What were the odds Hamen would be waiting for me in the parking lot with something more dramatic than a knife? From what I knew, the Slayers tried their best to stage their victims' murders as accidents, but I was at the top of their hit list. Maybe they would make an exception for me and kill me in broad daylight.

But if they wanted to kill me that badly, why had Hamen let me leave the fair bathroom alive? Maybe he was waiting for backup. Maybe they were expecting me to skip school. Maybe they were waiting until after the tardy bell rang to storm my new refuge and kill me here. If they didn't clean up their mess, Abigail would probably be the one to find me, and lord knows she didn't deserve that.

So, I put on my big boy panties and walked to school. In spite of the chill still present in the air, I was soaked from nervous sweat by the time I made it to class.

I kept my head on a swivel, scanning the hallways for Hamen or anyone who looked like they might be a secret murderer.

Turns out, he was waiting for me in Mrs. Wellborne's class like normal. He sat in his normal seat, doodling on the edge of his paper like he hadn't tried to murder me days before.

I froze in the doorway, debating whether I should turn tail and run. I mean, it wasn't like he was going to stab me in the middle of math class – right? And if I ran, he might follow me.

I took a deep breath and forced myself to walk in on my shaking legs and take my seat. Hamen didn't so much as look up at me. *What the actual hell – how is he acting so normal?* I wondered.

Abigail sat down beside me and smiled as Mrs. Wellborne started class. I copied notes while watching Hamen out of the corner of my eye. He made no sudden movements or incriminating glances. This guy was the master of his emotions. I wonder if Brian would've been able to break through that facade of calm.

Mrs. Wellborne dismissed us to work out the next few questions on our own. I ignored the worksheet on my desk and thought of ways to convince Hamen not to murder me.

I could only assume he had gotten all his information about me from Mr. Falcon, and if he was the one telling the story, it definitely didn't paint me in a good light. At best, Hamen thought I was the most dangerous siren on the planet. At worst, Hamen thought I was the most dangerous siren on the planet who had helped murder dozens of people. *If he could just hear my side of the story, maybe I could convince him to leave me alone,* I thought.

Before I had quite processed what I was doing, I was scribbling my plea on a note – explaining myself – explaining what had really happened – and throwing it at the back of Hamen's head.

He startled slightly before picking it off the floor, uncrumpling it, and reading it. I held my breath as his eyes slid over the page, and almost screamed in frustration when he balled it up again and shoved it in his book bag.

The bell rang, and Hamen swiftly gathered his things before vanishing down the hallway. And like a spectacular idiot, I followed him. I cornered him in the boys' bathroom. As soon as the door shut behind me, Hamen spun and glared at me.

"Are you trying to get killed?" he hissed.

I crossed my arms. "Did you even pay attention to what I wrote?"

Hamen walked towards me, his footsteps loud on the tile. He walked until he was right in my face. I could count the little pieces of stubble on his chin.

"If you're so innocent," he hissed. "Then why did you run? Why are you here?"

No words left my throat. He had a point. I was here for revenge – I wanted Mr. Falcon to face the consequences for what he did. But I still didn't want to *murder* him. I wanted him to serve justice the old-fashioned way.

The look on Hamen's face told me he would never believe me. Mr. Falcon had already gotten into his head.

"I'll prove I'm not dangerous," I whispered.

Days turned into weeks, which turned into months. Jack and I played together almost every day. Brian never came to bother us again. We did everything together. We would play from dusk till dawn, only taking breaks to eat popcorn and sandwiches prepared by my new guardians.

I had established a strange rhythm with them. I had stopped wrecking their house and treating them like shit, but I had no interest in being their son. Even though they were nice and took care of me in a way that my biological parents never had – they were still human – and I was not.

They could be my guardians, but nothing more. And strangely enough, they actually seemed okay with that arrangement. They never pressured me to call them mom or dad. They never talked to me about my original parents, and that was fine with me. I was trying to move past my grief and accept my new life as a pretend human. I was only myself in the dead of night, when no one else could see.

That got immensely harder when school started. Jack and I were in the same class – there was only one class of first graders after all – but all the other kids avoided me like the plague. They whispered and pointed their fingers at me.

I quickly found out why – Brian seemed to be in the middle of all the whispering. Jack pleaded with me to ignore them. The first time Brian had taunted me, it had broken the dam of sadness I had been trying to hold back. But I had mourned. All that was left was anger.

My first chance came in the hallway. Brian pushed me from behind, and I sprawled, spilling my color-coded folders everywhere. Brian and the other kids howled with laughter as I scooped up my fallen supplies.

I turned around, fists clenched.

"No one likes you," Brian jeered. "Why don't you just go back to where you came from?"

"Why don't you?"

Ten minutes later, Brian was sitting with a broken nose in the nurse's office, and I was being carted home by my parents. I stared at the floor, vividly remembering what had happened last time I had been taken home from school after getting in trouble. But instead of yelling or lecturing, Nichole and Robert said nothing.

Robert put his hand on my shoulder as we walked inside and sat me down on the couch. He held my hands in his and frowned.

"Cyan, what happened? You were doing so well."

My throat dried up. This was the first and only time they had ever brought up my previous behavior. They weren't mad; they were disappointed, and that hurt a million times worse.

"I'm sorry," I whispered. "It won't happen again." I had to figure out some way to control my emotions before they took over again.

I couldn't be evil.

EIGHT

I couldn't be evil. I shouldn't have left my pills. Maybe if I were still on them, I would be thinking straighter. Maybe if I got back on them, I could show Hamen I wasn't dangerous.

Your powers are the only reason you're alive right now. Those meds were a death sentence. Nichole and Robert should've never given them to you.

I swallowed as I walked down to Abigail's house, my bookbag heavy on my shoulders and my mind miles away from our project.

I'm not dangerous, I told myself. *I don't have to be on meds to not be dangerous. I'm safe to be around.*

The sound of the Slayer's body crunching against the street light pole played through my head.

That's different, I protested. *He was trying to kill me. I would never hurt anyone without a reason.*

"What did you say?"

I stopped, not realizing I had been muttering out loud, or that Abigail had been sitting by the pool, listening.

"Nothing!" I said quickly, throwing my bag down and getting out my papers. "Ready to get this over with?"

She covered her heart in feigned shock. "You mean you don't like spending time with me doing this ridiculous project?" She stuck out her lower lip, her eyes wide and pathetic.

I grinned. "I mean, there's other things we could be doing that would be a lot more fun."

She wiggled her eyebrows at me before hitting me with her textbook. "Maybe later. We've got to get this done."

We spent the next hour working in silence, the noise of the pool trickling in the background almost putting me to sleep.

"Okay, I need a break," she said, shoving her book across the stone. I shut mine, sighing in relief as I stretched out, the sun warming my skin.

"Can I ask you more weird siren questions?"

"Ask away."

"Do you guys have like . . . gender in the siren world?"

I raised my eyebrow as she flushed in embarrassment. "I mean, the other day you said you were bi. So, obviously, sirens have a grasp on LGBTQ stuff. Have you ever met another LGBTQ siren? Or is that just a human thing you learned being up here?" she asked.

I rolled my pencil between my fingers. "I'll put it this way . . . I've never met a siren that had too much of a preference about their partners, but I don't think I've ever met a trans one either."

"I guess if they were – they'd have to stay on land to get surgery or HRT," she mused. "So, do you have a preference? Men or women?" she asked. "I mean, if you don't mind me asking."

I smirked. "Yes, I totally mind you asking after spilling all the details about being a mythical creature," I teased.

Abigail blushed and shoved me. "Well, keep spilling then."

"I don't think I have a preference . . . but I think boys prefer me more than women do. Girls typically want a more masculine guy – and I can be girly at times," I said. "Last Halloween, I dressed up like a slutty vampire. Wore makeup, fake nails, and a crop top."

Abigail wiggled her eyebrows. "You've got to have a picture of that. Hold on – you've celebrated Halloween?"

Fuck, I probably shouldn't have said that, I thought.

"Yeah," I said slowly. "In the last town I lived in."

"Interesting. Have you ever . . . dated a human?" Her voice squeaked slightly as she asked the question. *Not for lack of trying, I* thought. *It's hard to date when it was ingrained in your mind as a child that no one could ever love you back.*

"Um . . . not really," I said. She raised her eyebrow, and my blush deepened. "But I *would* date a human. Or a siren," I added quickly. "What about you? Got a long list of ex-lovers?"

She scoffed. "I wish. You have no clue how much of a curse it is to be a trans girl who's straight. I had a crush on this guy back home, and you would've thought I chopped off his balls by his reaction. Apparently, I'm not a real enough woman for a cis guy to want anything to do with me," she muttered.

I laughed. "Are you kidding? You're gorgeous. I bet you could get a date faster than I could," I said.

"Yeah, okay, whatever."

I grinned. She paused in her writing, her face suddenly serious. She closed her book with a snap. "Okay, siren, let's make it a contest. There's a club for teenagers up here we could go to. But you're limited to girls only," she said.

"You serious? You want to have a contest to see who can get a date first?" I asked.

"You scared?" she teased. *Absolutely,* I thought, my stomach sinking. I definitely had an unfair advantage she didn't know about. *I just won't sing,* I told myself. *It's not like I can charm people if I'm not singing. It'll be fine. I can get a date the old-fashioned way.*

"Deal," I said.

We spent the next thirty minutes raiding her aunt's closet, searching for whatever might be acceptable at a nightclub for teenagers. I wriggled into a black suit that was definitely a little too big on me. I tried not to blush as Abigail walked out in a tiny green dress that sparkled in the light. She held up two pairs of shoes.

"Do I risk heels?" she asked.

I shook my head. "No. You'll be too busy dancing and seducing all the guys in the club." She rolled her eyes and threw the heels at me as she put on the flats. She burst out laughing as I attempted to wobble around in them, nearly tripping over a couch and impaling myself on the coffee table by accident.

We Ubered to the club, and she handed me a few bills before a burly bouncer let us in. We were immediately enveloped in fog and flashing lights. The bass thumped on speakers so loud it made my ears ring. Crowds and crowds of teens danced, spilling their drinks on the floor as they hooped and hollered.

My confidence suddenly wavered. I looked over at Abigail, who looked positively radiant in the low light. Her smoky eyeshadow made her look like a fae, and I was more than ready to dive into that trap.

You're here to get her some confidence, I told myself. *Leave her alone. Seduce literally anyone else. You don't have time for actual romance.*

She met my gaze and smiled. "Find me in half an hour. Good luck."

With that, she vanished into the crowd. I froze for a moment before I forced myself over to one of the bars. I settled down into a chair, flashbacks of Devin replaying through my head. I had been hungry and super desperate back then. Maybe my seductive voice worked better when I was desperate.

Come on, man, be charming. Be sexy, I told myself.

I looked down the bar and spied a group of girls chatting a few chairs down. I waved over the bartender and pointed down to the redhead in the center.

"Can I buy her a drink?" I asked, my voice cracking slightly. The bartender raised an eyebrow at me, and I blushed. *Come on, this always works in movies,* I thought. I offered him an awkward smile and passed him a ten. He nodded. He made the girl a drink and pointed down at me. I forced myself to sit up straight and nod my head at her.

Please let that have looked as cool as I thought it did in my head, I thought.

The girl's friends both scoffed, but the redhead smiled and slid off her chair to walk over to me. *Holy shit, that worked.* I pulled out the stool next to me and she sat down, twirling a strand of curly hair around her finger.

"Trying to seduce me?" she asked.

I blushed and decided honesty was the best policy. "Maybe."

She giggled. "Sorry about my friends."

"Don't be. They're just jealous that you're being flirted with and not them," I grinned. She giggled again and grabbed my hand, pulling me out onto the dance floor.

Dancing was one thing I knew I could do. I swayed in rhythm to the music, the notes sinking into my bones and vibrating in my blood. It felt like drinking cold water on a hot day. For a moment, I wondered if all sirens felt music like this, or if it was just me.

At one point, I spied Abigail dancing with another guy. It looked like the music could be in her blood, too, from the way she was moving. Her movements were slow and smooth. She oozed a confidence I had never seen in her before. I pushed down the surge of jealousy and concentrated on the girl in front of me.

The music suddenly switched to a more intimate one, and she wrapped her arms around my neck. I settled my hands on her hips and swayed her back and forth. Her hair smelled like strawberries. I found myself whispering the words to the song, and her body grew more fluid in my hands. She looked up at me, her eyes unfocused.

"We could get out of here if you want. My parents aren't home," she said, her voice slightly slurred. I stopped dancing. *Crap, I was singing,* I thought. *I just hummed a few words – was that how much it took? Did she sneak in liquor? Was she already drunk before I got close to her?*

I politely pushed her back, muttering something about going to the bathroom. I fought my way through the crowd, locking myself in a stall, trying to catch my breath.

Dangerous creatures. Don't know when to stop.

I know when to stop, I told myself. *I'm not going to take advantage of some poor human girl. I'm not dangerous. I won't be dangerous.*

I kept myself hidden in the bathroom until Abigail's meet-up time. I ventured outside to see her standing by the bar, the guy from earlier nowhere to be found. She smiled as I walked up and displayed her hand. A phone number had been hastily scribbled on her palm.

"Hey, look at you!" I said, high-fiving her.

She beamed. "What happened to that girl you were dancing with? She looked pretty into it," she said.

Guilt twisted in my gut. "Oh yeah, her. Um . . . she said she wanted to go back to her friends after a while," I lied, running my fingers through my hair.

Abigail nodded. "So, I guess I win! Want to celebrate with some food?"

A few minutes later, we had secluded ourselves in the back with a plate of cheeseburger sliders and fries. After a few minutes of scarfing, she groaned, pushing the plate away.

"I shouldn't be eating this. You would not believe how much weight I gained after starting the medicine," she whispered. "I used to be so skinny."

I pushed her plate back towards her. "Thick thighs save lives. Just eat it."

"Ironic for the guy who has an eating disorder." She pushed the plate back towards me.

"I do not!" I protested, helping myself to a handful of fries. She giggled as I chewed with my mouth open.

"You're so gross," she said, attempting to cover my face with her hand. She squealed as I licked her hand. "Oh, you're so going to pay for that," she said.

I swallowed my mouthful of fries and grinned. "Oh, am I?" I asked. Suddenly, her face was inches from mine, and the challenge in her eyes was doing things to my heart that I didn't think was possible.

Maybe she's the siren manipulating me, I thought.

"Dance off – now." She dragged me onto the floor, and we lost ourselves. I found myself staring, the club slowly narrowing until we were the only ones inside.

I let her drag me around the rest of the night until we were both too tired to move another step. She held her shoes in her hand as we waited for the Uber ride home. The driver kept raising his eyebrow at us as we whispered jokes in the backseat, barely managing to contain our laughter. After we were dropped off, we collapsed on one of the pristine white couches, still panting.

"That was so much fun," she breathed. "That's like . . . the most fun I've ever had."

I grinned, kicking off my shoes before putting my feet up on the couch. "Me too. You gonna call that guy?"

She looked at her palm. "Doubt it. The number sweated off."

I sat up, frowning. "Dang, that sucks."

She shrugged. "Nah. He was fun for a dance or two, but doesn't seem like someone I would want to date," she said.

I remained silent for a moment. "So . . . what is your type? Like – if you could have whoever you wanted in the entire world?"

She hummed as she pondered. "I'm not sure," she said eventually, avoiding eye contact. *Liar*, I thought. I rolled over so I faced her.

"Really? No celebrity crushes, no nothing?"

She rolled her eyes. "Why are you so interested in my love life?" she teased. *Because I desperately want to be a part of it even though I know it's a terrible idea*, I thought.

"No reason," I lied.

She narrowed her eyes at me. "I'll tell you mine if you tell me yours," she said. I had the sudden, intense urge to be completely honest. My tongue ached to tell her the truth.

"Fine, you really want to know who my secret crush is?" I asked. She nodded, and I lifted myself on my elbows before pressing my lips against hers. She pushed back almost instantly, and I nearly fell off the couch.

"What the hell, Jack?" she yelled, sitting up.

I covered my mouth, wishing the floor would swallow me whole. "I-I'm so sorry – I totally misread that situation – I'm so sorry -"

"Why the hell were you trying to get me to hook up with a random guy if you actually liked me?" she demanded, crossing her arms.

I blinked, confusion replacing my horror. "Wait . . . *that's* why you're mad? Not because I just kissed you?"

She groaned. "Are all sirens this stupid, or is it just you?" she asked.

My mouth fell open. "If you really liked me, why did you let me go flirt with other girls tonight?" I demanded.

She crossed her arms. "Maybe I just wanted to make sure you were actually into girls," she muttered.

I burst out laughing. "Why would I not be into girls? Did you think I just wanted you because you have a dick? That I have a trans-girl kink?"

She gasped, face turning bright red. I leaned closer to her. "Well, while we're exposing each other's fetishes – how do I know you don't just have a mythical creature fetish?" I asked.

She narrowed her eyes. "I don't have a mythical creature fetish!" she snapped.

"Well, I don't have a girls-with-dicks fetish."

She nodded, taking a deep breath. "Well . . . good."

We stared at each other in awkward silence. She cleared her throat, looking down at the carpet.

"So . . . you still want to kiss?" she muttered, flushing. I grabbed her by the waist and pulled her close. We melted into the couch, feeling each other's bodies like we would never have the chance to do this again. She tore off my jacket, throwing it to the floor. I was on top, and then she was. My heart raced, my skin clammy with excitement. A dull ache started to throb in my head, but I ignored it. I wasn't going to stop until she told me to or the world ended – whichever came first.

I was so tired of burying my feelings. I wanted to fall in love, have a family, have kids, have the life my parents had always told me I would never have. How could they be so cruel as to deny me this? I wanted Abigail more than I had ever wanted anything. And for the first time, I was going to take what I deserved, consequences be damned.

I was suspended from school for a few days, and I spent that time compiling ideas to keep myself in control.

I started by skipping meals. I couldn't attack anyone if I had no energy. As far as Brian, I had an idea for him, but I would have to wait for his next insult to see if my plan would work.

True to my prediction, his broken nose did nothing to deter his bullying. I could feel his cold, calculating eyes on me the instant I set foot on the playground. Brian and his biggest friend – I think his name was Henry – stopped me and made sure the teachers weren't watching before leaning into my face.

"You think you've won this fight?" Brian hissed. "No matter how many times you punch me, your parents will still be gone."

Familiar rage crept up. My hands balled into fists, but instead of sending them flying, I dug my nails into the tender flesh of my palm. I concentrated on the sharp bite of pain instead of his words.

"What's the matter, freak? Look at me when I'm talking to you." Brian slid a bony finger under my chin and forced it upwards. I recoiled, gritting my teeth.

"Don't touch me," I snarled. Brian grinned. *Stop reacting to him*, I screamed at myself.

"Don't tell me what to do," Brian snapped, grabbing me by the front of my shirt and shoving me backwards. I fell, smacking my head on the grass.

My vision went red as I scrambled back to my feet. I wanted to use my powers to drag the boy down to hell by his ankles. I wanted to throw him into traffic and record his screams. I wanted to carve the sick grin off of his face.

Instead, I turned and bolted into the school. I locked myself in a bathroom stall and took out the pair of scissors I had swiped from my teacher's desk.

I took a deep breath before sending the blade down my arm. It barely made a scratch. I had to saw for it to even break the skin.

I needed something sharper.

NINE

The next morning, I woke up on the boat, giddy with excitement. I could still taste Abigail on my tongue, feel her body wrapped around mine. I could still smell her hair.

It was almost enough to make me forget about the immense moral fuck-up the entire situation was. Did she actually like me, or had I just accidentally manipulated her like I had that redheaded girl at the club? My entire job here was trying to find justice for my dead parents – and all I had done was disappoint them.

My worst-case scenarios swirled around in my head, worsening my headache until I saw her at school. Then, they promptly vanished, and I practically ran over to her, all pathetic, needy smiles.

She looked just as flustered. Throughout science class, we kept stealing glances and wiggling eyebrows. I floated through the rest of the day and the entire walk to the boat. It really was the perfect setup – isolated enough from the public beach that I could swim without being spotted – and a five-minute walk to Abigail's mansion.

I didn't notice the person following me until it was too late. I spun around, heart hammering. Hamen stood at the other end of the dock, spinning his knife between his fingers.

Fuck, why wasn't I paying attention?

I put my hands up, taking a step backwards. "Please, just let me explain," I pleaded.

"I already know everything I need to know about you," Hamen said.

I swallowed, almost tripping over my own feet as I stumbled backward. "You can't kill me in broad daylight," I protested.

"There's no one here to see you." The knife sang as it flew through the air. I fell on my ass and hissed in pain as the knife caught my arm, carving a thick line of crimson.

Hamen hesitated, as if surprised his knife actually made contact. The water rumbled underneath me as I glared at him.

Don't hurt him, I told myself. If you can win this fight without hurting him, maybe it'll prove a point and he'll leave me alone.

He lunged for me again, his hands straining for my throat.

Drown him.

"Get off me!" I hollered, trying my best to knee him in the groin. It was no use. He had me pinned with my wrists above my head.

Drown him.

"Stop it," I growled. A wave rose from my left, enveloping us and dragging both of us under. I phased and wriggled out of his grasp, wincing as the salt stung my wound.

Hamen clawed for the surface, knife held between his teeth. I grabbed him, pinning his arms to his side as I ripped the blade from his mouth. He shrieked in pain as blood stained the water, writhing in my grip.

Drown him.

The thought was tempting. This was the second time he had attacked me, and I doubted it would be the last if I let him go again. But he was just a teenager – like me. He had probably been brainwashed by his parents into thinking this was right. I couldn't just kill him. I wasn't dangerous. I wasn't evil.

I hesitated too long. He kicked me away, pulled a hidden blade from his shoe, and wildly swiped at me again. I ducked and hit him with my tail, and he shrieked again.

Once the bubbles cleared, my heart dropped. My blow had sent the knife directly into his thigh. Dark red blood clouded the water. He clutched his leg, bubbles trailing from his mouth as he started to sink.

Damn it, why am I like this? I rolled my eyes before grabbing him under his arms and pulling him towards the surface. He gasped for breath as I swam up under Abigail's boat, realizing too late that it was probably not a good idea to take him where I was living. Oh well, the bed had been nice while it lasted.

I pulled myself up the ladder as much as I could and shoved Hamen over the edge before letting myself phase and climb up the rest of the way.

I landed on the deck to see Hamen curled up in a ball, shaking and clutching his thigh. I hooked my hands under his armpits once more and dragged him inside.

"Stay there," I said, rushing inside. Surely there had to be a first-aid kit somewhere? Thankfully, I found one in the bathroom that was well-stocked, if not a bit dusty. I ran back to the deck only to see Hamen attempting to climb over the railing.

"You've probably already attracted every shark in ten miles!" I warned. He ignored me, wincing as he grappled for the ladder. *For the love*, I thought.

I dropped the first aid kit and grabbed a fistful of his shirt before he could get away. I heaved him back into the boat. *Jeez, he's heavy*, I thought, gasping for breath.

He didn't give me a break for long. He lunged for my ankles, pulling me down beside him and making a grab for my throat. I kicked him away, and he screamed in pain. Tears rolled down his face as he reverted to fetal position, clutching his leg to his chest. *Oops, I definitely kicked his wound*, I realized. *So much for not hurting him.*

I got up, considering my options. There was no way he was going to let me treat his wounds like a normal person. And my conscience wouldn't let him escape only to be eaten by a shark. The thought of charming him made me sick to my stomach. I wasn't going to prove I was evil by messing with his head.

I took off my soggy t-shirt and used my teeth to rip it into strips. I held the fabric in my mouth as I dragged Hamen back towards the ladder. I forced his hands around the metal and used the t-shirt to bind his hands as tightly as I could. By the time I returned with the first-aid kit, Hamen was hysterical. Sweat dripped down his forehead as he thrashed against the ties.

"Don't touch me!" he screamed. His eyes widened as I approached him with a pair of scissors. He kicked out at me, which definitely did not help stop the bleeding from his thigh. "Get away from me!"

"Do I need to tie your ankles too?" I demanded. His eyes went even wider, and for a split second, I thought the emotionless siren slayer was about to cry.

I took a step back, putting my hands up. "Dude, I need you to relax. I'm going to cut out a hole in your jeans, pull out the knife, and clean out your wound. And then I'll let you go. Deal?"

"Like hell you are," Hamen panted. "I know what your kind does to their victims."

I crossed my arms. "If I wanted to do anything to you – I would've done it already," I pointed out. "Now will you please stay still so we can both get this over with?"

He didn't look any more trusting, but he didn't start kicking or screaming as I reapproached with the scissors. I quickly cut a patch in his jeans. Thankfully, the knife didn't look like it had gone very deep, and it hadn't hit major arteries; otherwise, he would already be dead.

I held a pad of gauze in one hand as I gripped the knife with my other. We both held our breaths before I yanked it out. Hamen bellowed, arching his back. I quickly stuffed the gauze into the wound before wrapping a bandage around his leg, tying it as hard as I could.

"There. All done. You'll make it long enough to reach an actual doctor," I muttered, ignoring the cut on his face. He took a deep breath, resting his head on the bars behind him.

I collapsed on the floor at a safe distance, debating the best way to untie him to give myself enough time to run when he spoke, his voice surprisingly soft.

"Why did you save me?" he asked, not daring to meet my eyes.

That's a good fucking question, I thought. *I really should have just let your ass drown back there.* But that's what everyone expected me to do. I wasn't going to turn into the monster they all thought I would become.

"I told you. I'm not dangerous," I said.

"Then why did you run?" he countered.

I raised my eyebrow. "Run from you? Because you're trying to kill me, Sherlock."

Hamen rolled his eyes. "Run from Tredecim, Idiot."

"Oh." I shifted, debating my next words. "I was scared. I didn't know where else to go."

"Why are you still here?" he countered. "If someone was trying to kill me, I would've skipped town by now."

He makes a good point, I thought. But I finally had a friend. I had found other sirens. I even had a vague notion of a plan to get revenge on my parents' murderer. I couldn't leave until I was sure the Slayers would leave me alone.

"I want justice for my parents," I finally said. "Mr. Falcon deserves to be in prison for what he did."

I waited for Hamen to smile and confirm that I was a horrible person, but to my surprise, all he did was laugh.

"That's *it*? You *don't* want to kill him?"

"I'm not like you," I said.

Hamen's laugh dried up immediately. He looked down at his feet. For a moment, I almost saw shame in his eyes.

"What are you going to do with me?" he asked.

I sighed. "Let you go, I guess. I don't exactly want to spoon-feed you or change your diapers."

He didn't laugh. "You know I'll just come after you again," he said.

"Why don't they send someone with more experience? Or let Mr. Falcon finish the job? No offense, but you're kind of bad at this," I said.

"I don't have a choice. If I fail, they'll just send someone else. There's no way you come out of this alive. I would run if I were you."

Not the Slayer trying to give me advice on staying alive, I thought. I stood up, shaking the water from my hair.

"I'll take my chances. I'm going to untie you and help you back to the dock. I would appreciate it if you waited until tomorrow to try and kill me again."

All Hamen could do was nod. He stayed surprisingly still as I unbound him and pulled him to his feet. He leaned heavily on me as I helped him climb the ladder back down to the dock. I kicked one of his fallen knives back into the water for good measure.

"You know, it would be way easier to get rid of me with a gun or something," I panted.

"I don't get a gun until I can prove myself," he said. "I have to make your death as painful as possible and burn the evidence."

Jesus fuck, what was wrong with these people?

Brian had said Mr. Falcon stabbed his parents before setting the house on fire. Had that been Mr. Falcon's first mission?

I swallowed, my throat dry. "Well, that's nice," I said, untangling myself from his arm and letting him support his own weight. He hobbled forward a few steps before turning around. I had never seen eyes look so heavy before.

"Like I said. I would run if I were you."

. . .

The next day at school, I was feeling surprisingly confident about running into my nemesis. There was no way my act of kindness last night hadn't touched him in some way. Maybe after a long night's sleep, he had changed his mind and decided not to brutally murder me. At the bare minimum, he was recovering from a stab wound. He probably wouldn't even be at school.

I frowned when I saw him walking down the hallway, favoring his leg. He slipped into class, and I walked right up to his desk as he sat down. My heart dropped as he looked up at me. A dark bruise that definitely hadn't been there yesterday covered the left side of his face. His eye was swollen and shiny. He looked almost worse than he had last night.

I replayed our fight in my head as he glared at me. I had never gone for his face. And even if I had – I was right-handed.

Who did this to you?

"Jack, find your seat, please. Class has started," Mrs. Wellborn barked. I scurried to my desk, my mind stuck. Had I hit him that hard by accident? How else could he have gotten that bruise? Had he tried to kill someone else after me?

His words played back through my head. *I don't have a choice.*

My stomach sank.

A piece of paper interrupted my thoughts. I looked down to see a crumbled ball on my desk. I opened it with shaking fingers.

Next time, leave me to the sharks.

The next moment my guardians were distracted, I snuck into their bathroom. It wasn't hard to find Nichole's disposable razor in the shower. I ripped out one of the blades with trembling fingers and shoved it in my pocket.

The next time I found myself in the school bathroom, I took out the razor. It sliced my skin like butter.

I hissed in pain as blood pooled along the cut, running down before dripping onto the floor. I quickly repositioned myself so it would fall into the toilet instead. As I watched it bleed, I pretended it was Brian's blood instead, that he was finally getting what he deserved.

It was only a matter of time before someone caught on to what I was doing – and that person ended up being Jack.

I was hiding in the bathroom like normal one recess, washing the blood from my most recent cut when Jack barged in, all wide eyes and face twisted in disgust.

"What are you doing to yourself?" he asked, his voice more upset than angry. I didn't know how to explain. Jack was my best friend in the world, but he was still a human. He couldn't understand how dangerous it was for me to be out of control.

Before I could say anything, he backed away. "I'm telling your parents!" he shouted before fleeing from the bathroom.

And he did.

TEN

The temptation to fall back into old habits was suffocating. Jack wasn't here to do a wrist check, but Abigail would certainly notice, and another lecture from her about my health was the last thing I wanted to hear. I settled for snapping a rubber band on my old scars as I contemplated what the hell was going on with Hamen and his black eye.

I was almost positive that it hadn't been my fault. And what was up with the *leave me to the sharks* comment? Did he really wish he had died last night? Were the Slayers that vindictive that they would dispose of their own members if they couldn't complete their jobs?

I had to try to talk to him, but I had the sinking suspicion that he would not respond kindly to a heart-to-heart with his mortal enemy, especially the one that had gotten him into trouble the night before.

I definitely did not have the good sense to run while I could. The thought of leaving Abigail made me feel like my legs were full of concrete.

You've only made out with her once. She's not that special.

But she was that special. She was kind, understanding, funny, and down-to-earth. She was something I never thought I would have. I couldn't just give that up, consequences be damned.

That night, I invited her to go swimming with me. She met me at the boat in an adorable pink one-piece and goggles.

We went to the end of the dock, hands clasped.

"I gotta be honest, I've only been in the ocean like . . . twice," she said, shifting. "You're not gonna let me drown or like . . . feed me to a shark, are you?"

"I was actually going to feed you to an octopus." She let go of my hand to punch me as I giggled. I took her hand once more and squeezed it. "I promise, I won't let anything happen to you. I got you."

She took a deep breath and slid into the water. I dove in after her and felt my body melt into my true form. I surfaced and gently swam behind her, gently supporting her by her hips. She giggled, kicking her feet.

"Your tail tickles!" she laughed, swatting me away.

"Oh, I'm so sorry." I dove under the water, leaving her to support herself. I sniggered as she swiveled around, trying to spot where I had disappeared to. I reached up and barely ran the tip of my finger against the bottom of her foot. She immediately shrieked, her kicks almost removing my hand at the wrist.

I surfaced at a safe distance, howling with laughter as she shot me the bird. "You are such a bitch," she gasped.

"Don't lie, you love me," I teased. She blushed, and I suddenly realized what I had said out loud.

"Love you, huh?" she asked, wiggling her eyebrows. We floated closer until her arms were wrapped around my neck.

What happened after that wasn't crystal clear. The more we kissed and explored with our hands, the worse my ever-present headache got.

But I didn't care. This felt better than any pill I had ever taken.

We went until our muscles gave out. I walked her back to the house and returned to the boat on cloud nine, giddy despite the pain festering in my skull.

Hamen was waiting for me in my living room, holding his usual weapon of choice. I sighed as I shut the door.

"Back so soon?"

"I told you to leave," he protested.

"Hamen, you don't have to do this," I said.

"Yes, I do," he whispered, his voice raw. "If I can't kill you, then I'm of no worth to anyone. I *cannot* go back empty-handed again."

How he got his bruise suddenly clicked.

"Did another Slayer do that to you?" I demanded. He shook his head, taking a step back. "Hamen," I repeated. "Who's making you do this? Who hurt you?" A tear slipped down his cheek. He whimpered as I walked towards him, refusing to meet my gaze. The knife trembled in his grasp.

"Hamen," I said, gently pulling his chin down so I could meet his eyes. "Who is making you do this?" More tears slid down his face.

"My father," he finally choked out. "He's the leader of the Slayers."

Nichole and Robert sat me down for a conversation as soon as I got home from school. They made me lift my sleeves and show them the cuts. They reacted the same way they did when I had broken Brian's nose.

"Why are you doing this?" Robert asked, his voice heavy.

"I don't know," I whispered. "I'm a bad kid. I just get angry."

They exchanged concerned glances. "Sweetheart, you're not a bad person. Everyone makes mistakes. Everyone gets angry."

"Not like me. Something's wrong with me," I insisted. "But when I do this, I don't feel as mad. I can control myself."

They exchanged another glance before pulling my sleeve back down. "You know, Cyan, we're both doctors. We've treated people who have trouble controlling their emotions. There's a pill you can take that might help you feel . . . feel more in control. Would you like to try something like that?"

I nodded. I was so sick of disappointing them. I just wanted them – someone – anyone – to think I was a good kid. That I wasn't evil.

Robert got up from the couch and returned with an orange bottle. "Just don't tell anyone, okay? Let's see if it works first."

I nodded before swallowing the capsule.

ELEVEN

I woke up with a blinding headache. I groaned, trying to blink away the dark spots in my vision. I could barely remember the day before, other than kissing Abigail in the water. What time was it?

I sat up only to hit my head. I swore, rubbing my nose. *What the hell?*

I was in the minivan.

I stumbled out of the car, blinking up at the sky. The sun was low. I checked my watch and my eyes widened in surprise. It was 4:15 – the next afternoon. I had slept all day. What the heck? Why had I gone back to the car?

Blinking against the harsh sunlight, I shut the door and started walking towards Abigail's boat. Maybe a swim would clear my head. Or maybe I just needed to buy some Advil. I felt in my pockets and took out my phone. Abigail had texted me asking why I wasn't at school, but other than that, there was nothing.

An hour later, I stepped up on the dock and headed towards the boat. I stepped into the kitchen to see Hamen waiting for me.

Something was very wrong. He stared at me like I was a poisonous snake, a mixture of fear and betrayal. Another wave of pain hit my head, and I hissed, clutching my forehead.

"Dude, what's wrong?" I asked. "Why are you here?" He didn't respond. The hairs rose on my arms. "Hamen? What's wrong? Why are you looking at me like that?"

"You lied to me."

"Lied about what?"

"Don't do that. You're not fucking with my emotions. Not this time," he snarled, yanking a knife out of the back of his pants. I put my hands up, skittering backwards.

"What are you talking about?" I demanded.

"Don't pretend like you don't remember," Hamen rasped. "He's dead." He threw the blade, and I ducked. I felt the wind pass over my shoulder.

"What?" I racked my brain, but couldn't remember talking to Hamen at all the day before. And who died? Did he think I killed somebody?

He rushed me, knocking me backwards and kicking me hard in the stomach. I wheezed, acid crawling up my throat. He kept his foot planted on my chest, the knife pointed at my heart. I gawked up at him, wondering what the hell was going on.

"Hamen! Talk to me, what is going on?" I pleaded.

"Stay out of my fucking head!" he screamed. He sent the knife hurdling for my chest, and a shield of water barely managed to assemble itself in time to prevent it from tearing my heart open. My head screamed, and I knew I wouldn't be able to do the same again.

"Hamen, you don't have to do this. I know you don't want to," I slurred, dizzy with pain.

"I should've killed you a long time ago," he said, tears flooding his eyes.

END HIM.

I shivered as I banished the intrusive thought from my head. I would rather die than become the stereotype he obviously thought I was.

KILL HIM.

My vision blurred at the edges. I clawed at my hair, trying to relieve the pressure, but it only grew worse.

DO IT.

"Cyan?" Hamen asked. I tried to talk, but all that came out was a gurgle of pain. My head, my head, what's wrong with my head?

Fine, I'll do it myself.

I woke up the next morning with my head in a fog. I nearly tripped over my own feet getting out of bed. It took an extraordinary amount of concentration to get the cereal spoon to my mouth without spilling it on the floor. When Robert asked how I was feeling, I slurred something affirmative before he drove me to school.

The whispers and pointing fingers of the bullies felt like they were on a different planet. I doodled on my folder as the teacher taught.

At recess, Brian and Henry came up like normal. Jack stiffened beside me, waiting for me to blow up or take a blade to my wrist. I stared at Brian like he was a character in a movie, something far away, something not real. Was I even real?

"Hey freaks. What, not hiding in the bathroom today?" Henry sneered. I switched my gaze to his, which was difficult because he towered over me. My perspective gave me an excellent view of the underside of his nose, where a booger the size of Texas lurked.

I burst out laughing. Everyone turned to me, faces furrowed as I howled, wiping tears from my eyes.

"You–you need to go blow your nose," I chortled, almost falling over. Mystified, Brian and Henry walked away, leaving me with a very concerned Jack.

"Dude, are you okay?" he asked. "Why are you acting so weird?" It must be the pills, I thought. They're doing something weird to my head. I'm not angry at all . . . this is the closest to happy I've felt in a long time. This is incredible.

I'm never going to stop taking these.

TWELVE

My skull felt like it had been cracked open like a walnut. A groan escaped my lips as I struggled to make sense of the swirling colors in front of me. I smelled copper and felt something scratchy around my wrists. The last thing I remembered was . . . I had no idea. Trying to think felt like biking uphill on a mountain made of pudding.

Maybe it was the excruciating head pain, but as the colors slowed, I could've sworn I was tied up in Abby's foyer. Two figures stood in front of me, both holding knives in their hands like their lives depended on it.

"What'sss going on?" My words came out slurred. One of the figures inched closer, and I squinted, trying to make them out.

Again, maybe it was the pounding in my skull, but it looked like Hamen was crouching before me. He wore his normal frown and curly blond locks. His white t-shirt was soaked through with blood. Was that normal?

"Cyan, is that you?" he asked.

I raised my eyebrow. "Who else would it be?" I laughed, my head rolling. Hamen stood up, and the other figure stepped forward. A bright smile lit up my face.

"Abigail! I feel like it's been forever since I've seen you!" I slurred. Hamen's frown grew deeper. Abigail gnawed on her fingernails.

"Why is he acting high?" she whispered.

"I don't know." Hamen's voice sounded raw, like he had been screaming or crying. Or both.

"Cyan, snap out of it!" Abigail shouted.

Her voice sounded like a gun going off. I gasped, the spinning suddenly grinding to a halt.

Holy shit, I'm tied up in Abigail's foyer.

Holy shit I'm tied up in Abigail's foyer.

"Guys, what's going on? Why am I here?" I struggled against my bonds, but the rope was thick and tight. I tried to stand only to discover my ankles were bound just as tight. My heart pounded in my ears. Was this Hamen's final murder attempt? Why was Abigail here with him?

Wait, had she called me *Cyan*?

"What do we do?" Abigail whispered. "You can't just kill him if he doesn't know what he did."

Hamen crossed his arms. "I definitely can," he muttered. "That is literally exactly what I am supposed to do."

"Guys?" I asked, my voice squeaking. "What is going on? Let me go!"

"Stop moving!" Abigail snapped. I froze as she walked up to me. "Cyan," she said slowly. "What do you remember?" I racked my brain, but my memories still felt like sludge.

"I-I don't know. Everything is foggy. I think . . . I was coming over to work on our project? Or at school maybe? Wait, how do you know my real name?"

Hamen reached into his pocket and threw a plastic baggie at me. "Recognize these?" he demanded.

I leaned forward to look at the bag. "Blue contacts? Why would I buy blue contacts? My eyes are already blue."

"See? He doesn't remember," Abigail said, walking away from me. "We need to wait for Reece."

I resumed struggling against my bonds. "How do you know who Reece is? Guys, what is going on?" I shouted.

Abigail swallowed. "Cyan, Hamen told me everything. We know what you did. You're . . . not well. Reece is on her way now to help."

My stomach lurched. Abigail knew I had been lying to her.

"Whatever he told you, I promise I'm not dangerous!" I pleaded. "Please, you have to believe me!"

Abigail's eyes filled with tears, and she turned away. Hamen put an arm around her like a shield. White hot anger flashed through me, and I bared my teeth at the Slayer.

"Did Hamen include how he's tried to kill me? Several times?" I hissed. "I'm not the dangerous one! I didn't kill anyone!"

"Cyan, please, calm down," Hamen whispered. "You're . . . you're just sick."

"How am I *sick?* How do you know who Reece is? Guys, just talk to me!" My voice was a scream by the end. Hamen and Abigail took a cautionary step backwards, their grips tightening on their knives.

I could hear my heart echoing in my head. It felt like someone was trying to drive an iron through my forehead. I groaned, bile racing up my throat.

"Let me go."

"Cyan, please!"

"*Let me go!*"

Water raced up my wrists and down my ankles, slicing through the rope. I staggered to my feet to almost immediately fall back over.

"Shit," Hamen whispered.

A car screeching into the driveway outside silenced all of us. The door opened, and Reece jumped out, heels clicking on the concrete. She looked just like she had the last time I had seen her – dark curly hair, stony eyes, mouth pinched shut. She reached under her skirt and pulled out a pistol. She surveyed the scene, her face expressionless. Her gaze landed on me.

"Cyan, get in my car. We're leaving."

"I'm going with him!" Abigail protested. My head swam. I stumbled to the side, biting my lip to keep from screaming. The world tilted.

"His eyes! It's happening again!" Hamen warned.

"Cyan. Car. Now," Reece commanded. I tripped again, clawing at my hair. I could barely hear her over the pressure pounding in my head. I vaguely felt myself hit the hardwood.

The world slowed down around me. Colors mixed. Sounds felt like they were miles away. All I could feel was my head exploding. I think I might've screamed.

Hamen lunged towards me with his knife. Abigail grabbed him, yanking him backwards. Reece shouted at them to stop.

KILL THEM ALL.

I jumped in surprise, looking behind me to see who had spoken. Hamen threw his knife, but it went wide. Abigail screamed, and Hamen threw her to the side. She hit the floor hard, sliding into the wall with a thud. Fury filled my veins, hot as lava. Hamen advanced on me once more, a wild look in his eyes.

The pounding in my head vanished. The pipes in the walls groaned. Hamen stopped, the color draining from his face. I curled my fists, feeling my eyes burn.

"You're going to pay," I whispered, narrowing my eyes at Hamen. The ceiling exploded, water raining down from the pipes. It curled around my fists. Hamen backed away from me, hands in the air.

"*You're going to pay!*" I screamed, pointing at him. The water rushed towards him, picking him up and flinging him outside the door like he was no more than a weak stuffed animal. He landed on Reece's car. The metal crumpled around him, glass shattering. Hamen dropped to the ground, groaning.

Out of the corner of my eye, I saw Reece shoot at me. I blocked the bullet with a simple wave of my hand as I stalked Hamen. I dragged him towards me by the ankles, straddling him as I wrapped my fingers around his throat. He pawed weakly at my hands as he sputtered. A grin worked its way across my face as I felt the life begin to leave his body.

YES FINALLY KILL HIM.

A force hit me from behind. I turned to see Abigail pawing at my shirt, her grip strong despite the tears streaming down her cheeks. Hamen lay almost lifeless on the concrete, his chest barely rising.

No matter, I'll come back for him, I thought. I turned my eyes on Abigail, running my tongue over my teeth. She took a tentative step away from me as I got back to my feet. I gathered more water around my fists and swung. She screamed and ducked at the last second. My fist went through the car window, glass shattering.

"*You bitch!*" I seethed.

"Look in the mirror!" she screamed. I turned to yank my hand out of the jagged window and caught my reflection in the shards. I stopped breathing.

My reflection stared back at me, but it wasn't me. It smirked, eyes glowing red.

"*Hello, Cyan. Long time no see,*" it said. I yanked my fist out of the car. Blood dripped to the ground from my shredded knuckles. The water splattered to the ground, lifeless.

"Brian? What are you doing here?" I whispered. My reflection smiled.

"*What am I doing here? I've been here, right in your little head. You've been quite a nice host,*" it said. "*I could have never accomplished what I did without you.*"

I reached up, feeling at my eyes. My reflection did the same thing. My knees shook. "No, no, no," I whispered. "You're not in my head. My eyes don't look like that."

"*I guess this would all make more sense if I let you remember,*" Brian said.

I walked up to the secretary at the high school, all confident smiles and humming under my breath. *"I need to be enrolled."*

She handed me some forms, but it wasn't my hands that took them, or my eyes that read the papers.

I was on the gym floor. Red liquid dripped down my chin as the ball rolled away. The coach yelled at me to get cleaned up, and I shuffled to the locker room.

"Finally."

The hands that weren't quite mine shoved a wad of tissue up my nose and fished a pair of blue contacts out of my bookbag. The hands rummaged through the other students' bags, shoving every granola bar and bag of chips they found into my face. They showered my body and wrapped a towel around my waist as the others filtered in.

Hamen was already getting dressed. His eyes caught mine in the mirror, but he quickly turned away, his cheeks slightly flushed. But I was more interested in the kaleidoscope of bruises decorating his back – like he had been thrown across a street and into a metal pole the night before.

"I know you're a Slayer." The vibrations came from my throat, but it wasn't my voice.

"I don't know what you're talking about."

"Where are the rest of you?"

I was running my fingers down his bare chest, humming under my breath. *"Aw, come on, I'm sure there's some compromise we could come to."* He slapped my hand away, but not before his cheeks turned red.

"Falcon told the rest of you about me, didn't he? Is he here?"

"Leave me alone."

"I don't want to hurt him. Just tell me where he is."

Hamen was sobbing on the kitchen floor, his face buried in his hands.

"My father," he choked. "He's the leader of the Siren Slayers. But I never wanted to be involved. He made me."

My hands wrapped around his as his body trembled.

"I can't do it. You're too fucking nice. I know you didn't kill all those people. If I were in your shoes, I would've killed me forever ago. You're a better person than I'll ever be, and I just can't . . . I can't kill you."

"Shh . . . don't cry. Come on, let's get you cleaned up."

My hands were in his hair, coaxing him up the stairs and onto my bed. They summoned a glass of water and urged him to drink until he had stopped gasping for breath.

"Please, you can't let me go. He'll kill me if I fail. He'll keep sending Slayers after you."

"Then let's leave. You and me. I'll protect you. But I'll never be safe until I can frame Falcon."

"You promise you won't hurt him? You just want him to get arrested?"

"Of course."

"I'll tell you. But we have to leave tonight."

"I promise."

The hands cupped his cheek, the fading bruises still hot under his skin. Our lips met naturally. Why did closeted boys always give the most desperate kisses? My vocal words hummed and whispered sweet nothings until he drifted away, but not before he murmured an apartment complex and room number.

I was back in the minivan, driving to the address I had used my real siren voice to get. Falcon stopped dead when he saw me grinning on his porch. My hands waggled their fingers and stepped into the room, shutting and locking the door.

"You found me," he said, pulling a gun from a holster on his waist.

"You don't sound too surprised."

"You ruined my family." He pointed the gun at me as I laughed.

"I ruined your *family? I beg to differ."* A stream of water oozed from the bathroom, silently snaking through the carpet. Before Falcon could blink, the tentacle wrapped around his feet and toppled him. The gun flew from his grasp. I stepped over him as he struggled.

"The Slayers will find you eventually," he said. "You'll never be free."

"I already am." The hands plucked the blue contacts from my eyes. Falcon's face went white.

"You-you-you're supposed to be-be," he sputtered.

"Dead? Oh, I know." My hands latched onto his throat as I settled myself on his chest, squeezing. His white face began to turn red.

"Do you have any idea what kind of torture you put me through? You would've all been better off if you just let Cyan be. He only wanted to get you arrested. He wouldn't even kill that stupid blond you sent to murder him."

Falcon gaped for air, clawing at my hands.

"Cyan was trying to show you mercy you never deserved."

"He's a monster," Falcon wheezed. "All of you are."

"Of course! But he still thinks being a monster is something to be ashamed of."

I let go of his throat, leaving him pinned to the carpet. I pulled out one of Hamen's old knives from my shoe and flicked it open.

"I'm going to get his revenge for him."

Thoughts that weren't mine – *or were they?* – circulated through my head. I had had ten years to fantasize about how this would go. I wanted to watch him squirm in panic. I wanted to hear his muffled pleas for help no one else would hear. I wanted to slice him into pieces until I saw *regret* in his eyes. I wanted his death to last like an expensive bottle of wine.

I gagged him so his screams wouldn't alert the neighbors and started with tourniquets, which were painful enough, but that wasn't the point. They would prevent him from bleeding out too fast. I started with his hands, humming as I worked. It took some muscle to cut through the bones, but I was in no hurry.

I wanted the *regret.*

Half a leg later, I saw it. Tears dripped down on the carpet. I paused, standing above him, my hands dripping in his blood. He sobbed quietly, shivering. Grown men still cried like children.

"Do you get it now? Do you finally feel bad about what you did to them?"

He nodded frantically, hope slowly creeping into his eyes. He thought there was a chance I would spare him. That an apology was all I wanted. He could still survive at this point – albeit without his hands or his right leg. He could still be redeemed. Wasn't this repentance enough?

I leaned over him, my red eyes shining. *"I'm not Cyan. And I don't forgive you."*

I left him to dig through my bag. Falcon's moans turned into shrieks as I poured the bottle of gasoline over his body. I flicked open my lighter and let gravity do the work. A wave of warmth hit my face as the kitchen ignited. I stood back and watched from a safe distance.

The smoke alarms started blaring, but it didn't take long for the fire to do its job. I washed my hands in the sink and pulled out my phone, snapping pictures of what remained of Falcon. I texted them to Jack.

I was back at the boat. The news had traveled fast. Hamen's face was streaked with tears.

"What did you *do?*" he screamed.

I dragged him towards the bathroom, covering his mouth with my hand. I threw him to the tile, stomping on his back. I unbuckled his belt and secured him to a handle on one of the cabinets. He started to struggle. I could feel him shaking as I grabbed his chin and forced him to look at me.

"Cyan, what are you doing?"

"Oh, I'm not Cyan." I ran a tantalizing finger down his chest. He stopped breathing. *"But I believe Falcon told you about me."*

"You're the one from that town. You're the one who killed everyone. You're the one who killed Mr. Falcon. What did you do to Cyan?"

"Oh, he's here. Just on a little vacation. But if it makes you feel better, he was never the one kissing you."

Hamen let out a sob and thrashed against the belt. I traced his knife over his Adam's apple, still slick with Falcon's blood.

"If you're gonna kill me, just get it over with."

"You're not worth killing. I've got bigger plans. Your daddy might not care about you, but if he gets word that I'm holding Cyan's little slut hostage, he'll show up with his minions in a heartbeat. Then the Slayers will be the extinct ones."

Hamen managed a dry chuckle. "Out of all the humans in this town, you're gonna use Abigail as bait? Jealous much?"

I hissed at the smirk on Hamen's face.

"Cyan is my puppet, not hers! Besides, you're going to be the jealous one by the time I'm done with you."

I held the knife in my teeth as I ran my fingers along the bottom of his t-shirt. His breath hitched again as I slowly lifted it, scraping the center of his chest with a fingernail. I held his shirt in place at his throat, displaying his pale chest like a canvas. I crawled into his lap, pinning his hips to the floor. I took the knife and gently dug the blade into his skin, just enough to draw blood. He cried out and tried to jerk away from me. I laughed, tightening my grip.

"The more you move, the more this will hurt. But you're welcome to beg."

Hamen swallowed. "Cyan, please, if you're in there, if you can hear me, stop this!" he whimpered.

I tsked, running the knife down several inches. Hamen screamed, thrashing against me as I finished the first letter. By the time I was done, blood dripped down his heaving chest, staining his jeans. Hamen sobbed, somehow sounding more pathetic than Falcon did.

"Too bad Daddy will never get the message."

I was knocking on Abigail's door. She frowned when she saw me. She was smarter than Hamen. "Why are your eyes red?"

"It's about time we met." I shoved her backwards.

"Who the fuck are you?"

"If you knew Cyan very well at all, you would know exactly who I am. But I guess everyone has their secrets." I twirled the bloody knife between my fingers. She finally had the common sense to look scared.

She lunged for a flower vase. I sidestepped, and it shattered on the spot where I had been standing. I grabbed her by the shirt and threw her down to the floor. She flipped and crawled backwards, eyes wide. I could practically hear her heart pounding in her chest. It sounded delicious. Maybe I would carve it out for Cyan to find. The hope left her eyes as I raised the knife above my head.

"You've caused a lot of trouble for me! Cyan is mine!"

"Jack, if this is a joke, now would be a really good time to stop it."

My shadow fell over her body. She closed her eyes, bracing herself for impact.

THIRTEEN

I was back outside by the car, blood still steaming from my knuckles, broken glass sparkling in the moonlight. The memories glitched through my head, choppy yet crystal clear.

Mr. Falcon's body going up in flames.

Hamen screaming as I carved letters into his chest.

Abigail looking at me like I was a monster.

You were a perfect puppet.

My stomach rolled. Tears dripped down my face. I shook my head. "No, no, no." I slammed my fists into the window. The glass shattered, but the reflection only multiplied into a thousand tiny copies. They all laughed at me.

"*You finally got your revenge!*" they shouted. I clawed at my head, falling to my knees.

"GET OUT OF MY HEAD!" I screamed.

Abigail ran up to me, grabbing my face and forcing me to look at her. "Cyan, Cyan, you're gonna be okay. Talk to me, okay?"

Another scream rent my body. I threw Abigail to the side.

"*DON'T TOUCH HIM, HE'S MINE!*"

Reece kept her gun trained on me. *Shoot me*, I begged. *Please shoot me. Don't let me hurt anyone.*

Abigail reappeared, her soft fingers digging into my scalp, her legs pinning my body to the ground. I wailed and thrashed and begged her to let go, her fingers scalding.

"HE'S NOT YOURS, HE'S MINE!" she screamed.

The pain in my skull was blinding, worse than it had ever been, but pleasant emotions filled my head.

Holding Abigail's hand.

Cuddling on the couch.

More than cuddling on the couch.

My body went slack. The pain vanished, along with the visions.

I looked at Abigail, who was trying her best not to cry. I reached up and wiped away one of her tears.

"Why are you crying? What's wrong?" I asked. Warm salty drops fell on my face.

"I'm okay. Just stay with me, okay?"

I nodded, although my head felt too heavy to nod properly. It lolled to the side. I didn't know what I was agreeing to, but I would do anything for her.

"Did you know that your eyes glow, too?" I mumbled.

ABIGAIL

ONE

Have you ever ridden in a car with an unconscious siren, assassin, and diagnosed sociopath? Because I have. It wasn't fun. The broken glass kept falling out of the windows, and the wind was so loud I could barely hear.

I had gotten one side of the story when Hamen had shown up in the nick of time to rescue me, covered in blood and screaming *that's not Cyan* over and over again. After he had subdued Cyan – or Brian, whoever he was – he had explained who the Slayers were and why he was there – all the way back to where Cyan was from and what had happened there. The story seemed so fake, so outlandish, so horrifying, I had a hard time believing him. Another siren who could fuck with people's emotions – *and apparently their thoughts now* – had *possessed* my boyfriend?

I had searched through Cyan's phone and called the only contact he had besides me: someone labeled IN CASE OF EMERGENCY. Reece had picked up the phone and demanded we stay put until she arrived to retrieve him.

She demanded that I tell her every word Hamen and Cyan had said to me while I babysat their unconscious bodies in the backseat. I did my best but my mind was still spinning from all the siren lingo that had been shoved down my throat. Blue Powerline, Red Powerline, Slayers, mind-control, charming, glowing eyes.

All terms that applied to me. Because I was apparently a Siren. A Red Powerline Siren. I had been manipulating people's emotions my entire life and hadn't realized it. I had the same special abilities as the serial killer who had murdered dozens of people. The father I had never met had been a mythical creature.

And yet Cyan is considered the dangerous one, not me? Make it make sense.

How could I have not have noticed? I had always attributed my differences to being trans – not to being a *damn siren*. I thought I had a hard time making friends because people were transphobic, but what if something deep in their psyche had warned them I was dangerous? What if they thought I was a freak because they could've *sworn* my eyes turned red sometimes?

Whenever I trailed off, Reece cleared her throat, which made the pit in my stomach grow even deeper. I had only known her for a few hours, but she already terrified me. Her icy, unbothered stare had a special way of making me feel guilty for everything that had happened. As if I could've known that Cyan – *whose real name I didn't even know until Hamen told me* – was being controlled like a puppet in a sick play.

By the time my words had fizzled out, we were driving into a dilapidated town. Reece pulled over in front of a police station that looked like it had seen better days. A massive teenager stood out front, his arms crossed and mouth drawn in a thin line. "That's Henry," Reece said, opening the car door.

Without a word, Henry scooped up Cyan's body and carried him into the station. He laid him down on a bench inside a cell and locked the door behind him. He did the same with Hamen. I didn't think Hamen was going to try anything, but when I tried to speak up, Henry muttered something about *damned fucking Slayers*, so I decided not to push it.

It smelled like copper and desperation. Sweat ran down between my shoulder blades. I tried to keep my eyes trained on the ground, but my gaze kept skipping to Cyan's limp body. He was still covered in blood. Broken glass glittered from his knuckles.

"What are we going to do?" I whispered.

"Wait until he wakes up. See if he remembers anything," Reece said.

"What if he's just pretending to have amnesia?"

I spun around to see Hamen blinking slowly, his voice still slurred. He didn't look surprised to be locked in a cell. Maybe he had been awake in the car, listening to our conversation.

"Maybe this was his plan all along to get back here. So, he could kill all of us in one go," Hamen continued, leaning his head against the stone.

Fury coursed through my veins. "None of this is his fault," I spat. "*You're* the one who's been trying to kill him."

"For good reason! You've known him for what, a week?" Hamen argued. "You just saw what he was capable of. You should get rid of him now before he does any more damage."

Before twenty-four hours ago, I wouldn't have been able to imagine Cyan doing anything scary. The thought of him terrifying a whole town seemed ridiculous. Then again, he had tried to stab me.

"You don't know him like I do," I said. "He was happy with me. He was normal." *And funny. And kind. And caring.*

"He was only happy and normal with you because you were controlling his emotions for him," Hamen argued. "That's why Brian wanted to get rid of you so bad." My throat went dry. *No, please don't tell me that. The boy I had started to fall in love with couldn't be a mirage. He had to be real.*

"We won't know what's really going on until he wakes up," Reece said. "So, both of you can shut up until then."

We lapsed into silence.

Cyan groaned awake around two in the morning. The rest of us immediately sat up, tense, barely breathing. Cyan's hands went to his head, pulling at his hair. Reece stood and crossed her arms as Cyan pushed himself up, blinking slowly at the room around him. He swiveled and stared stupidly at Reece through the bars. I stayed out of view with the others, holding my breath.

"Reece?" he whispered, his voice dry and cracking. "Is that you?" She nodded, squinting to look at his eyes. They were blue. "Why . . . why am I here? I have the worst headache." He stood up, wobbling so precariously that I thought he might fall to the ground. He balanced himself against the wall and rubbed his eyes.

Henry got up and took a protective stance behind Reece, not that she needed it. Hamen watched with interest from his cell across the hallway.

"Who are you?" Reece asked.

Cyan tilted his head. "I'm . . . I'm Cyan. You know that. Guys, what's going on? Am I back in Tredecim?"

"What do you remember?" Henry asked.

Cyan winced and stared blankly at us. "Remember . . ." he muttered and trailed off, pacing around the room.

"Does the name Abigail ring a bell?" Henry asked. At my name, Cyan froze. He spun around, the color draining from his face.

"How do you know about her? What's wrong? Is she okay? I don't remember – my head –" My heart shattered even more as he clawed at his hair. His pacing became more frantic. "What did I *do*?"

"Just tell us what you remember," Reece said. Cyan slammed his fists against the wall, dragging his palms against the rough stone. Unable to hold back, I ran into view.

"Don't let him hurt himself!" I shouted. Reece grabbed me by my shirt, yanking me backwards as Cyan flew against the bars, his arms clawing at me, teeth bared.

"*You're dead!*" he spat, face contorting in a snarl. I retreated, barely breathing as Henry shoved me behind him. Cyan let out a low rumbling laugh. Brian's red eyes bled through Cyan's blue.

"*Nice to see you, Henry,*" he purred. He draped himself across the bars, running his tongue over his teeth. "*Putting people in cages now, are we?*" he asked.

"Where is Cyan?" I spat.

Cyan tapped the side of his skull. "*Oh, he's in here, watching, enjoying the show. Well, probably not enjoying per se.*"

"Has this been your whole plan? Possess him and use his body to keep on your killing spree?" Reece asked.

He grinned. "*Pretty smart, right? Being able to control emotions is cool, but these water powers are so much better.*"

My fists trembled with rage. "You bitch."

Cyan covered his mouth in mock shock, giggling. "*That's not very polite.*"

"We'll figure out a way to get Cyan back," Reece threatened.

"*I'll just keep coming,*" he threatened. "*You can't get rid of me forever.*"

I glared. "Wanna bet?" I looked at Henry and Reece. "Hold his arms down. I know how to reach him. At least for a little bit."

They strode forward and pinned Cyan's arms to the bars before he could skitter away. He fought and pulled back, spitting curses and kicking. I summoned all the bravery in my small body, marched up, and grabbed him by the front of his shirt, pulling his head towards mine. *It's always been me*, I thought, flashing back to the moment in the driveway where I was able to banish those horrible red eyes.

He screamed more curses, but I reached through the bars, grabbed a fistful of hair, and forced his lips against mine. I searched my newly realized powers, concentrating on every single positive memory I could muster up, and screamed them into his head. Cyan's body spasmed and then went slack.

I stepped back and saw blue eyes once more. I nearly collapsed in relief. He panted against the bars for a few moments before bursting into sobs. Henry and Reece released him, and he stumbled backwards, falling to his knees on the ground.

"I remember everything," he sobbed. "I'm so sorry."

TWO

It was easy enough to piece together. Brian had been living in Cyan's head for the past month, using him to track down Mr. Falcon and murder the Slayers. Meanwhile, regular Cyan had been none the wiser, using his time to search for other sirens and frame Mr. Falcon for his parents' murder. I had been unknowingly keeping Brian at bay by holding the reins to Cyan's emotions whenever he was around me. That was why Brian wanted to kill me so badly. I was the competition. I was the only one who could let Cyan be in control of his own head.

Is Cyan really in control if I'm the one keeping Brian at bay? I wondered. The ethics of the situation made my head spin. I sat against the wall, trying not to cry or panic as I concentrated on Cyan's fragile string of emotions.

Keeping Brian away before the big reveal had been so easy; I hadn't even realized I was doing it. But Brian has been hiding back then, biding his time, taking control at specific opportunities to finish his sick game.

Now the secret was out, and there was no need for subtlety. Holding him back felt like balancing a spinning basketball on the tip of my finger. I couldn't use brute force, but I could feel the strain. I had no idea how Brian had managed to brainwash an entire town for years on end. He must've been the most powerful siren on the planet.

Cyan had stopped crying, but hadn't moved from his spot on the floor. His arms hung limply, as if the gravity was twice as strong in the cell.

"Cyan, you need to tell us everything that happened. Everything that Brian made you do," Reece said. He looked up at us, his eyes heavy as his arms and black with despair.

"He . . . I . . ." He swallowed. "We killed Mr. Falcon. I . . . I cut his body up into pieces. And lit him on fire. I texted the pictures to Jack." He drew up his legs and placed his head between them, rocking back and forth. My stomach lurched. *It wasn't Cyan that did that*, I told myself. *It wasn't Cyan that tried to kill you. It wasn't Cyan that carved that horrible message into Hamen's chest. It was Brian. It was all Brian.*

"Did you kill anyone else?" Henry asked.

Cyan shook his head. "Just him."

"Did you try to kill anyone else?"

"He wants to kill everyone," Cyan whispered. "Where is Jack? Does he know?" he asked.

"Well . . . he got your text . . ." Henry said quietly. "But he doesn't know what's going on. I'm sure once we explain – he'll understand."

"Where is he?"

"We don't know," Reece said.

Cyan lay back against the floor. "He probably wants me dead," he whispered. "You should let him kill me."

"Absolutely not. This isn't your fault!" I protested.

"There's a serial killer stuck in my head. Getting rid of me is exactly what you should do. Before he comes back. Before he gets out of this cell and kills all of you too!" he shouted.

"That's what I said," Hamen muttered behind us.

"Getting rid of you isn't an option!" I retorted. "I can keep him away! It's working right now!"

"So, you're just going to be my puppet master for the rest of our lives? What if you forget to kiss me one morning and I go berserk and murder the whole town!" Cyan shouted. "It's not feasible! You need to get rid of me!"

"We're not putting you down like you're a sick dog!" Henry chimed in.

The look in Cyan's eyes grew desperate. "You have to!" he begged. He crawled towards the bars and wrapped his pale hands around them. "Please?" he whispered, looking at Reece. From the little I had heard about her, she was probably the only one with enough guts to actually do what he was asking.

"He's probably right," Reece said.

"Are you fucking kidding me? We're not even going to try to save him first?" I shouted.

She ignored me. "Cyan, do you trust my judgment?" she asked coldly.

He nodded.

She turned to glare at me. "Then *I'll* decide if or when he needs to be put down. I'm the only one here who can't be manipulated by sirens. I'm the soundest mind here."

Henry frowned. "She's got a point."

I sagged. "Fine," I whispered.

We walked back up to the front desk.

"We need to find Jack and tell him what's really going on before he does something reckless," Henry said.

"I'll go with you," Reece said. "Abigail, are you okay to watch them for a few hours?"

I nodded. The others filtered out of the room, leaving me to babysit the two murderers.

It felt like I was the one in a cage. Brian had me more trapped right now than he had the night he had shown up on my doorstep with a knife. If I dared let up for a moment, we were all toast. I was the only one keeping this town from being puppeteered by a serial killer.

I sat on the floor down the hall, out of view, while I played games on my phone to keep myself awake. I doubted I could keep Brian at bay while unconscious. I could hear Cyan's footsteps echoing off the concrete.

"You know, I don't think pacing is going to help you break out of there," Hamen drawled.

"I don't want to escape," Cyan said. "Why did they even bring you here? You didn't do anything."

"They're afraid I'm going to kill you. And they should be."

Cyan winced as if he had been burned. "I'm so sorry," he whispered. "I didn't mean to hurt you."

"You didn't just *hurt* me," Hamen snarled. "You . . . you . . ." he trailed off for a moment, his words stuck in his throat. "You promised we would run away together. That you would keep me safe. And then you left me in your bed to go murder Mr. Falcon."

Hold on, has Hamen had a crush on Cyan this whole time?

Hold on, they shared a bed?

I clenched my fists, but then promptly felt terrible about being jealous. Cyan wasn't the one who had lured the vulnerable boy on.

Cyan swallowed. "You deserve someone better than me anyway. You'll have the chance to have a real boyfriend in the future."

Hamen shook his head. "When I was ten, I had a friend over for a sleepover. My dad caught us holding hands. At the hospital, he told me that he would do way worse than break my wrist if he ever caught me doing something like that again. With anyone," Hamen whispered. "So, no, I won't." *Jesus,* I thought. *These Slayers are some real psychos.*

"That's horrible," Cyan said.

Hamen wrapped his arms around his legs. "I really should've killed you."

Cyan sighed. "Yeah. You should've."

None of this is his fault! Just because he has powers doesn't make him dangerous, I thought. *I apparently have powers, and I'm not dangerous. Right?*

I thought back to everything I had gotten away with as a kid. Being able to live by myself in a huge mansion. Convincing my doctor to give me HRT. *Have I been manipulating people my entire life?* I thought. *Did I make all that stuff happen?*

"I don't know how they're going to keep Brian out of my head. But maybe I can convince them to let you go home," Cyan said.

"Don't," Hamen snapped, his voice cracking. "You're not leaving me now. If the others don't want to keep me here, just tell them to kill me."

Cyan nodded. "For the record, you're not a coward."

It was hard to tell, but the noises coming from Hamen's cell sounded like he was crying.

It took me another hour to get up the courage to talk to Cyan face-to-face. I felt like the boy I had started to fall in love with had never existed. I might as well have been confronting a stranger, and I hated talking to strangers.

But I couldn't sit there forever knowing that Cyan had lied through his teeth throughout our whole relationship. I wanted him to beg for my forgiveness, promise that the kisses had never been one of his deceptions, swear to never keep another secret.

But what if he didn't? I had spent the better part of my teenage years pining for Mr. Right. And right when I thought I had found him, everything was falling apart. I didn't know if I would survive the fall if he didn't try to catch me.

I walked in front of the bars and sat down, fiddling with my fingers. Cyan looked terrified to see me.

"You lied," I said quietly. "About everything."

He sagged. "Yes," he whispered. "I did."

I glared at him. "You told me that sirens migrated." Across the hall, Hamen sniggered. I ignored him. "You told me your parents lived in the ocean. That you were just out exploring, trying to figure out where to live your best life."

"I didn't want you to find out about what really happened-"

"And the real zinger is that you lied to me when you were in your right mind!" I hissed.

Cyan shrank away. "I'm sorry," he whispered.

"Sorry doesn't cut it!" I snapped. "I could've helped protect you! I told you everything about me! It was a fair trade, remember?"

"I know."

I sniffed back tears before getting up and stalking away. Once I was out of sight, I let my tears fall. I wanted to go back in time. I wanted to feel Cyan's hand in mine. I wanted everything to be like that night we kissed for the first time.

But it never would be. Brian was living in his head, Mr. Falcon was dead, and the only person preventing Cyan from continuing his murderous rampage was me.

THREE

Reece returned by dinnertime and stayed the rest of the night with me. Her search for Jack had been futile. By sunrise, I couldn't force myself to stay awake any longer. I could feel Brian's excitement growing, like spiders crawling on the edges of my brain. As soon as I was out, he would have the opportunity to break free again, and who knows what he would make Cyan do. Those bars weren't strong enough to hold him.

Henry returned to the police station with a grim face. I had resorted to jogging up and down the narrow hallway to keep myself conscious.

"I've searched the whole town. No one has seen Jack except Rick," Henry said.

Reece swore, but I was too tired to ask her who Rick was.

"What are we supposed to do?" I gasped, sweat running down my back.

"I have an idea. But it's going to be difficult," Henry said. He pulled an orange prescription bottle out of his pocket and jiggled it in front of Cyan. Immediately, my head seared in pain. I cried out, clutching my forehead, acid rising in the back of my throat. Whatever was in that bottle, Brian didn't like it.

"Are those my pills?" Cyan asked.

Henry nodded. "I'm hoping Brian will have a harder time waking up if you're on your calm-down supplements."

Cyan reached through the bars and took the bottle. He unscrewed the cap and threw the bottle back, swallowing the pills dry. Henry's jaw dropped as Cyan threw the empty bottle to the side.

"Dude! How many of those were you supposed to take?" Henry demanded.

"Just taking one won't be enough to block him out. He was still able to manipulate my feelings back in the day when I was on it," Cyan rasped, coughing.

"He also can't take advantage if you're dead from an overdose!" Henry protested, turning to Reece. "This can't be good for him!"

I wanted to join in and say my piece, but I could feel my willpower slipping. I stumbled as my eyelids fluttered.

Just a second . . . I'll close my eyes just for a second . . .

I startled back awake to find Reece shaking me. I had fallen to the floor. Cyan was heaving in the corner of his cell. I watched in dismay as he vomited the pills he had just taken. Reece cursed, and Henry sighed in relief.

Cyan looked up at us with bloody red eyes, grinning his usual manic smile. I quickly snatched my control back. The red eyes fizzled out, and Cyan almost stumbled into his pool of puke.

"Well, that didn't work," Reece muttered.

"Maybe we can force-feed a *normal* dose," I said.

Henry shook his head. "Those were the only pills I could find in his room before his parents got home." I sagged in desperation. I physically couldn't keep this up much longer. What were we supposed to do?

Reece sighed and pulled something else out from under her skirt. "Time for Plan B then," she muttered. She unlocked Cyan's cell and walked inside.

"What's Plan B – *ahhhhhh!*" Cyan screamed as Reece tased him. He fell to the ground, twitching and moaning. Henry's jaw dropped as Reece locked the cell behind her, pocketed her taser, and pulled out her pistol instead.

"Abigail, go take a nap. If Brian so much as twitches, he won't be twitching for long," Reece said. I could barely nod before I succumbed to unconsciousness.

. . .

I woke up with a start on the office floor, bathed in sweat and gasping for breath.

"Is he okay?" I demanded, scrambling to my feet, the last image in my head was one of Reece standing over him with a taser. I bolted down the hallway to see Reece had barely moved from her station, a cautionary hand still on her gun.

"He's fine. Still snoozing."

Cyan was indeed still slumped on the floor, looking almost peaceful. I sighed in relief.

"So . . . is this the plan? Just keep tasing him so I can sleep? That can't be good for him," I said.

"Got another idea?"

I pursed my lips. "It can't be that hard to get more of that medication. Y'all got a pharmacy around here?"

"Actually . . . we do. Cyan's adoptive parents are doctors. They may have some extra in the Urgent Care. We could break in, try to steal some," Henry said.

"The last time we tried to break into Urgent Care didn't go that well," Reece muttered. "But hell, it's worth a shot."

Hold on, they had broken into an Urgent Care before?

I followed Henry out of the jail and down the street. I took a moment to really look at the town for the first time. There was nothing special about it – it looked like any downtown area from any small town. Most of the storefronts were abandoned and collecting dust, except for

Rick's Gun Store and the Sweet Treats. I briefly thought about grabbing Cyan a cone on the way back. Maybe if we hid the medication in there, Brian wouldn't try to make him puke it up.

Henry scanned the dark streets before sliding down an alleyway. We found ourselves in front of a steel door. He pulled a key from his pocket and opened the door.

"Why do you have a key to the Urgent Care?" I asked.

"Long story." The heavy door slammed shut, and I shivered in the darkness.

I followed the bouncing beam of Henry's flashlight down the hallway, trying not to think of corpses waiting in the dark.

"Now, if I were a mood stabilizer, where would I be hiding?" he mused, walking into a room that looked like an office. Cabinets lined the walls, and he started throwing them open at random and looking through them. I did the same, watching Henry out of the corner of my eye.

He was massive, at least six feet tall, with giant muscles to match. He looked like he could be drafted to an NFL team the next weekend. I wasn't surprised he had killed Brian the first time.

The lights above us suddenly flickered to life. We spun around to see two figures standing in the doorway. They were tall and skinny, wearing lab coats and gaunt faces. For having caught two teenagers in a place where they definitely weren't supposed to be, they didn't seem surprised to see us.

"Mr. and Mrs. Hartzfield!" Henry piped up, shutting the drawer behind him and trying his best to put an innocent smile on his face. "I can totally explain what we're doing in here."

"Save it," the strange man said. "Take us to see our son."

Henry's jaw dropped. I nudged him with my elbow. "Who are these people?" I whispered.

"How do you know Cyan is here?" Henry demanded, ignoring me.

"We know a lot more than you think," the woman said. "And we are all running out of time. Please, take us to him."

Henry clenched his jaw, and for a moment, I thought he was going to bulldoze over them and make a run for it.

"Fine," he said. "But I don't know if you're going to like what you see." They nodded and moved out of the doorway so we could head towards the exit.

"Henry, who are these people?" I demanded as soon as we were out of earshot.

"Cyan's adoptive parents," he whispered back.

We entered the jail. Cyan had woken up, but I didn't feel Brian itching for control. He must've been too weary of Reece standing at attention with her pistol. Henry motioned for Cyan's parents to wait out of sight as we walked up. Reece didn't take her eyes off her target.

"Did you find any medication?" she asked.

"Not exactly," Henry said. I took back control over Cyan's head, and Reece finally looked down the hallway and furrowed her brow. "They know he's here," Henry whispered. "They wanted to see him."

They stepped in front of Cyan's cell. Their son blinked, as if he was trying to read something in another language.

"Are you real?" he asked.

"Yes, Sweetheart, we're real," Nichole whispered.

He swallowed and crossed his arms, looking down at the ground, his lips pressed in a thin line. It wasn't quite the reaction I thought he would give. I would've been crying tears of relief if I saw my family after going through so much hell. I guess they hadn't parted on the best of terms.

The last time they had seen their son, he was fist-fighting a serial killer and stole their car to disappear for a month. It wasn't like his parents looked overjoyed to see that their son was safe. Or at least alive. How did they even know he was here?

"What are you doing here?" Reece asked, her stare suspicious.

Robert looked down at the ground, then at Cyan, then the ground again, as if he were debating whether or not to jump off a cliff.

"We knew the whole time you were a siren, Cyan," he blurted.

Cyan's head snapped up, his blue eyes wide. "No, you didn't," he protested. "I kept it a secret. You never saw me."

"We knew before we adopted you," Nichole said. Her face twisted like the next words were burning her insides. Tears filled her blue eyes. "We used to be Slayers."

Cyan made a noise like he was being strangled. Hamen's jaw dropped. Even Reece looked surprised. I winced as Brian beat against the edges of Cyan's psyche. Guess he didn't know as much about the Slayers as he thought he had.

"This was never supposed to happen," Nichole continued, tears now streaming freely down her face. "We knew your family were the last ones, and once they were gone, the water powerline would be extinct. There would be no need for Slayers anymore." She wrapped a hand around the bars. Cyan recoiled back like she had burned him.

"Mr. Falcon, of course, was the one assigned to do the job. He informed the rest of us that the Blue Powerline was gone, and we thought that was the end of it. But then the Leader contacted us.

"He had been watching to make sure the job was done. He watched you get thrown from the car and not use your powers to save your parents and decided . . . you had potential. He had never seen a siren restrain themselves in such a way, and he wanted to see how far you could be pushed before breaking."

"He asked us to take you in and care for you. He wanted to see if a siren's nature could be fixed if they were raised in a normal human family. We changed our names, moved to the most desolate place we could find, and adopted you," Robert explained, his voice raw.

My mind spun. It sounded made-up. Too insane to be true.

"Cyan was an *experiment?*" Hamen demanded. "An experiment my *dad* told you to conduct?"

They nodded. Cyan shook his head. "I don't believe you," he sputtered. "This is - this is crazy. This is just Brian messing with me again. You're not real, this isn't real . . ." He sank to the floor, fists buried in his hair.

"Hold the fuck up. If you were really Slayers, why the *fuck* didn't you kill Brian?" Henry growled, hands curled by his sides.

"The same reason Mr. Falcon didn't. We didn't know Brian was here and got trapped in the same fog as everyone else," Robert said. "Our focus was on keeping Cyan safe and regulated. And he was, until he stopped taking his pills and started using his powers."

"We knew something was wrong, but we had no clue how *wrong*," Nichole said. "We were so worried. And when you disappeared after the fight and our car was gone . . . we had no choice but to alert . . ."

Static filled my brain. A strangled laugh suddenly left Cyan's curled-up figure on the floor. His body shook, and tears streamed down his face.

"Holy shit. You're really not lying." He threw his head back into the concrete bricks. "So . . . so this *entire* time, I've just been a piece in a sick game all of you have been playing? A *puppet*?" Cyan spat.

"Cyan, it's not like that! We love -"

"*You* were the ones who told the Slayers I had run away. *You're* the reason they knew I was there. *You're* the reason I had Hamen trying to kill me," Cyan seethed.

"We had no choice -"

"*You're* the reason I was drugged. *You* saw me hurting myself and not eating. *You* saw all of that and let it happen."

"We saved you!" Robert shouted.

"You *knew* my parents were murdered and you never said anything!" Cyan screamed. "How much time did I have to adjust and be normal before you decided you would throw in the towel and dispose of me, too?"

"But we didn't!" Nichole protested. "We figured out the medication. You didn't use your powers. You were kind, you had friends. You turned into a good person. The experiment *worked*." She stretched her hand through the bars only for Cyan to bare his teeth and skitter backwards.

"Don't fucking touch me," he growled. "You're not my parents!" She recoiled, lower lip trembling. Robert took a deep breath and clenched his jaw.

"We're sorry," he said quietly.

"I hate you!" Cyan spat. "How long did I have to prove myself before my time was up? Huh? *Answer me*."

For a moment, I was tempted to let Brian free so Cyan could tear them apart.

"It was never up to us," Nichole said. "We made reports to the Leader and followed his instructions. He was very pleased with your progress until you ran away. We tried to convince him to spare you, but he said it was too risky to let you live."

"But now that we know what's really going on, everything's okay!" Robert said. "He knows it wasn't Cyan acting that way – it was Brian. Brian is the one who needs to die."

"I don't know if you forgot, but I killed Brian," Henry said.

"He needs to die again. And we think we have a solution," Robert said, looking at Cyan. "The Leader agreed that if it works, he'll let you live. He's on his way here now."

"If *what* works?" I growled.

Nichole and Robert exchanged a look, like they were about to light a bomb. "We need to give him brain damage."

"I'm *sorry?*" I demanded.

"Cyan's medication targeted his amygdala – the part of the brain that controls emotion – the part of the brain that probably controls his powers. If we damage that specific area, on purpose, we might be able to get rid of Brian's ability to control him," Nichole explained. Jaws dropped all around the room.

"You think you can kill Brian again by cutting open Cyan's head and stabbing a needle into his brain?" Henry echoed.

The gravity of what he was suggesting crashed onto my shoulders.

"Absolutely not! You are not lobotomizing him!" I protested. The room dissolved into silence. I could only hear my own ragged breath and my heart thudding in my ears. *This is crazy,* I thought. *His parents literally just admitted to using him as an experiment, and we're going to listen to their advice?*

"It's not reasonable or safe to expect Abigail to hold Brian back for the rest of your lives," Reece finally said. "If you don't want to die, this makes a lot more sense."

I gawked at her. How in the hell could she think this was the solution of all things?

"However, you might wish you had chosen death once you have to go through the rest of your life pretending to be normal," Reece pointed out.

"I've already been doing that," Cyan said flatly.

"Cyan, tell them this is crazy! What if they stab the wrong spot! They could turn you into a vegetable! You could lose all of your memories!" I cried.

"This is the compromise we've come to," Nichole said. "If we try the surgery, Cyan has a chance to live. If not, the Slayers will come here and kill him themselves."

"We don't want to lose you," Robert protested, eyes full of tears.

"Fuck off," Cyan spat. "My real parents would've raised me to be a good person. You stole that chance from them." He slowly got to his feet, his fists clenched by his side. "I'll do it. Give me the brain damage."

"Cyan, no!" I protested.

"I'm so sick and tired of people being in control of me," he said. "I want my body back. I want my life back." He narrowed his eyes at his parents. "But I have a condition."

"Anything," Nichole said.

"You're going to leave this town. I never want to see you again."

His parents sagged. "And you're leaving Hamen here with me. His father doesn't get to lay another finger on him."

Across the hall, Hamen's face dropped in shock. Nichole and Robert exchanged a long look before finally nodding. "Very well."

"I don't know exactly what my ancestors did – but what I do know is that what humans have done to us is a thousand times worse. Brian's right about one thing. Humans are the evil ones," Cyan said.

My protests died on my lips. As much as the idea terrified me, Cyan had a point. He had been a puppet in someone else's game for far too long. It was time for him to hold his own strings.

FOUR

There was no time to lose. I made sure I had tight control over Cyan's head as we marched him to the Urgent Care. I could feel Brian's anger curling at the side of my head like smoke from a fire. He was definitely not happy about our plan to get rid of him or the new revelation from Cyan's parents.

Get over it, I thought. *You weren't the experiment.*

I followed Nichole and Robert and watched from the corner as they donned surgical gear and sterilized their equipment. Cyan trembled like a leaf beside me.

"You don't have to do this," I whispered.

"Yes, I do," he whispered back. "Just . . . if I die, make sure they keep their promise."

"We're ready," Nichole said, motioning him over. Cyan took a deep breath and walked over to the table. I concentrated on keeping Brian away as they strapped him down. Leather cuffs were tightened around his ankles, wrists, and head until he looked like someone who had tried to escape from a psych ward. He stared at the ceiling, unable to look at me as his parents snapped on their gloves and pulled masks over their faces.

Cyan, talk to me, I thought. *It's okay if you chicken out. Just speak up.*

He didn't speak.

My fingers curled involuntarily as Robert picked up a giant needle and hovered over Cyan's face.

"This is to numb you for when we cut into your skull," he said. I swallowed back vomit and couldn't help but turn away as the plunger was pushed down.

Meanwhile, Brian raged. It felt like someone was squeezing the middle of my brain. I ignored it. Nichole took a razor to Cyan's head and shaved a clean patch before rubbing it with iodine.

Aren't surgeries, especially brain surgeries, supposed to be in a super sterile environment? I thought. *I'm not even wearing a mask. What if he gets an infection? Are they making this unsafe on purpose?*

I turned away again as Robert brought out something that looked like a drill with sharp teeth on the end of it. The pressure in my head tripled as the machine whirred and screamed, and for a moment, my vision blurred as the tightness grew unbearable.

Go the fuck away, I thought. *You're just mad because you know you're going to die.*

I forced myself to look. A tiny piece of Cyan's skull sat on the table next to me. It looked like a nickel – if nickels were white and porous. The world wavered in front of me as I tried not to throw up. I doubted that would be very sanitary.

Robert ran his finger around the opening he had just cut. "Can you feel that?" he asked.

"No," Cyan whispered.

"This is your last chance to back out," I blurted.

"Do it," Cyan said. Nichole nodded, picking up what looked like a metal skewer one would roast marshmallows on. I averted my eyes once more, whispering a silent farewell to the siren I might have loved.

Goodbye, Cyan.

I didn't have enough time to grieve before a loud thud sounded in the hallway. Cyan's parents jerked their heads up as an unfamiliar shape kicked open the door, a gun in his hand.

"Oh my god," Nichole whispered.

"You can't be in here!" Robert shouted. The figure raised the gun.

"Get out of my way," he said. "You're not the one I want to hurt." Cyan's parents locked hands over their son. Cyan tried to lift his head to see what was happening, but the straps prevented him from doing so.

I instantly tried to break into the stranger's emotions, but all it made me feel was like I had just run into a brick wall. Whoever this was, he was furious, and I wasn't strong enough to control Brian and whoever this was.

"Jack?" Cyan finally whispered. "Is that you?"

Jack laughed, a strange barking sound, and drifted closer into Cyan's field of vision. The skin under his eyes was black, the whites of his eyes bloodshot. Stubble graced his face. Shaking fingers swiped greasy hair out of his face.

"What are you doing here?" Cyan asked. Jack ignored him and turned his gaze back to me and Cyan's parents.

"Get on the floor," he said. I slowly slid to the floor, hands still by my sides. Nichole and Robert didn't move.

"Jack, I know you're upset, but you have to let us explain," Nichole said.

He lifted his gun.

"If you're protecting him, that's all I need to know."

The gun popped twice. Two bodies fell to the floor. I covered my mouth to muffle my scream. Cyan didn't make a noise.

"So, you decided to come crawling back here after what you did," Jack seethed.

I tried desperately to hack into Jack's head and make him feel calm, peace, anything, but nothing worked. His mind was like a steel trap. He was so full of anger that no matter how loud I screamed, he couldn't hear me.

I tilted my head to the side and watched as Jack walked over to the gurney, knuckles white on his gun. Tears streamed down his face.

"I fucking hate you," he seethed. "I should've helped my father kill you a month ago."

Cyan said nothing to defend himself. I tried to swallow, but my throat was too dry. "He's not the one who killed your father. Brian is," I shouted from the floor.

Jack laughed. "Last time I checked, Brian was a blondie."

"Brian possessed him. He hasn't been in control of his actions for months. Brian made him do it."

"Then why isn't Brian making him do anything right now?" Jack asked. I lifted my head, letting my eyes glow red.

"Because I'm holding him back. But I don't have to," I threatened.

"Abigail, don't you dare!" Cyan shouted.

Jack turned the gun towards me, his jaw hardening. "You think I won't shoot you, too?"

"I'd love to see you try," I hissed, getting to my feet.

"Abigail – don't you dare!" Cyan shouted, struggling against his restraints. "Jack, don't!"

I lunged for Jack's ankles. He toppled over, the gun falling out of his hands and skittering across the floor. We both lunged for it, wrestling over the barrel.

Let me go.

"Don't you dare!" Cyan screamed.

I hesitated. Cyan literally had an exposed hole in his head. Who knew what Brian would do? What if his brain fell out?

Jack wrenched the gun out of my hands and took aim. I didn't have much of a choice.

I let go of my control, and the pressure in my head instantly vanished. Cyan immediately tore through the cuffs, grabbing for whatever he could reach on the table beside him. The color drained from Jack's face as he perched on top of the gurney, clutching a fistful of surgical tools.

"*Hi, Jack,*" Cyan grinned, eyes glowing bloody. Jack stumbled backwards, chest heaving.

"Why – how are your eyes red?" he whispered.

I got to my feet. "I warned you," I said. Jack shook his head.

"Th-that's impossible," he whispered. "Brian's dead!" Cyan lurched forward, swiping at Jack's head, laughing as he wobbled and missed.

"*Not quite as dead as your father,*" Cyan taunted. I waited until the fistful of surgical tools was an inch away from Jack's face before snatching my control back.

Cyan blinked for several seconds, wobbling slightly. He dropped the tools on the ground and stumbled back to the gurney, groaning. He tried to hold his head and nearly stuck his fingers into the hole in his skull. For the first time, Jack looked uncertain. His eyes flashed between me and Cyan.

"Explain. Now," he whispered.

"Brian somehow got into Cyan's head. He hid there, waiting for an opportunity to kill your father. Cyan had no clue what was happening. I've been the one holding Brian back. We were trying to get rid of him for good when you decided to barge in and ruin everything!" I seethed.

Jack's eyes flickered. "No . . . no, no, no. That can't be true. Are you lying to me?" he shouted.

"You literally just saw it!" I shouted.

"How do you even know this brain thing would work?" he asked.

"We don't," I said. "But we had to try something."

Jack paced, muttering. "This is insane. This is fucking insane."

"*I want to talk!*" Cyan screamed, eyes flashing red. I cried out as the pain in my head surged, stumbling to the floor. Jack reached out for me, trying to steady me. I gasped as my vision winked out.

Cyan, Jack, and I were standing in a living room that would have been cozy if it weren't for all the screaming.

A tall blond man hollered through a gag as he thrashed against the ropes that held him to a kitchen chair. A woman sat tied next to him, silent tears streaming down her face. In the middle of it all, a little blond boy stared at a bulky man wearing a black hockey mask and spinning a knife in his hands.

Holy shit, is that Brian? I realized, staring at the little boy. His cheeks were fat and rosy, his lower lip stuck in a confused pout as he stood in front of the Slayer.

The woman who must've been Brian's mom wrestled the gag out of her mouth. "Please, not my son. Let him go. He's not dangerous – he's a good little boy. He's only three!" she begged.

The man in the mask walked up to her, almost moving in slow motion. He tilted his head as if he were considering her request.

Little Brian screamed as he sank his knife into her stomach.

ONE a voice whispered in my ear.

"Brian . . . run . . ." the mom gasped.

Brian ran for the door, straining for the handle, only to be yanked backwards by his hair.

I watched in horror as the Slayer threw Brian to the floor, stomping his foot on his back. He grabbed his wrist and pulled until it popped. Brian screeched, tears pouring down his face.

"You bastard, get away from him!" the mom screamed. The Slayer left Brian wailing on the floor and silenced her with another stab to the abdomen. She went still, head hanging listlessly. Her long blonde hair was stained red.

TWO

Next to her, the father sobbed, straining to reach for her despite the ropes that held him bound. The Slayer walked over to him next. This time, the blood sprayed so hot and fast it stained the hockey mask.

THREE, FOUR

He kept stabbing, even after the dad had gone quiet.

FIVE, SIX, SEVEN, EIGHT

Blood covered the furniture, the floor, the Slayer's arm, Brian. He went back to the mom.

NINE, TEN, ELEVEN, TWELVE

The Slayer turned towards Brian, who lay frozen on the ground.

Run! I tried to scream, but my voice made no sound here. I was a captive audience. This had already happened – there was no going back and changing it.

THIRTEEN

The Slayer left the knife imbedded in Brian's foot, pinning it to the carpet. As Brian screamed, the Slayer whistled, opening a bottle of foul-smelling liquid and spraying it over the living room. He pulled a matchbook from his pocket.

He didn't bother giving the room a backwards glance as he threw a lit match onto the floor. Flames raced, smoke filled the air, and little Brian started to cry.

I covered my mouth, the vision starting to go hazy. Through the smoke, I saw Brian tug at the knife in his foot until it came out, freeing himself moments before the flames reached him. He crawled to the door on his hands and knees, coughing. This time, he reached the handle.

FIVE

I woke back up on the hospital floor. Cyan sat quietly on the edge of the gurney, red eyes filled with tears. Jack hovered above me, his eyes hollow.

"I tried to get over it. I really did," Cyan whispered. *"But I had nightmares every night. I was so angry. I couldn't forget. And I couldn't forgive."* Cyan turned to Jack. *"The Slayers was going to spare Cyan if they could just get rid of me. You just ruined Cyan's only chance of survival,"* he said. *"Congratulations."*

Jack's face was white as a sheet.

"Jack, I'm sorry. I know he was your dad, but *Jesus fucking Christ* did you see what he just did? You know as well as I do, he would've never gone to jail or been punished for what he did!" I shouted.

Jack looked up at me, jaw slack.

"I'm not saying that everything Brian did was right," I whispered. "He wanted revenge, not justice. He killed people who had nothing to do with your father. But *Jesus*, Jack. Your dad stabbed his parents *thirteen* times and left their son to burn alive at three years old! I'm sorry, but he deserved what he got!"

Jack deflated.

We all froze as a cell phone rang from the inside of Nichole's pocket.

"Get it," I hissed to Jack.

Grimacing, he crawled towards Nichole's body and fished the phone out of her coat and handed it to me. The caller ID simply said LEADER.

I swallowed, throat suddenly dry, and answered it.

"Well?" The voice on the other end was cold and mechanical. I could only assume he was asking about Cyan's lobotomy.

"Um . . . yeah about that. Nichole and Robert are . . . They are no longer able to do the surgery. We'll have to get someone else to do it."

"I'm afraid that's just not possible, Abigail. They are the only ones qualified of all of my men, and well, we can't just take this to a normal doctor."

My heart froze. *How the fuck did this guy know my name?*

"Then . . . then let me try." *How hard can it be to do brain surgery? I just have to stab him, right? They already did the hard part.*

"No, I'm afraid that's not possible. You could injure the wrong part of his brain and make him more dangerous." He sighed, like he had just lost his car keys. "It's unfortunate, this was a fascinating experiment, but all good things must come to an end."

Tears welled in my eyes. I was not going to lose him, not after all of this.

"We won't let you," I said.

"Then we will simply have to kill you too. See you soon."

The line went dead. I dropped the phone. I turned towards Jack, vibrating with rage.

"You're going to fix this!" I snarled.

We left behind Nichole and Robert and slapped a plastic cap over the hole in Cyan's head before we ran to the police station. One very hasty explanation later, we had barricaded ourselves inside and gathered every possible weapon we could find.

Spoiler alert: there weren't many to be found.

Henry stood right by the door, Reece and Jack not far behind him. I sat next to Cyan, normal Cyan, on the bench in his cell, fiddling with his thumbs. His eyes were empty, as if the needle had already been struck through his brain. He looked too tired, too overwhelmed to care that we were all about to die.

Hamen stood beside us, looking like he was going to vomit. He held Jack's gun with a sweaty hand. Reece held hers at the ready. Cyan halfheartedly held the scalpel that had been used to carve the skin from his skull. While rifling through the front desk, I had found a plastic fork still in the package. Maybe if I prayed hard enough, I could give one of the Slayers a cut with it before they splattered my brains across the wall.

Cyan stared at the wall, his expression blank as the stone. I wanted to talk to him, comfort him, but what was there to say? *I'm sorry your parents (who only adopted you because you were an experiment) got murdered by your best friend (because he thought you killed his dad). I'm sorry your one chance at possible survival was just ruined.*

Who was I kidding? We were all about to die in this jail. The Leader was moments away with god-knew how much backup. We were five teenagers with two guns and no extra ammo. We were fucked.

My fingers found his hand, and to my surprise, he didn't flinch away. *At least we'll go out with a fight,* I thought.

We held our breath as car tires screeched to a halt outside the front door. Cyan tensed.

We all jumped as the door shattered open. The Leader strode in, all poise and perfectly manicured suit. Half a dozen other men stood behind him, hands clasped behind their backs – no weapons in sight.

"Reece," the Leader said. "I've heard a lot about you."

"No one pulls a weapon or they die," Reece spat back, taking her time to make eye contact with every Slayer.

The Leader's icy eyes landed on Hamen. "I'm very disappointed in you, Son," he said. Hamen winced as if he had just been hit with a belt.

The Leader's eyes slid over to Cyan, who stared back as if this man was any other stranger on the street – and not someone who had been secretly pulling the strings his entire life.

"I'm very impressed with how you turned out," he said. "It's a shame we have to stop the experiment."

"Yeah. A shame." Cyan stood to his feet, wobbling slightly before taking a few steps forward. "I don't know if Nichole or Robert had time to inform you of my conditions."

The Leader raised his eyebrow. "Your conditions?"

"I'll go quietly. But Hamen stays here. You don't get to lay a finger on him ever again."

The Leader cracked a smile, a wide hideous thing. A low, rumbling laugh shook from his chest.

"You may be pretty, but I'm the one who owns him," he sneered. "Hamen." The blond jerked to attention, his lips drawn. "If you want any chance of forgiveness, kill him now."

Hamen, don't you dare. We've got your back, I thought.

We all stared, wondering who he was going to listen to. I knew he had a crush on Cyan, but was that enough? If he didn't join his father, he would die with the rest of us.

"I'm not a coward," Hamen said. He turned the gun towards his own temple and pulled the trigger. Blood splattered across my face. Chaos descended.

I jerked Cyan behind me as one of the men grabbed Jack, shoving him against the wall. Reece and Henry descended on the men, the pops of the guns and screams deafening.

Cyan trembled against me as I tried breaking into their minds, but only felt the same sensation of running into a wall. Whoever these Slayers were, they had perfected the art of blocking their emotions.

The Leader didn't so much as blink as he watched his son bleed out onto the carpet. He pulled out his own gun and pointed it at me. *Fuck*, I thought. *Fuck, fuck, fuck. Here is where it ends.*

"Let Brian go," Cyan whispered. I turned to him. He grabbed my hands. "Please," he begged. "I can fix this. I can end them – forever." *He wants me to let Brian lose so he can kill all of them.*

I knew it would work too. But I also knew that Cyan would never forgive himself if he killed another person. Tears streamed down my cheeks.

I let go.

Cyan tore his hands out of my grasp and waltzed out of our hiding place. The Leader hesitated as Cyan waved.

"*Nice to meet you,*" he said, holding his scalpel like a baseball bat. I turned my head away, unable to watch.

Screams filled the station. Flesh tore and bodies thudded. Liquid spurted. Some landed on my face. Two minutes later, the station was silent.

I forced myself to open my eyes to the bloodbath. Someone's hand lay on the carpet in front of me. I tried not to look at the other pieces scattered around me as I looked to see who was still alive.

Henry dry heaved in the corner as Reece surveyed the chaos with her typical stoic face. Jack covered his mouth with his hands as he trembled against the wall. Cyan stood in the middle of it all, a huge grin covering his face.

"Happy now?" I asked. "They're all dead. You killed them all." Cyan nodded.

"*Almost.*" He turned and sank his scalpel into Jack's gut. I screamed as Jack stumbled backwards, hand closing around the handle.

"*Now I'm done,*" Cyan said, grinning. Jack narrowed his eyes at him, blood trickling out of the corner of his mouth.

"So are you," he said. He pulled the knife out his gut and slammed it into the hole in Cyan's skull.

SIX

It was hard to remember what happened after that. I screamed as Cyan stumbled backwards, the knife sticking out of his brain, blinking in confusion. Jack fell to the floor. Reece and Henry were shouting something, but all I could hear was the blood rushing in my ears.

"Cyan, Cyan, can you hear me?" I demanded, holding his shoulders. All he did was blink at me, looking slightly confused. *Oh my god, he's gone,* I thought. *His entire personality just got erased. His wound is going to get infected. He's going to die.*

I collapsed, sobbing on someone's shoulder. They carried me out of the police station and everything faded to black.

I woke up in a clean linens. It smelled like fabric softener. I pushed myself up, wincing as my head wobbled on my neck. Reece sat at a desk against the opposite wall. She was wearing a pleated blue skirt and white button-up and was typing on a laptop. Upon closer inspection, it was a page of math problems.

I wanted to scream. How on Earth could she casually be doing math problems right now?

She looked up and nodded at me. "You slept for a long time."

"What happened? Where are we?" I asked.

"At my dad's house. Cyan is in the hospital. He's alive. We still need to clean up the police station though." My stomach twisted. I doubted any amount of cleaning could get rid of the blood and bits of brain matter that had sunken into the carpet.

"Cyan's alive? Can I see him?" I asked.

"Probably too soon. He's still unconscious." Reece put down her math homework and turned to face me. She studied my face. "Are you okay?" she asked. I almost laughed. It was the nicest thing I had ever heard come out of her pinched lips. My hands trembled.

"No."

She nodded. "Neither are the others. But we're alive. We won," she said.

Not all of us are alive, I thought. *Cyan's going to kill himself when he wakes up. Brian made him murder his best friend.*

Stupid fucking Brian. He couldn't be satisfied until every semblance of the Slayers were gone.

"The Slayers are all gone, aren't they?" I asked. "Every last one?"

Reece nodded. "It's over. Cyan – Brian – whoever ended it for good. The sirens are safe." She tilted her head. "Actually, Hamen survived. He's in the hospital too. Totally blew up his eye."

How does Hamen survive a gunshot to the head when Jack bleeds out after one stab to the gut? It's not fair. None of this is fair.

I made my way out to the kitchen. A motherly figure stood at the stove, stirring something in a pot. She turned and smiled as I shuffled to a chair at the table.

"You must be Abigail. I'm Marie – Reece's stepmom."

"You know about all of this?" I asked, motioning around me as if that made my question any more specific.

"Everyone in Tredecim knows what happened. It's hard to keep things quiet here," she said, sliding a bowl in front of me. She rubbed my back as I picked at the bowl of grits. She whispered kind phrases that went in one ear and out the other.

All I could think about was if Cyan would ever wake up again – and who exactly would be waking up. She agreed to take me to see him even though he was basically a vegetable.

We rode bikes to the hospital – which seemed oddly scenic and picturesque for what we had just lived through. On the way down the hallway, I heard voices. I peeked my head into a room and saw Hamen and Henry. The entire right side of Hamen's face was covered with bandages, but he was sitting up and alert. Henry sat beside him, and for a moment, I could swear they were both laughing. I leaned against the door.

"Dang, you are a really bad assassin," I said.

Hamen turned and smiled – perhaps the first genuine smile I had ever seen from him – and nodded.

"He couldn't even kill himself," Henry joked.

My jaw dropped, but Hamen giggled.

"Guess I'll have to find a new job," he said. "One that doesn't require 20/20 vision."

"I'm glad you're okay." I meant it. Hamen's abusive family was gone. He was finally free.

I walked away from the room and headed down to Cyan. He looked part cyborg with all the tubes and wires attached to his body. Someone had reattached the piece of bone from the front of his skull and sewn the skin back over it. He looked like Frankenstein's monster, but at least he was alive.

He might not feel the same way when he wakes up, I thought. I sat by his side, placing my hand over his, careful not to nudge any of the tubes. His skin was cool to the touch. Had it always been like that? I had never noticed.

If you had asked me how well I thought I knew him a week ago, I would've answered confidently. When I hadn't been pestering him with questions, my tongue had been down his throat. *Of course* I knew everything about him.

But turns out, even Cyan didn't know much about his own life. Both sets of parents had lied to him. His brain had been governed by medication and psychic powers. The different versions of Cyan everyone had seen were just acts played by various puppeteers. The boy I thought I had fallen in love with had never really existed.

I wiped a stray tear from my eye. Maybe . . . maybe this was for the best. If he survived the brain injury – if it had actually disabled Brian's influence – he would truly be free to figure out who he was. Maybe I would fall in love with that version, maybe I wouldn't. But until I figured it out, I would be here.

I stayed until my eyelids began to droop. On my way out, I couldn't help but notice that Henry hadn't left Hamen's side.

The next few days took eternities to pass. Reece, Henry, and I went to the police station and attempted to clean it. Reece had already taken the liberty of removing the bodies, and I didn't ask where they had been buried. It wasn't like anyone would come looking for them.

We ended up ripping up the carpet and repainting the walls, but I swore I could still smell the blood under everything else. I found myself hoping it would catch on fire and burn down. The place had to be haunted – and I was not interested in dealing with any other vengeful spirits.

On the third day, Henry called me to say that Cyan was starting to wake up.

I rushed over to the Urgent Care. He lay on a hospital bed, looking smaller than he ever had. He blinked up at me, his blue eyes distant. I welded my jaw shut, refusing to cry as I held his hand.

"Cyan? Can you hear me?" I whispered. He hesitated before nodding. I laughed in relief, resisting the urge to throw my arms around his neck. Cyan experimentally squeezed my hand before lifting his hands. He stared at them for a few moments before looking around the room.

"Abigail," he whispered. "You're still here."

"Of course I'm still here."

"Jack is dead, isn't he?"

I swallowed, squeezing his hand. "Yes. But it's not your fault. Brian did it."

He stared off into space, brows slightly furrowed. "Is Brian gone?"

I blinked, surprised that he took my word as fact without arguing with me.

"I haven't felt anything," I said. "Have you?"

"I – I don't think so." He felt the bandages on his forehead. "I don't know what to feel."

"It's okay," I whispered. "It's over. It's all over."

SEVEN

Cyan sat next to me on the newly repaired dock. We watched Annie and her friends splash in the water out in the distance. The setting sun warmed our backs, casting an orange and purple glow on the water.

Behind us, the smell of hot dogs and hamburgers floated by on the breeze. My stomach growled, and Cyan turned. "Hungry?"

I nodded, taking a moment to admire the sunset illuminated in his eyes. The shaved patch of hair on his forehead still hadn't grown back all the way, making it look like he had a very awkward reverse mohawk.

He had officially been discharged from the hospital a few weeks ago. Reece's family welcomed him with open arms, although they seemed perturbed by how quiet he was. A series of brain scans showed that his amygdala was obliterated, macerated by the scalpel.

Dr. Davis theorized that damaging Cyan's already overactive amygdala was just enough to bring him back to normal levels – just like how Nichole and Robert had intended with his brain surgery to begin with.

Of course, explaining all of that to Cyan didn't make much of a difference. Whenever I tried to push for how he was feeling, he would just shrug. He stared off into space whenever someone mentioned Jack or his parents. He seemed to feel nothing, but I knew that couldn't be true. He had to feel something – right?

"Come eat!" Steve yelled from the backyard. The kids started paddling for shore. I turned back to Cyan after they were gone.

"Do you want to try one more time?" I asked. He shrugged and halfheartedly stretched his hand over the water. He closed his eyes and furrowed his brow, but nothing happened. He had tried several times earlier that day, and many times in the past days.

"I think my powers are gone," he said, lowering his hand.

"You're not upset about your family's power-line being gone?" I asked.

He shrugged – like he normally did. I buried a flash of frustration.

"Cyan, please, you can talk to me," I pleaded.

"I mean, I could in theory pass the powers down to my kids," he said. I blushed and turned away. We both knew I wouldn't be having anyone's kids.

"You know that's not what I meant," I said. "How are you *feeling?*"

He stared into space. My heart sank lower to my toes. All remaining hope I had for My Cyan coming back was gone. He hadn't laughed, flirted, or joked once with anyone. I kept telling myself that Cyan being an emotional zombie was better than being manipulated. He was alive, and that was more than I thought I would get. But I still missed him. How could you mourn someone that was sitting right next to you?

He suddenly covered my hand with his.

"I don't want to make you upset," he said. "I want you to be happy."

My throat closed. I squeezed his hand. "I just want you to be okay," I whispered.

He took a deep breath, and for the first time, a smile stretched across his face.

"I feel . . . fine," he whispered. "But I shouldn't. My best friend is dead, both sets of parents are dead. I absolutely train-wrecked my first ever relationship. I *should* be devastated, angry, upset. But it feels like all that stuff happened to someone else. This feels like the first chance I've ever had to be . . . myself. Not Jack or Cyan just . . . me. It feels like I'm finally going to get a chance to live a normal life."

It was the most words he had uttered about the subject in weeks. His words were equal parts a relief and depressing to hear.

Cyan had spent his entire life feeling too much, buried in a whirlwind he had no control of. Maybe this was a tender mercy. It was selfish of me to want the old Cyan back when it had caused him so much pain.

I smiled and squeezed his hand. He smiled back, hope softening his face in a way that our rollercoaster rides and kisses had never quite accomplished.

"You deserve to be happy," I said.

"So do you. And we know from experience that plenty of straight guys see you as a catch," he said, winking.

I flushed, but his hope was infectious. Maybe if I went back to that club, I could find the guy whose number had sweated off my palm.

"Guys, come eat!"

We joined the line for food and sat down on the grass to eat. Cyan ate like a normal teenage boy for once. He was already starting to fill out.

A shadow interrupted our dinner. Reece stood above us; her lips pinched in a thin line.

"You'll never believe what's on TV," she said. We followed her into the living room. Hamen stood here, arms crossed, what was left of his face pale.

On the screen was jerky footage of a teenage girl kicking a woman into a fountain. The woman's body wavered and morphed into something else entirely.

"Oh my god," I said. "Is that . . ."

Hamen shook his head. "It's not a siren. Look at the markings on her face." The footage switched to a different teenage girl, blabbering at the camera. I didn't catch any of her words. It switched back to a man in a white lab coat, promising something about a reward and saying something about dangerous creatures.

"If it's not a siren, what is it?" I asked.

"She must be a mermaid," Cyan said. "Brian mentioned them once. Roger thought they could sense others' feelings instead of controlling them. Said they were shy."

"Who's Roger?" Hamen asked.

"Are mermaids dangerous?" I interrupted.

"Humans are dangerous," Cyan said, like he was reminding us to be home before dark. The room went silent for a few moments as the newscaster droned on.

"Well, whatever it is, the humans definitely think it's dangerous," Reece said.

My gut churned. That wasn't good. We had permanently solved the problem of sirens, but the rest of the world didn't know that.

"We can't just let them hurt the mermaids if they're not dangerous," I said. My protest was met with uncomfortable silence.

Reece crossed her arms. "And pray tell, how would we clarify the difference?"

"Even if we showed people what real sirens are, humans would still panic. We would have Slayers all over again," Hamen said. "And the mermaids still probably wouldn't be safe."

I swallowed. As much as I hated to admit it, they were right. Hadn't we done enough saving one species from extinction? Hadn't we been through enough? We couldn't save everyone. Cyan was the closest to being okay for the first time in his life. I wasn't about to drag him into another war.

I looked around at the others. Cyan was biting his knuckle – a new habit since the brain injury. Reece seemed to be trying her best to look aloof and unbothered, but something was raging beneath her dark eyes. Hamen had crossed him arms, but he didn't look scared.

"We can't intervene . . . of course," Reece said, her words slow and deliberate.

"It would be too risky," Cyan agreed, eyes shifting between all of us.

Hamen nodded. "They'll have to fend for themselves."

"We do nothing," I finished.

I had no way of knowing if I was the only one lying.

HAMEN

seven years later

There was a ghost on my doorstep. It blinked, and I realized the ghost was still alive. He had downy white hair and almost pink eyes. He stared at my face, but his gaze seemed to go past me, which made sense when I saw the cane gripped in his pale fingers.

"I'm looking for Abigail," he said.

That was probably the last thing I would've expected anyone to say. I furrowed my brow, suddenly weary of the stranger, even though he couldn't have been more than sixteen years old.

"Why are you looking for Abigail?" I asked, bracing myself for a fight.

"Who are you?" he asked, ignoring my question. For a moment, I could've sworn he sniffed the air. Who does that?

"Who are you?" I retorted.

He hesitated, shifting on his feet. "My name is Daniel," he said finally. "Cyan told me I could find her here. That they were old friends."

I almost laughed, wondering if I was dreaming.

"You found Cyan?" I asked.

Daniel raised his eyebrow. "You know who Cyan is?"

I chuckled. It had been years since I had seen my old friend. Foe? To this day, it was hard to decide. "Sure do."

"So, do you know where Abigail is?"

"She moved away from here a long time ago. Why are you looking for her?"

Daniel's pink eyes flashed red. "Because I think we have some things in common."

I invited him in. He navigated the trailer easily, barely using his cane to tap on the floor. He flopped down on a couch and put his feet up on my coffee table like we were old friends about to catch up.

"Forgive me for badgering you with questions, but you've got a lot to explain," I said.

"I was hoping you would be the one to explain things to me," Daniel said. "Cyan refused to give me any details. Said he didn't like to talk about what happened in Tredecim. He just told me to ask a woman named Abigail. I still don't know who you are, by the way."

"My name is Hamen. Did Cyan mention anything about me?" I asked.

Daniel shook his head. I wasn't sure if I should be offended or grateful that Cyan hadn't talked about me. Maybe he still felt awkward about what had happened between us. Lord knows I did.

Daniel tilted his head. "You have some . . . history with him? Were you mates? Partners – I mean?"

I flushed. "It was . . . complicated." I paused. "Wait, how did you know that?"

Daniel grinned. "I am merfolk," he said. "I can feel it on you." He extended an arm. Narrow translucent fins stretched from his skin, needles glinting in the afternoon light. My mouth fell open. I had to resist the urge to stretch out a hand and feel them. I had never met a merperson in real life – just seen the countless news reels and YouTube videos about their Rebellion.

But wait, then why did his eyes glow red?

He seemed to sense my question before I could ask it. "I always knew I was different than the other merfolk, that I could do things to people that they couldn't. I've been trying to find out why, and my search has led me here."

"Your parents never told you?" I asked.

"My mother is a normal merfolk. I never met my father," he said.

There it is, I thought. His father must've been a Red-Powerline siren. What were the odds?

"Daniel, do you know what sirens are?"

He shook his head.

Footsteps sounded around the corner. Henry walked into the living room, his hair still dripping wet from his shower. As normal, my heart skipped a beat upon seeing him.

He frowned and pointed at our unexpected guest. I motioned for him to sit beside me, and he did so, scattering droplets over the couch. Daniel sniffed the air like a dog, his eyes shifting over to Henry.

"This must be your Mate," Daniel said.

I flushed again as Henry shot me a quizzical look. I placed my hand over his.

"Henry, this is Daniel. He came looking for Abigail. Cyan sent him," I explained.

Henry's eyes widened. *Why?* he mouthed.

"What are sirens?" Daniel demanded.

We spent the next hour telling the story Cyan had refused to relive. The murder of Brian's parents to the massacre at the police station that ended it all. Every time I tried to smooth out a bloody detail, Henry nudged me. This kid deserved the truth - all of it - every nasty, horrifying, terrible piece of it.

By the end, Daniel somehow looked even paler.

"Jesus that's fucked up."

"Yeah. It is," Henry agreed.

"It sounds like your father was a siren from the Red Powerline," I said. "That's why you can manipulate people's emotions."

Daniel was quiet, his brows still furrowed.

"I don't get it."

"I know it's a lot to process but -"

"No, I understand what happened. What I *don't* understand is how a whole town knew that sirens were a totally different species from merfolk . . . the ones who were actually responsible for the myths . . . and you did nothing when my kind was being trafficked and sold."

His words hung heavy in the air. I shifted. Guilt and apprehension had kept me up for many nights since we had spoken the decision to not intervene out loud.

"Daniel, I -"

"I mean, for god's sake, you had people capable of forcing people to change their feelings! Why did no one help us?"

"Merpeople can tell when humans are lying, correct?" Henry asked. "Or is that a rumor?"

"It's true," Daniel said.

I leaned forward. "Then listen to me very carefully. I, of course, couldn't intervene, couldn't make anyone change their mind. But . . . Abigail left town pretty soon after your kind was revealed. I have no clue what she was up to or might have done, and she never bothered to share specifics."

Daniel blinked. "So . . . you don't know for sure if . . . *intervention* happened or not?" he asked.

"Nope," I said. "And I never want to. If anything like that *did* happen, it would only put sirens, only put people like *you* back in danger."

I had my favorite theories that I had shared with Henry. What were the odds the Supreme Court had *really* changed their minds so quickly? What were the odds that so many humans decided to put their own lives on the line to help an alien species?

Of course, maybe she had done simpler things behind the scenes – made a fisherman a little more forgetful than normal, or given a human-passing merperson more benefit of the doubt than they deserved.

Maybe she had done nothing. Maybe she had done just enough to help but stay hidden. After all – who would suspect someone without a tail?

All I knew was that the day their species had been voted free, she had sent a postcard with the simple message *mission accomplished* scrawled across the top.

At the end of the day – I would never know. And I didn't want to.

Daniel stayed quiet for a moment, mulling over my words.

"I think . . . I think I would like to ask her myself," he said. "Do you know how to contact her?"

"We can give you her number," Henry offered. He scribbled down her number on a sticky note, realized Daniel wouldn't be able to read it, and sheepishly added her contact to his cell phone instead.

"You're welcome to stay the night, if you want," I offered.

Daniel shook his head, already headed for the doorway. "That's okay. I need to get back to my Mate or she'll worry."

I walked him to the porch, the screen door slamming shut behind me.

"Did Cyan say how he was doing?" I asked. Part of me was afraid to know the answer. He had been a puppet his entire life, people fighting over the strings. How did someone heal from that?

"He said it took a while, but he's moved on," Daniel said. "He's happy."

I smiled, relief making my knees weak. My heart still ached for the siren I was supposed to kill. He had been dealt the worst hand in all of this. All he wanted was to be in control of his own life. Part of me still missed him, but if vanishing into the ocean was what it took for him to get his life back, then so be it.

I didn't know why his ancestors drowned humans, but he had spared my life too many times to be counted as one of them. He had the power of the seas at his command, but never wanted to use it to hurt people. He had tortured his own body for years, done everything in his power to break free from the terrors we had all instilled in him. Terrors that would've never come true had we not been so fearful. He had never been the real monster.

In the end, we couldn't save him. The blue powerline was dead, and there was nothing that could be done to fix it. Cyan being okay was the smallest consolation.

Daniel paused before tapping down the stairs. He turned around.

"Cyan . . . is happy," he repeated.

I nodded, not sure why he was repeating himself. Daniel shifted, as if he wasn't sure if his next words should be spoken.

"You're not a Slayer anymore, right? You would never kill another siren again, no matter what? I'll know if you're lying," he reminded.

I chuckled. Even if I had the desire, there was no way I would be a good shot with my one remaining eye. "I was never a Slayer."

Daniel smirked before turning around once again. "Cyan has a family."

It took a few seconds for the meaning of those words to sink in. My mouth open and closed, my brain sputtering as it tried to form words. *Family* could mean anything. Maybe Cyan lived in a pod of whales or had moved back to land and gotten a boyfriend and puppy. But it could also mean he had a wife. A child. *Children.*

"You mean . . ." I sputtered.

Daniel smiled a shit-eating grin. "I can't *confirm* anything of course, secrets and keeping people safe and such – but the blue powerline *may* or *may not* be dead after all."

THE END

or is it?